ONLY
HER MEMORIES
ARE LEFT

VINAY SINGH PARIHAR

RIGI PUBLICATION

ONLY HER MEMORIES ARE LEFT

BY

VINAY SINGH PARIHAR

Copyright © VINAY SINGH PARIHAR 2023

Originally Published In India

ISBN: 978-93-95773-71-3

Published by RIGI PUBLICATION

777, Street no.9, Krishna Nagar

Khanna-141401 (Punjab), India

Website: www.rigipublication.com

Email: info@rigipublication.com

Phone: +91-9357710014, +91-9465468291

DEDICATION

In the Loving Memory of

My Dearest Aaji Shrimati Chandan Devi & Babba Shri Aadhar Singh Parihar

My Dearest Nanaji Shri Ganga Singh Baghel

ACKNOWLEDGMENT

My special dedication to my beloved pets Angad and Ashwatthama whose presence makes my life worth living.

With this book I would like to offer my gratitude to my parents, **MR. MAHENDRA SINGH PARIHAR & MRS. NEELAMDEVI PARIHAR.** For always supporting me with my life's decisions and always enlightening my path during all walks of life. I would further like to extend my gratitude to my elder sister and her husband **MRS. KALPANA BHADAURIYA & MR. UTTAM BHADAURIYA** With this book I am introducing myself as a writer before the world. Being an avid reader, I have always fantasized about writing my own story and through this book my dream is turning into reality. Every first holds a special place in our hearts so is this book, this book being my debut as a writer, it has my heart in it, I have been working on it from a long time and after all the sleepless nights and tiring days my hard work is finally compiled in these pages and I am able to present it before you in the form of this novel.

It hasn't been an easy journey rather it has been an arduous one filled with quandary and self-doubt it wouldn't be possible for me to turn my story into this book if I hadn't had the support of the most amazing and supportive people on earth who accompanied me on this adventurous ride full of joy, celebration, struggle, frustration and a lot more, but they stood by me and kept saying I can do it, which has resultantly brought us here today.

I would like to thank few people who have cleared my turbid thoughts and have influenced me for writing this book. To begin with my two little nephews **LUCKY & YASHU,** also my younger brother **MR. SHAILENDRA PARIHAR,** all of them deserve all the love in the world they have been my pillar of strength who helped me to keep pushing my limits and working harder day by day to reach where I am today.

My special mention to my brother in law **MR UTTAM BHADAURIYA**, he is currently serving in INDIAN ARMY 44 armed cops unit, he taught me the biggest trick to succeed in life is to give your hundred percent and never quit something you have started, there were times where I lost my zeal but he taught me and encouraged me in all facets of life be it my engineering, my business and now with this book he always kept his assurance on me and his voice echoed in my ears "VINAY YOU CAN DO IT".

My LATE GRAND PARENTS their blessings have always been upon me, I was from a very mediocre family where everyone worked for survival, we have had seen days with financial scarcity but I still recollect the time of my grandmother's demise when I prayed before her corpse saying *"aaji jaa toh rahi ho, garibi leke jana"*. And from that day I believe it's my grandmother's blessing that I have been able to take my family out from that financial debacle and have been able to set up my factory **SHREEJI MACHINERY PVT LTD. SHRREJI E EVOLUTION PVT LTD, M S BUILDCON, ARMOURED COP SECURITY, MECH TEA CAFE, P MART** And looking forward to enter into other business ventures in the days to come. From nowhere, today I stand before you all as an entrepreneur, the boy who was once unemployed is providing employment to other people. I have come a long way only by the blessings of my elders.

I would further like to extend my gratitude to my dearest friends who hold special place in my heart they also played their part in persuading me for writing this book, they actually add soul to this story without them this story would not have existed. **KOSHLESH PANDEY, VIJAY PANDEY, MANOJ PANDEY, A. RAJPUT, RANJEET PATEL, VIKAS PARIHAR, AVNISH PARIHAR (A K SINGH) the** euphoria of being with them has led me here to write and relive all the glorious moments we all have once spent together. During our academics my entire life revolved around my friends and now due to unforeseen circumstances we hardly share a word with one another.

Last but surely not the least a special mention and a word of thanks
to the person without whom these incidents would not be compiled
into this book, **POOJA,** she was the one who motivated me in
writing this book and it's the result of her motivation that has led
me here writing this book. She is the **U-TURN** of my life, had she
been not there in my life I cannot even imagine how my life would
have been.

VINAY SINGH PARIHAR

PROLOGUE

Sitting in a lonely room away from the glitz and glamour of this world, vinay was hoping to get some sunshine into his life and was praying before the Almighty to bring back his good olden days, he was all alone with his reminiscent from the past to haunt him in that dark room, the notification light was constantly blinking on his phone lying adjacent to him, as his friends were trying to reach him for knowing about him whether he was alright, apart from this blinking light the entire room was wrapped in darkness.

All he was begging was for a fresh start a new beginning which he very well knew cannot be attained, his loss will never be compensated after this day. He was brooding over what had adversely gone wrong in his life. Sobbing over her death he was constantly blaming himself, little did he know that even though he knew about her ailment he would not be able to save her from leaving the world anyway but he was endlessly ranting about it that if he knew she would have recovered from her illness. She took her last breath before his eyes and even after hours he was not coming in consensus with the reality of his life. He was totally numb and was unable to feel his limbs he was in total denial of the reality and felt extremely helpless before the destiny he wished life also had a delete button so that he could permanently delete that dark day from their life alas! Life doesn't work that way, and thus blaming his fate was the only thing he could possibly do. His mind kept on telling him that all that was a nightmare and for waking himself from that disaster he kept on banging his head on the wall, but every time he banged himself his faith was shackled as he realized it wasn't a nightmare and resultantly, he banged himself harder the next time in order to punish himself.

While he was struggling with his thoughts a message popped on his mobile and the notification sound brought him back to his senses for a little while, for once he thought it was her message but by the time, he rushed to grab his phone he realized that now he will never receive any notification from her number. There was a constant downpour of tears from his eyes which has blurred his vision he was only able to read the message after wiping his tears, it was a message from Aditi:

"I know whatsoever I do or try to console you words would not be enough to help you heal, I am neither trying to sympathize nor I am trying to give you any sermon about the reality of life all I am trying to do is to be by your side which I very well know that you need solitude but unless you vent out your grief I can't just leave you like this, no one can fill the void in your life created by her loss but you will have to accept the fact not for anyone else but for yourself. You loved her bits and beyond and would have never thought of this untimely separation, but this is the undeniable truth which you will have to accept and move on and unless you do that you are not going to get out of this trauma. I just want you to know that I am just a call away, I can provide you with the shoulder to lean upon if you like. By doing this I can only be a partner in your pain but you have to overcome this all by yourself. You can do this vinay, this time shall too pass"

The constant trail of tears was rolling down from his eye while he was reading the message, night had never been this long for him every second felt like he was caged under a time loop for centuries and the night became endless. He could feel his heavy breaths as if with every breath he was pulled down by tonnes of weight over his chest. Just two days ago he was enjoying his life like no other, he was thrilled to have secured his dream job and was ready to face the world from the first date of upcoming month. As soon as his last exam ended, he rushed to his pg. and grabbed his luggage which was packed already as he had been planning for this day. when he boarded the train, he tried calling her relentlessly only to get no response from her end. He was impatient during the entire journey, his impulse was not allowing him to rest or sleep, he had his castle of thoughts surmounting him all the time until he fell into deep sleep with one such delighting thought of being able to finally meet her, and was woken up the next morning by the cry of tea vendor across his berth.

When he reached house everyone in the family was delighted to see an engineer walking into the house. The twinkle in the eyes of the proud parents was enough to say how much happy they were to see their son come back home. Now it was Pratiksha's turn when he was about to meet her after a long time and for that matter, he picked his black shirt the one most praised by Pratiksha, she always asked him to wear black as according to her he looked irresistible in that look. He made sure that he wore everything of her choice and for that matter he also used that perfume which she once gifted him and since then he has been using the same titan skinn fragrance as she always asked him to wear it when he came to meet her on their regular dates, he also made sure to carry some roses and carnations for her as a greeting gift along with some dark chocolates.

He was taken aback on reaching her house when he saw the big lock on the front door of her house, he tried reaching her through her phone call but all his efforts went in vain as the mobile he was trying to reach was unavailable. He was a bit curious to know about her unavailability but was not ready to hear what was coming his way. A lady from the neighbourhood saw him struggling to reach the family and thus came to help him with the information she had,

"Whom are you looking for son"? asked the lady.

"I am here to meet Pratiksha, but unfortunately her house is locked and also her mobile is unreachable" replied vinay.

"Then why you came to her house, she is in the hospital son battling for her life may god bless the poor child may she recover soon from her ailment" said the lady with pity in her eyes.

"What happened to her? Is she alright why didn't she tell me about this? where is she admitted do you know about that? vinay began a trail of questions before the lady.

She is in the city hospital from yesterday precariously fighting for her life the lady replied. Before she could add anything vinay ignited his bike engine and sped towards the hospital, and while he was riding towards the hospital the moments they shared together replayed before his eyes not allowing his tears to stop.

INDEX

1.	BACK TO SCHOOL	13
2.	THE FIRST SIGHT	20
3.	NOW COMES THE TROUBLE	27
4.	GARBA NIGHT	30
5.	NEW BIKE	39
6.	FAREWELL	42
7.	AFTER YOU ALWAYS	49
8.	CALLING TO SAY HELLO!	59
9.	DECISION OF REGRET	66
10.	BHOPAL	79
11.	OLD FRIENDSHIP, NEW BONDING	86
12.	QUESTIONABLE MOVE	94
13.	FOCUSING ON THE POSITIVES	101
14.	FOUND A FRIEND IN HER	109
15.	GIFT	118
16.	BOOMERANG	129
17.	ARE WE MEETING?	143
18.	THE PROPOSAL	153

19.	VALENTINES DAY	163
20.	INTERNSHIP PERIOD	170
21.	THEY ARE STILL CONNECTED	181
22.	BHOPAL HERE SHE COMES	185
23.	AUDITION: FAIL, DATE: PASS	191
24.	WHY SHE HAD TO RETURN	199
25.	UNVELING TRUE COLOURS	208
26.	ANOTHER DITCH	219
27.	I THOUGHT SHE WAS MY FRIEND	224
28.	CAMPUS 3 SELECTION	234
29.	GHOSTED	239
30.	SAH	245
31.	GONE TOO SOON	252

BACK TO SCHOOL

JUNE 2009

"Have you plugged in cotton into your ears? Your phone is constantly ringing right next to you, come-on answer it someone from your class must have the news regarding your SSC results declaration. Don't act like a scared kitten, be brave and be confident. You have already played your part nothing is going to change now I very well know you are petrified about the uncertainties of your result you are rigorously thinking about the adverse result but my child how can you forget how hard have you worked for these exams so how can the result be adverse, and even if it does this is not the end of your life, results only give you grades but what actually matters is what knowledge do you possess." Said maa in order to console her timid son.

Her words gave me a sense of courage to face the day and then I picked up the phone it was harsh my classmate on the other side of the call with trembling hand I picked up the call,

"Hey! Where are you man I have been trying to reach you from a long time… by the way the results are out have you checked yours or not?" asked harsh

Responding him with a lame excuse for my unavailability I said I was busy doing some household chores although I was not, then further asked him whether he checked his own results.

"Yes! I did, I secured 68% I wasn't expecting to get such good marks as my exams didn't go so well, but I am very happy with my results" replied harsh joyously.

"Great! man congratulations, allow to me to check my result and then I shall get back to you" I replied.

I sat with my laptop then to check what fate was in store for me, I filled in the required details on the official website of Gujarat state board and pressed the enter button with shivering hands my parents sitting behind me waiting in desperation to celebrate, while the website was buffering, I was trying to lure God with everything I could possibly think of to get the grades in my favour. Within seconds the result flashed on the screen. My pupil expanded as I could not believe my eyes... I had secured 79% although I was expecting between 70-75 but 79% was a surprise for me too.

My parents, overjoyed with my performance began announcing my result to the relatives and to the neighbours holding their head high with pride. Indeed, parents are always overwhelmed and proud with even the smallest achievement made by their offspring's. exuberance filled in our family and sweets were distributed in the locality. Every member of the family showered encomium on my success, For the next few hours I was engaged on phone discussing results with my classmates and taking blessings from the relatives as SSC exams are till now treated as herculean task which if you pass with flying colours get good recognition amongst your cousins and relatives. By now this mentality is partially changed but back in 2000's it was a very big matter. I was relaxed as I got good grades and had not to go through all the humiliation and strange looks from the relatives which one gets on scoring low.

This relaxation hardly lasted for couple of hours, and was halted when the time came to discuss which stream should I take admission in, my inclination was towards the science stream as I wanted to become an engineer but my father had other plans for me. This point of difference became my source of anxiety and worry, although my father was very liberal but when it came to academics, he had altogether a different personality. I had constant nervous jitters about how would he react if I tell him that I wish to take science stream, and my nightmare came to life when I told him about my plans to pursue engineering course later in life to which he clearly denied. Although he was not against science as a subject but somehow, he had no confidence in me that I could do well in science background and this mindset was my ultimate enemy back then. My glorious moments hardly lasted for 3 hours and again I was left with nothing but anxiety which ultimately resulted in a sleepless night.

Next morning, I received a call from a dear friend Priyanka she was a family friend and we bonded pretty well if I ever had a dilemma, she was my confidant who enlightened my path in taking toughest decisions easily. She took no time to gasp that I was not feeling what I was trying to show, she knew me very well and thus was very vell accustomed with my fake smile and joy.

What is the matter, tell me? she asked me straight.

"Nothing! Why are you asking me this, everything is great" I replied

"There is no need for you to hide anything from me so stop overacting and come to the point what is bothering you?" she said with a stiff voice

"Nothing! Everything is fine" I replied but this time a bit more consciously so that she believes me.

"So, you are not going to tell me, you want to throw some more tantrums. Alright meet me at Mech tea engineering café sharp at 12pm" she ordered.

"I can't I am sorry I am already occupied I will catch up with you some other day" I replied in order to avoid facing her as if I did go to meet her, I would not be able to hide and will surely cry.

"I am not requesting you to come, I am commanding that you have to be present there at the stipulated time, and if I don't find you there,

I will be at your house by 1pm, now the choice is yours what do you want" she replied angrily.

"Dear I cannot come please try to understand" I begged before her.

She was in no mood to listen "if I do not find you at 12 in the café be ready to see me at your house" she reiterated and disconnected the phone.

I was left with no other choice but to go if I do not then she would bump into my house which I certainly did not want that day particularly.

I was on time, although I was in a chagrin mood the ambience of the café helped me appease, the café had the interiors of equipment's and subtle music was being played which was very soothing the entire place had a very positive vibe to it. I ordered myself a coffee frappe as Priyanka was on her way and she was about to take 15 more minutes to reach. She reached the café before I could even finish my coffee and began complaining how could I order without her being present for which I apologised giving the excuse that I could not resist myself from ordering, as I liked aroma of freshly brewed coffee making the entire place fragrant.

"First things first, a big congratulations to you for scoring so good dear! You have exceeded everyone's expectation I'm really very happy for you…" said Priyanka beatifically.

I replied with a confounded smile.

"Now will you speak what has been bothering you?" asked Priyanka frowning her brows at me.

"I want to get into science stream and pursue engineering for my future, but my father does not seem to be consensual about my plan, and upon this decision my entire future depends so is this a trivial matter to not worry" I said resting my forehead in my hands.

"Stop worrying you will have to come up with a solution for this catch 22 situations, and that is the reason why both of us are sitting here, to drive a solution and not to mourn" said Priyanka authoritatively.

"I know what are we here for, but I am unable to figure out any bright light behind this tunnel" I replied with a heavy voice.

"That's what you believe, but unlike you I have a brain which actually works and I have an idea to share with you," said Priyanka

"Idea!" I said this time with a hopeful tone. "What is it?" I added.

"Why don't you approach your tuition sir, maybe he can convince your father as I know he has always liked you as a student and your grades are also good enough to ask him to convince your father. Not only that he has taught you over the years he knows very well whether you can take science or not." Replied Priyanka.

"I believe it is an excellent idea but I still have a doubt in my mind" I said

"Now what" replied Priyanka

"Only thing that is taking a toll on me is that what if Soni sir also agrees to what my father thinks then I will have no other option than to take commerce" I said biting my fingers with anxiety.

"Well, if this happens than without giving a second thought go with what the elders around you are suggesting. They are not your enemies their opinion is always for your good" replied Priyanka trying to cheer me up.

"I think you are right, before landing on my thoughts I should once try and leave the rest upon the mercy of God! Thank you for decluttering my mind. I owe you a treat for this… you have really helped me with clearing the ambiguity and helped me to think positively, I really fortunate to have you in my life." I said in a grateful manner.

"Are you going to Thank me entire day over here or you will go to meet your Soni sir, we can celebrate some other day, do what is most important for today" Priyanka said.

Thanking her once again I headed to the tuition classes, most of the students have gathered at the classes that day as they wanted to thank their teacher for helping them gain good marks.

I was also there but some different reasons. I waited for other students to leave. Soni sir gasped from my facial expressions that something was not okay with me and thus once all the students left, he took me inside his cabin to ensure that if some other student comes in, they may not hear what we were talking about to ensure our privacy.

"What happened Vinay beta? Is there something bothering you? soni sir asked

"Yes, sir I need your help", I replied and told him about my father's decision.

"Maybe your father needs to look towards a different perspective, you need not worry I shall talk with your father and will try to make him bend his decision" assured soni sir.

Having taken of the load from my shoulders I then went back to my house hoping my efforts bear some fruits and my father changes his mind.

I was desperately waiting for soni sir to call my father for convincing but till he did not make one, negative thoughts engulfed me believing that my efforts were abortive.

He kept his promise and the same evening he called my father, but unfortunately being outside for some work I could not hear their conversation, but he ensured that my father was convinced for me this was absolute prodigy. For me it was an uphill task but for sir it was a piece of cake, my father had his faith on the assurance of soni sir but most importantly his faith was on my calibre.

When I returned home, I saw a throng of my family members waiting for me in the living room with poker face. I thought I landed at the wrong time, in order to avoid any confrontation with my father I began walking towards my room in a taciturn manner. But I was stopped by my father in a bold and loud tone.

"Kahan chale hone wale engineer sahab," said my father

I turned with zest when I heard him, I could not believe my ears what he just said was still a dream for me. But it turned into reality when I saw everyone in the family spreading their smiles at me. No wonder the happiness I found at this moment was unmatched.

It had only been possible because of soni sir, the next morning I went along with soni sir to secure admission In RASHTRABHARTI HINDI HIGHER SECONDARY SCHOOL. And voila my wish became a reality for which I was enthralled in every bit. Although it was not a blue blood school but I have always wanted to study from that school as it had a high reputation amongst other schools of our area. And also, I had a lot of hopes with this school that it may help me in sculpting my future. Although my father was a little reluctant at first but I knew I could convince him on that.

THE FIRST SIGHT

JULY 2009

My new journey began in the new school, I was complacent enough to have school as per my desire but the initial days seemed to be a little daunting as I had no companions with me for which I was mentally prepared, as I was an introvert since childhood and I sucked at approaching people so I was completely in my shell trying to ameliorate my learning skills even during the lunch breaks, this was also purposely done in order to prevent myself suffering from ennui.

One day during the lunch break I was engrossed in practising a practical sum taught by the teacher in the previous lecture when a voice from the back door caught my attention, I tried not looking back and being laser focused towards the physics problem which was right in front of my eyes but I could not help myself but turn back. It was a girl calling her friend from our class, their bonding seemed to be of long years friendship, possibly they were classmates till 10 and stream section made them part their ways.

I was unable to glance at her as there were few students standing and talking in the passage which blocked my vision to see her, but her constant cry for her friend's name made me very curious to look at the face behind that melodious voice. I had never been so much attracted towards any voice like that before. I stood up from my seat and began walking towards the corridor to have a glimpse of her. She was at an angel where I was able to see her back so I began moving further to see her face and I was awestruck to find how gorgeous she was, I have never seen someone looking so pretty. No adulation is enough to describe her beauty. Her deep dark brown eyes to which she applied kohl was enhancing their beauty, her perfectly aligned teeth gave her the picture-perfect smile, her cheeks were so plum that needed no additional blush they already had their natural pigment which added glow to them, her hairs were thick and long of which she made a braid with a white coloured ribbon at the top, which was mandatory in the school and it complimented her look so well. She was the epitome of beauty; I had never felt such felicity which I felt on seeing her.

While I was busy admiring her beauty with myself, I saw a boy from our class giving me cold looks, he was none another than the stud of our class having the most masculine body back then.

"don't you dare think of doing what you have in your nasty brain" the guy said in an aggressive tone.

His words were enough to intimidate me but somehow, I managed to put up false courage and replied "think what? A person cannot stand in the corridor, or do we need to take a special permission from you whether can we stand here or not"

The moment I said this all eyes were on us including the two most beautiful eyes of the world. In order to prevent ruckus, the companions of that boy took him away saying "we shall see him after school".

I took a sigh of relief when they left but by that time the girl had already left, but as she left, she also left with a part of my heart with her I wanted to know more about her but then I recollected about that stud of our class who was after her thus I ended up busting my bubble of hope to know more about her and rested to focus on my studies.

Days went by I heard her often calling for her friend during lunch breaks, some days I bid defiance at her and then there were days when I secretly glanced at her from the corner of my eyes, as I did not want it to look obvious that I was so crazy after her. But could never gather the courage to encounter her or initiate a friendship with her.

On keeping an eye on her I noticed the guy who tried intimidating me earlier was crazy after her and never allowed any other boy to even to look at her, he followed hooliganism to prevent others. But one more thing was clearly visible that she was really uncomfortable with him being around I saw her warning him multiple times to stay away from him. Few days passed, I felt like I should go and help her to complain before the principle about the teaser. But then thought she might not mistakenly take me to be one of them thus stayed aloof but kept argus eye on her to be there if she needed me anytime.

As days went by, I also became familiar with few students and found two gems from our class koshlesh and vijay we became very good friends in a very short span of time and luckily, we hailed from the same area and thus we began pooling our bikes to come to school. This extra time which we got, curated our bond stronger. I began enjoying going to the school these amazing people became the reason for me to never miss my school. Entire semester went by but I was not able to know what was the name of my crush! My friends were well aware of feelings and they several times took a dig at me for this reason but coincidently they also had crush on two girls who belonged to the same class as her and they were friends too, we often sat and laughed at how three of us became friends and our crushes were also friends. But none was ready to bell the cat and approach them, we wanted to become their friends but never approached them, all we did was to gaze them silently as the selenophile gazed at the moon.

I began enjoying going to school during the Diwali vacations I literally counted the day left for the schools to reopen so that I could once again be with my friends and my crush. Every evening I induced plans of how I was going to approach her to at least befriend her. When I told my friends about the plans, they always laughed at me as they knew although I made plans, I was not going to execute any of them, but thanks to talking to them my vacations passed with an ease as I had someone to share my feelings with. Being an introvert, I never expected myself to have such loving and caring friends. Although the vacations were almost 25 days long but every single day, I could hear her saccharine voice into my ears her thought became an integral part of my life.

***

My exile ended when the vacations were over but this came up with the news of upcoming examinations for which I worked my fingers to the bone in order to get good grades as I had the huge responsibility to prove that I could do well in science stream soni sir backed me when I needed him know it was my turn to deliver the desired results, although I was crushing over her madly but I did not allow it to come in way of my studies.

One day when all three of us friends were sitting during the lunch break when koshlesh said

"Are we living in stone age or what? It has been more than 6 months and all three of us are silently gushing over the girls and we know nothing about them not even their names, all we know is they are from our school, we are so stupid that we don't even know which division they are in?"

Vijay and I nodded our heads in agreement

"What can we do now to know more about them?" asked vijay.

"Let's try to befriend them, our intentions are not to harass them all we want is to become friends with them nothing wrong" replied koshlesh.

"You both can try your luck; I will abstain from doing so because if I approached her and what if that moron summit again tried becoming a stud instead of accepting my friendship, she will begin hating me forever…" I replied hopelessly

"Well don't worry about him, earlier all of us were freshers here and thus got intimidated by his false hoax, now the ball is in our court as we all very well know that she hates to see him around her, this can be taken as an advantage if we get her out from this summit's daily torture, she will finally begin to notice you positively" replied koshlesh

Vijay nodded in agreement.

I don't see this working in our favour, but let's just put heads together to find an apt way." I spoke

For next couple of days all we three of us had the same topic to discuss but did nothing coz we were worried to not paint ourselves in a corner.

Maybe God was hearing us framing strategies every day and thus decided helping us, a recent renovation work in the school brought our classes next to each other such that even if they had to go anywhere, they had to cross over our class, this resulted in seeing her often crossing the corridor, I choose the seat closest to the window thanks to which I never missed spotting her coming and returning. I reached school before time to ensure seeing her beautiful refreshed Sunkissed morning face.

Our school had an arrangement were we had to go into the computer lab for practical class barefoot, one winter morning it was her class's practical lecture when I saw her classmates leaving I fixed my eyes at the window to catch her glance as our teacher has not come yet, when I detected her voice from behind I knew she was coming when I saw her walking on her toes saying to one of her friend, "yaar ye farsh kitna Thanda hai (how cold is this flooring)

I swiftly responded to her commenting "dekhna kahin aapke piar na gal jaye "(be watchful of your feet catching frostbite) I haven't expected this level of sangfroid from myself.

Hearing this her friend smirked and she irefully gazed at me and gave a tough expression.

This was the time when we had our eye contact for the very first time, and may be my all stars were in my favour that day, a friend of her came running from behind pushing her in a hurry " Pratiksha yaar we are already late stop walking like a sloth hurry up, sharma sir is very punctual and dislikes students arriving late for his class"

Oh my god! Her name was Pratiksha which means wait and indeed I waited a lot nearly 7 months just to know what her name was. And finally, my crush was no longer fairy angel the names which I gave her in my fantasies but was Pratiksha… I was on seventh heaven I felt like the genie was ready to grant me anything I thought for and that was the reason within 5 minutes our eyes met, she noticed me and most importantly I now knew what her name was. It was a cherry on the cake, I could not thank God enough to give me those perennial moments in my life.

when she was returning to her class wrapping her lecture I saw her taking notice of my presence, and ever since then everyday she took notice of me sitting by the window and I never missed this opportunity to share an eye contact even for a micro milli second my love for her was sacrosanct it was ubiquitous although she was unaware about my genuine feelings but one day she will surely understand, this ultimate thought kept the flame in me alive with my unilateral love for her I hoped one day she will align with my ulterior feelings. My friends called me crazy when they saw me frantic even for the dumbest things. days passed our eyes often met but unfortunately, I could never gain that courage in me to stand before her to speak my heart out. Although I was crazy for her but keeping myself aligned with my studies was equally important for me, and while surfing in these two boats my first year in new school ended giving me a lot of memories and I prayed every evening before God to get our friendship started to at least a nascent stage so that she is no longer nonchalant of my existence. My prayers did not bear any fruit than and the entire year passed with exams and other practical's keeping us engaged to spare time for all this cute school romance. And once again we were at the door of long unending vacations which almost seemed like a villain to me as they were the reason why I was away from Pratiksha for nearly 45 days, but the only thing that helped me pass this exile was my tuition classes where I could meet vijay and koshlesh daily. As all three of scored good in 11th annual examination our families were content to see us doing justice with the options we took.

NOW COMES THE TROUBLE

JUNE 2010

I spent the earlier night sleepless, my curiosity kept me wide awake I kept building castles of my dreams about her, to be honest I was more thrilled to see her than for my studies, although my career was very important to me but her thought got an edge over it, her impression on my brain was indelible. It took longer than usual for the night to end that's what I felt like as soon as the clock struck 6 in the morning I was up from my bed and into the shower, I did not want to miss the sight of her coming to the school and for that reason I left the house early. On reaching I waited for my friends to come at the parking ground of the school and began looking for, as I could not dissipate that beautiful morning of our new class without seeing her eternally beautiful face.

As the prayer bell rang, I began walking towards the classroom with sluggish footsteps, when I heard a voice coming from the backside,

"kesi hai yaar" it took me no time to recognize that it was none other than the girl of my dreams, as there was a huge crowd of students walking I had to struggle to reach where she was standing, on reaching I saw her talking to a girl who was facing backwards to me so I could not see her face, on walking closer I realised the other girl also sounded familiar to me therefore I began to walk further to have a look was she really the one whom I was not expecting?

It was a shocker for me to find out that the girl was none other than Aditi, Aditi was a family friend our family shared great bonds together we have had been friends from couple of years and I had also heard from one of our friends that she had silently always liked me which I also felt by, how she behaved when I was around. I have always liked her company as a friend but never thought to pay any heed to her feelings as I could not reciprocate the same for her, I pricked up my ears to hear their conversation which sounded that they were very good friends which was absolutely a surprising news for me, I walked backwards in order to not catch her eyes. I was not really ready for this surprise cum tremor while walking down to my class room I kept thinking whether it was god's conspiracy or what to bring all three of us under the same roof, is this going to translate into a love triangle or is it going to destroy my chance of being with Pratiksha. Most ridiculous thought kept me engaged all throughout that day. That scene from the morning kept on playing in my head presenting the weirdest possibilities that were never going to happen but my anxious thoughts kept my rationality at bay, I could see nothing but my love nest being destroyed. Although Aditi was my very good friend but here in same school, she looked nothing more than an enemy to me.

Aditi was a very bold girl and she had insights about me in the school I tried hard to keep myself hidden from her during breaks but it was like writing on the wall, she knew my class and despite of my efforts she easily found me sitting in the corner hiding, even I was also frustrated with this monkey business of hiding and peeking so I decided to act normal such that she could know nothing about my feelings for Pratiksha. I did not want to have my feelings become the apple of discord between her and me. Along with that I even asked koshlesh and vijay to not utter a word about Pratiksha before Aditi.

I managed to continue this acting before Aditi for few weeks but only I knew how difficult was it for me to keep myself aloof of Pratiksha. This situation was absolutely opposite of what I have planned during the vacations but maybe it was god's will. I envisaged a scene where I and Pratiksha were spending quality time together but it was all a day dream nothing factual. This was the longest time ever since I took admission in that school where I did not admire her in the school the fear of being caught by Aditi encircled me always, what I feared the most was she may spill the beans of my cute love before my family. I also made sure to not be seen more often with her as it may give impression on Pratiksha's mind of us being together which was not at all true at least from my end.

While juggling with all these situations months passed and now it was the time of the biggest festival of Gujarat for which this state is famous worldwide. The festival of dance, fun, enjoyment, food, sleepless nights, and much more the festival of NAVRATRI. In Gujarat the Navratri are celebrated with GARBA a folk dance usually performed in large groups in circular motion during the evening till late night time. This festival is 9 days long where goddess Durga is worshiped and to take the blessings of deity people perform garba around the idol of goddess. People wear tradition dress specially curated for this festival for women it is called chaniya choli and for men it is either kediya or kurta payjama.

I have always wanted to see Pratiksha in the traditional attire and this time our school has organised one garba night thanks to which my desire of seeing her in chaniya choli would come true. And the best part about this garba fest was that it was organised coincidently on my birthday. I believed it was god's way of fulfilling my desire on my birthday. Ever since I got this news, I was super thrilled again my imagination was riding at the bullet speed. I had been ignoring her for over a month but that day nobody could dare to stop me I was over the moon I only wanted from God to grant me one wish that Pratiksha shall not miss this event as my sole purpose of attending that fest was to see her and nothing else. God has really been kind upon me to grant me what I direly prayed for.

GARBA NIGHT

I reached that evening to the school way before the stipulated time to not miss looking at my dearest Pratiksha, she was a bee in my bonnet I could not stop myself from thinking about her, I also decked up my newest pair of kurta and pyjama to rock the garba night, although I was never into dance and garba but the only thing fuelled my excitement was her presence. As it was my birthday and most of my friends and class fellows were aware of it, they came to offer me their greetings but the only greeting I prayed to get was hers but it was next to impossible as for me she was my world but for her I hardly ever existed.

"Ahha! Brother you seem to be full of joys of spring today" said koshlesh elatedly…

"Yes, why not after all its my birthday today" I replied cheerfully.

"of course, it's your birthday but the main reason for your cheerfulness is someone else which we very well know" replied vijay banteringly.

"Stop making fun of me guys, I am already very nervous today" I said.

"Nervous for what?" asked koshlesh with amusement

"What if she did not turn up today? All my imagination will be busted in air" I replied chipping my fingers

"Stop being a scared kitten, she will surely come, she loves to dance how can she miss this day. Don't lose your hope she will be here anytime soon". Replied vijay.

"Yes, you are right I should not be thinking negatively let's check out what are the arrangements and by the time she will be here" I replied and we began moving to see the arrangements for the garba night.

As we moved further, we saw a table at the centre of the ground decorated with lights and flowers, with the idol of goddess Durga around which several lamps were lit. traditionally this arrangement is done and is called as Gabbar. People do garba in a circle around this Gabbar and the songs chosen are especially created for garba which has anecdotes of goddess Durga and other Gods.

On the other side of this arrangements there were refreshments stall like a Chinese food counter, pav bhaji counter, south Indian food counter, pani puri counter, ice cream counter. And many more to add in the list. Our mouth was watering thanks to the aroma that has enchanted our brains to dine in to try the food.

The orchestra was doing their final checks with the mic and speakers for their performance, the vocalist was locally very famous for their melodious garba's which they sang, they wanted to make sure that the show goes uninterrupted due to any technical glitches and thus the ensured double checking of all their instruments. I was never a huge fan of garba night but this entire set up made me very eager for the programme to begin. Koshlesh and vijay were giving a hand with me in exploring the venue and waiting for the diva to walk in. As every minute passed my curiosity grew higher and it became next to impossible to wait more.

Students kept coming in and within no time the entire ground was filled with students decked up in traditional attires almost all the girls opted to wear Chania choli. My heart was sinking by seeing the clock ticking, the time was running by and there was absolutely no sign of her presence nor her close friends can be seen which kept enhancing my restlessness.

As per the schedule the programme for the evening began to start with the prayer to the deity which was performed collectively by our principal and trustee. Although I was physically present in the hall but my eyes were glued to the entrance looking for her, I kept praying to God to give me the present of her presence on my birthday. Finally, my wait was over, God answered to my prayers. The moment I saw her my body was sent to chills I had goosebumps over my body like someone moved a feather around my neck.

She looked drop dead gorgeous in her black and red chaniya choli, which was elegantly decorated with beads and cowries there were mirrors all around her skirt which reflected like diamonds as the light contacted them. With intricate embroidery work her skirt which added extra bling to her entire costume, the thread work had minute kutchkali art work demonstrated on the attire, her dress transformed her into the walking diva. She chose minimalist makeup with bold Smokey eyes and nude lips. Although she needed no makeup but the way she accentuated her eyes with indigo blue eye liner made her look beyond gorgeous.

I have always seen her dressed simply in the school uniform but her transition to this gorgeous diva seemed like a spell casted on me. Her oxidised choker with matching earrings and bangles suited perfectly with her eye makeup but the best part about her glamour was the twinkle in her eyes. I was floored to see her in this traditional avatar I adored her with argus eyes to remember even the smallest detail about her as if I had to appear for some examination on my observation skills. My friends tried to bring me back to my senses but I was not ready to leave her sight.

I was then forcibly taken by koshlesh around the food counter as all of my friends wanted to celebrate my birthday, they had set up a cake for me which was a total surprise for me. Seeing the table decorated with cake and candles I was touched by the loving gestures of my friends. That was indeed a pleasant surprise for me but I my heart was still wanting to leave the celebration at once and be back to the place where I was deeply indulged in appreciating her beauty.

Aditi also came to wish me and joined us in the celebration. I opted to talk less with her as I did not want Pratiksha to get any wrong signals for me, I felt guilty of bidding defiance at her but nothing else seemed more accurate for me back then. She was smart enough to gauge my awkwardness with her proximity and thus she chose to leave my side. I was very ashamed of my pretentious behaviour towards her but then I chose not to come up with my emotions driving my reactions and opted for a stone look at her.

Everyone was enjoying the evening so were we, koshlesh and vijay even went on the floor to do garba and insisted me to join them but I was enjoying the sight more and also, I had no history of ever going to the dance floor thus the thought of doing garba before a whole bunch of people petrified me. I saw Aditi giving me cold looks from the corner of my eyes but I took no cognizance of her and thoroughly enjoyed myself but relishing the snacks and treating my eyes with Pratiksha's killing dance moves. She had the looks to die for not only me but there were several other boys trying to catch her sight but she did not paid heed to anyone of us which kind of attracted me more towards her.

With every twirl she did her skirt flared with all those mirrors reflecting the light and the beads and cowries making the sound on being collided with one another I could pen every detail of her movement the sound of her anklets with every step she took, took away my heart. Everyone else present on the venue looked so plain as compared to her impeccable beauty. I enjoyed every microsecond of the evening till she was before me, but my heart sank to my stomach on hearing the announcement of the function being wrapped up. I was not ready to take that, I wanted it to last forever but hardly lasted for couple of hours. I saw her leaving the premises

I even secretly followed to escort her to her father's car waiting outside for her. And my wonderful reality and the wonderful evening ended.

My friends brought in cake for me to cut on my birthday and they had gathered ready with the cake when I saw the cake in their hands, I felt precious because it was the first time my friends had brought in cake for me. That was the best birthday I have celebrated with my secret crush not only that my friends surprise added cherry to the cake.

The only guilt that followed me back home was my inappropriate behaviour towards Aditi. I knew she had feelings for me and had always hoped for me wellbeing but during the cake cutting when I tried avoiding her, I could see the disappointment in her eyes. She chose to not confront me for my behaviour and acted normal before everyone else, however I knew this matter will again be discussed this time may be face to face. I was not ready to take that stress for the day and instead I chose to focus on all the wonderful memories of the evening and slept peacefully.

I was still in the hung over of her memories the next morning when I received a text from koshlesh:

"Hey I am extremely sorry dear, I forgot to give your gift and I guess I have lost it somewhere last night"

"it's okay dear your arrangement for the cake was more than enough, I need no other gifts than your friendship" I replied

"You are getting me wrong; I did not buy that gift for you. Aditi brought that for you yesterday but she did not give it to you in person instead she gave it to me to hand it over to you" koshlesh descriptively replied.

"What she had a gift for me? And she gave that to you? But why would she do that? Why did not she give it to me directly if she brought it for me?" I replied

"There is nothing to be perplexed at this, don't you remember how you ignored her I wonder why did not she smashed your face with that gift there itself" said koshlesh

"You are being so mean; you know very well why I behaved the way I did." I justified myself

"Let it be, I just wanted to inform you that last night Aditi came to me and asked me to give you the gift wrapped in a beautiful decorative paper, and she was very hopeful that you would like the gift very much, but as I was so engrossed in garba, therefore I asked vimlesh to keep it with him and return me as we returned, bit unfortunately both of forgot about the gift and it remained with him. I recollected about the present and called vimlesh only to know that last night his bicycle broke down returning home and while getting it fixed, he forgot it at the cycle repair shop and now upon re visiting that shop he could not find it. I am really feeling very much ashamed as she very responsibly handed me that box thinking that it would reach you, instead it was lost midway before reaching the real owner." Replied koshlesh

This entire conversation sent me on a guilt trip, I was already ashamed for my behaviour towards her and this fact that she thought for me and brought a present for me but hesitated to give me directly due to my ignorant behaviour towards her made me feel even worse for myself.

The way I treated her it was apparent that she was not willing to even see my face or talk with me and that's what I deserved but I felt sorry for my behaviour and thought of rectifying my error and to allay the matter. And thus, I decided to make up for my mistake by asking her out for a coffee.

Without wasting a moment, I sent her a text asking her to meet me at mech tea engineering café at 11am.

"Why?" she replied.

"I will tell you everything once we meet, kindly be on time" I replied and began getting ready.

I was not really very sure whether she would come or shall refuse to come because of the previous night.

The atmosphere at the mech tea engineering café was as usual sanguine, the place was perfect for hangout with friends and family not only that their flavoured teas were all very nice, Aditi loved drinking tea and what better place could I find for her to seek her apology. I saw her entering, but I could not make out from her face about her mood I was guilty but showed up with a confident face.

"Yes, why did you call me here?" asked Aditi without sitting on the chair.

"I will tell you everything but before that please be seated and, make yourself comfortable I said while pulling up a chair for her.

She gave me a very strong gaze while sitting…. Her eyes had a lot to say but she preferred silence.

"Why are we here what is the matter" she asked again

"I will tell you everything but first allow me to order something for you, masala tea and cheese chilli grilled sandwich will do?

She nodded in agreement.

I placed the order and then decided to talk about the elephant in the room.

"Thanks for your present Aditi" I said

"Ohh! So, you got the present. Did you like it?

"Not actually I haven't got the present, koshlesh told me about it but unfortunately he lost it somewhere so I have only got the news that you brought something for me but I could not get it though." I replied

Paroxysm was all over her face and it turned red. Very thoughtfully I picked that present for you and he lost it. How careless can a person be? She replied with dejection

I know dear I am sorry please forgive koshlesh for his carelessness and treat this as a peccadillo. Please don't hold any grudge against him.

Why not he deserves a retribution replied Aditi

Well, if that is the case then I also must be awarded with some retribution, because my behaviour towards you was also not apt yesterday. I spoke

Ohhhh! So, you did everything on purpose. But why and if everything you did was intentional than why are we here please throw some light upon what is going in your mind… Aditi replied in ambiguity.

I did not want my friends to tease me or either you but calling one another's name and thus I acted cold yesterday. You know we have been friends outside the school and we already have family relations but most of the people in the school are not aware about this and because of this I did not want to grab their attention and be the teased by names. you know how everyone in the school combine names to make fun of and or create fake pairs and that thought kept me stone cold yesterday to not gather eye balls on us. I seek your apology for that please forgive me, I was not trying to be pejorative towards you, only thing was I was trying to ward off stupid people. I replied in my defence.

Although this was not the absolute truth but she believed me and then we decided to talk less in the school premises to which she agreed. I did not want to let go her as a friend because we shared a very good bond but it was too early to unveil the secret of my attraction towards Pratiksha to her as I was not sure myself how would she process that information and thus kept it with me.

By the time our tea and snacks were finished she was back to being normal at least with me but was furious at koshlesh for misplacing the present for which I pacified her and she was happy again so was I to save my friendship.

She even took her enrage over a text to koshlesh blaming him for displacement of the present but was soon pacified when he sought her apology, though she was a bit cranky with her short temperament but was very genuine and very humble to forgive us.

I was happy to return home as the baggage on my shoulder of having done injustice to a friend was released and was feeling very light and happy to have all the puzzle pieces sorted as per my will.

Days passed by and now again the villain of our happiness, Diwali vacations were back, and my school romance was again brought to a halt and we were back to our mundane routine of going to classes appearing for tests and doing the practice for the upcoming board examinations.

NEW BIKE

I worked on how the way I looked during the vacations and took resort from certain personality enhancing videos to improve my personality and to look attractive I wanted to ensure that my looks matched with Pratiksha's eternal beauty, although all these thoughts were sown in my brains garden, still I wanted to do every bit to make her feel I did all these efforts for her. She was always in my thoughts in my prayers in my dreams I could not get over her. It is rightly said love makes you crazy and I had truly gone crazy.

Vacations were over I was super thrilled to see her again but it came as a surprise for me to see her coming on a new scooty pep plus whereas I came on a broken bicycle my naïve mind pulled me back to approach her thinking that she would judge me on the basis of my broken bicycle. I had one perception in mind back then that your status truly matters if you want to approach a girl which was an absolute bullshit, but still it mattered to me back then. I focused my ears on her conversation with her friend who was congratulating her for her new vehicle. To which she replied I promised my father to work hard for my studies and this is what he awarded me with, my first ever personal vehicle. I am so happy for this. Her smile was enough to tell the level of excitement she had.

On reaching home I raised a request before my father to buy me a bike and to support my demand I gave him reasons like I have to study hard and riding the bicycle to school and tuition kills a lot of time and also causes fatigue which adversely impacts my productive hours of study. My father found my demand appropriate although he had already agreed to buy me a bike for my college but then he agreed to by it 6 months prior to help me with my studies. My father had always been a very benevolent person but he was also a very responsible father before providing me the bike he made sure I got my learning license ready with me. He had always believed in inculcating lawful attitude in us, so within a week I also got my very first bike BAJAJ DISCOVER DTSI black and blue in colour, I was curious to flaunt it before my friends and classmate but more than anyone else I wanted to show it to Pratiksha.

Immediately after taking the delivery and getting the initial veneration of my vehicle done by mother, I took my younger brother for a ride; I was over the moon while riding the vehicle. My next destination was our tuition classes where I met vijay and koshlesh who were equally thrilled to see my new bike as. After the class ended all three of us went for a ride, koshlesh and vijay also drove the vehicle one after another to get their hands on.

I was very happy for my new bike I also wanted to never let down my parents' expectations they made sure to provide the best education and best facilities for me and in return I wanted them to be proud with my good grades for that I assured myself to push even harder with physics and maths to get the best results.

By now Pratiksha had realised about my craziness for her and she had caught me red handed multiple times admiring her to which she never objected neither gave any signs of discomfort, if at all she would have I would have instantly prevented myself doing anything which she disliked.

I took my vehicle on the next day to the school and parked It adjacent to hers, I had already made up my mind that as far as my bike was concerned it will always be parked adjacent to hers no matter whosoever parks besides her, I will pave a way to park my bike next to hers so that our vehicles will give us an opportunity to share proximity at the time of leaving the school. Not only this from the time she got her hands on her new scooty she had stopped being in the lobby during the recess and instead she preferred to sit on her vehicle which gave me a food for thought that someday she would grace my bike by sitting on it.

My mother being a firm believer of God tied an amulet on my bike to ward off any evil and prevent any accidents. I secretly brought one such amulet to tie on her scooty as well. One day without being caught by anyone I secretly tied the amulet to her vehicle such that it was not easily visible to anyone not even Pratiksha.

God was kind with his mercy upon me as he was fulfilling my petty wishes day after another. And very soon my desire to see her sitting on my bike was fulfilled, during the break when I was walking down the lobby towards the canteen my eyes caught the sight which by then I had only imagined and never saw it happening in reality. But it wasn't an imagination any more she was actually sitting on my bike with her one arm resting on the handle. I was on cloud nine to see she was touching something owned by me… I felt like a superstar had given me an autograph even more happy than that. Koshlesh was passing by when he noticed me giggling at the wall on his closer inspection, he got to know the reason for my happiness and he took no time to tease me asking for a treat. These small progress with my attraction were big things for me and my buddies celebrated even the smallest thing with me.

After the school ended, I came to my bike joyously feeling it everywhere Pratiksha was sitting and the handle at which she rested her arm there was still her fragrance felt at the surface of the bike. I touched it as if I was touching some fragile glass thing very cautiously that day, I became a little mean and did not allow my friends to come along on my bike as I wanted to feel her presence more and take her aura on the ride with me at which my friends were a little miffed with me, eventually they understood my emotions and granted my wish to drive alone.

She began sitting on my bike quite often as if it was a cryptic message for me that she liked me too but none of us had initiated any sort of communication between us and this brought us to the end of our school life. The principal announced for the farewell which was due to take place in 10 days for which if anyone was willing to perform the registrations were open. Although I was aware that our bond was about to end but was not ready for this to end so early. Days passed like the sand in hand and we were left with nothing but the final goodbye.

FAREWELL

I suggest you all to not miss farewell function as this is one such memory which you will be cherishing forever and taking along with you while parting away from this school. Advised the principal after the assembly on the day prior to our farewell. Although we were not going to miss this very special day but this announcement made our decision firm. Certain events are such in life which remain with us forever and I was hopeful farewell was going to be one such event for us.

The function was organised in the school auditorium, followed by dinner at the school campus. This was a tradition of the school to bid adieu to its students by hosting them a dinner party along with some entertainment right before the exams to provide the students with a time being relief from the exam stress and anxiety. It was also probably the last day when all the students were seeing each other as after this day reading vacations begin and only those students will come who have some doubts.

I could not miss this last chance of seeing her in the school, this thought of separation anxiety was killing me deep within this farewell was a weal and woe for me because on one hand I was happy that school were ending and we were on the last stage of completing the school and entering the world of college and real professional life after but alongside there was a pain which was hard to explain as I was not very sure will I ever be able to meet her again.

Like all other functions organised till then I reached way ahead of the time and began looking for her. I was curious to know if she had a performance to make. The auditorium began to fill up with students coming in. as our principal insisted all the students to not miss the event mostly all students made it to the event but my eyes were looking for that one familiar face which was enough to summarise my two years in that school. I grabbed a seat near where her friends were sitting hoping that she would probably sit next to her friends, finding me sitting there koshlesh and vijay joined me. Wating was in my fate she did not turn up on time even that night, meanwhile thoughts such that what if she was not going to come surmounted my brain, the trail of my thoughts was put to a halt when all the students stood up from their seats to welcome the principal who was on the stage to host the evening for us.

He welcomed us to the event and began thanking us for accepting their collective guidance provided by him and the teachers. He along with the trustees ignited the lamps and the function began with the prayer sung by students followed by short speeches from our teachers. All the teachers took the opportunity of guiding us once again for the life ahead. Till the time a student is in the school they are bound by a discipline of school and as soon as one enters the college the entire system changes flexibility is provided in terms of attending the class which mostly lures the students to bunk more often and they can be easily deceived by this fake freedom of choice which although is very appealing but may end up distracting them from their goals and that's when this valuable advice from the teachers steps in to be our guiding light and help us preventing getting derailed from our passion. It was very pleasing to hear from the teachers they sounded more like a friend and guide than the strict teachers which they have been in all those past years. All the students began cheering the teachers as their such friendly attitude towards us was very novel for all of us. Their words of wisdom made us all little emotional. School is not just the place to learn academic lessons it's the place where we grow over the period of 14 years it's a place which teaches us not only reading and writing but also instils values in us to transform into a responsible Smartian.

These emotional words of advice made me forget for a while about Pratiksha and then when I overlooked at where her friends were seated, I saw her sitting alongside them. She might have come when I was totally engrossed in listening to the teachers, I was glad to see her. She dressed simple but she looked magnetic effortlessly. God might have taken extra time while creating her personified features, her smile was so pure and magical that just by seeing her smile all your pains can be healed. Her glimpse was enough to take away all my worries, I had never felt so deeply in love for anyone like that before. Initially I also took that attraction as infatuation which usually occurs during adolescence. But this was hitting me differently, I had planned my future in my head along with her yet had not talked to her once in the past two years. I was brought back to my senses with the round of applause made by everyone for the words of wisdom shared by the teachers.

The contestants began their performance one after another, while we were having a great time letting ourselves loose of all the pre exam stress, the host for the evening announced the name of the next performer which brought me to surprise as it is was none other than Aditi, by the end of academic session all my friends were well aware that Aditi was the sister in law of my elder cousin and thus everyone took that as an opportunity to tease me, they have all noticed the awkwardness we shared if ever we crossed our ways in the school, we all were in that adolescent age were being teased by a girl's name meant nothing but some smoke of a brewing relation, back than even friendship was categorised as an affair this was the main reason why I ignored her as I did not wished to be linked to anyone apart from Pratiksha.

The lights went dim and she took her position at the centre stage and then the focus light was shifted at her, her ethnic attire which she donned was shimmering with the lights focus, she chose to wear a black golden sequined skirt with a matching blouse, her blouse was an embroidered one with ruffled sleeves and a contrasting dupatta which added the glamour to her dress. To ease her movements her skirt had a thigh high slit and she wore a colour coordinated leggings to cover her legs from exposing.

Her makeup was minimal yet radiant enough to make her glow in those dim lights. She accentuated her eyes with Smokey eye look and matching jewellery to add to her look. Her hairs were tied neatly in a bun and wore a head gear to complete her look her entire look made her different than usual. This was probably the first instance when I actually noticed her. She looked very pretty, when I was busy appreciating her beauty the beats of the song began playing.

It was one of the most popular chartbusters which was a recent release and was on every youngster's playlist, the song was the title track from the movie JHOOM BARABAR JHOOM it was an upbeat song which was on the lips of everyone present. The moment beats of the song began students hooted at their loudest pitch.

What an energetic performance it was! She danced like a professional dancer her moves were killer and she even mastered the hook step for the song, by far her performance was the best amongst all for that evening.

Koshlesh whispered in my ear "bro! she is so good at dancing. You haven't told me this before?"

"It the first time I am seeing her performing, although I have heard from my cousin that she dances well but never got the chance to see her performing, I am equally as shocked as you" I replied.

She brought down the house because of her dance performance. By the end of her performance all the crowd in the auditorium was dancing along sitting at their respective seats.

Even after her performance ended it was the talk of town for the evening. The host of the evening concluded the programme soon after all the remaining performances were over Aditi's name was once again called, although it was not a competition but to regard her efforts the principal awarded her with a present for performing with such grace, this sweet gesture from the principal was appreciated by everyone.

Later we were directed towards the area were the food and refreshment stalls were kept, I had my eyes on Pratiksha as I had especially brought the camera to the school to have her picture as I was pretty unsure to see her ever again after that night. The Romeo in me could not let my Juliet fly away without any photograph to cherish for lifetime.

I devised a plan along with koshlesh and vijay and asked them to help me getting the perfect picture. they asked me to stand in proximity with her without being noticed and they would pretend to capture my picture and shall secretly take her as well. The idea sounded full proof to me I thought this way I can get her picture and if I was lucky enough, I would also get a picture of us together, but it wasn't as simple as it seemed to be.

she was surrounded by her friends so were we, as it was officially the last day of school all the classmates were together reliving the memories of the school. And we lost the track of time while being with all our friends. Someone said perhaps this is the last time when we are seeing each other and after this day we will be sailing in our life's journey alone, hardly a few of us will remain in touch and the rest will forever be a part of memory.

Hearing this I recollected my wish to capture her image but by this time I have lost her sight. I scanned the entire venue tracing her when I saw her heading towards the girl's washroom where it was impossible for me follow her. I thought of waiting for her in a corner, when koshlesh came searching for me "what are you doing here?" I have been looking for you from a long time. I can't find Pratiksha has she left or what?"

"No, she has gone towards the washroom, I have seen her going that way and that is the reason why I am standing here" I replied

"Have you gone mad or what? Why are you making it so obvious with your acts that you are after her, doing so will make her furious, let's go from here we will think something different way to get the picture" replied koshlesh furiously

He then took me towards the lobby area where vijay was already present with a plan in his mind. He asked us to wait at the parking area as we have already had our dinner he said "no matter what she will surely come at the parking area let's just wait for her there by doing so we can surely get her picture".

We were really happy to hear such an excellent idea, immediately worked at it. A small mischief came in koshlesh mind. He asked us to move Pratiksha's vehicle to a different location doing so will ensure that she spends extra time at the parking area and this way we will get enough time to get the pictures clicked.

I was sceptical to bring this plan into action as it may invite troubles for us and especially for me as I wanted to have a good image in her heart and not the image of the boy involved in eve teasing and harassing innocent girls. I tried defending my stand before my friends but they were in no mood to listen. They hurriedly lifted her scooty from both ends and took it from one corner of the parking to the other, while denying them to do so I kept an eye if anyone was seeing us doing such mischief. Although my heart was screaming to not do anything to baffle her or make her furious but I joined the cult thinking that this might be the last chance of having an interaction with her or having her a memory of me even if it was a bad one.

We sat on her scooty and began taking pictures, not of her but of us seating comfortably at her vehicle this way we at least had a piece of memory with us, but this wasn't enough for me although I was picturising a scenario where we both were seated comfortably on her vehicle. I was brought back to the reality by the murmuring of my friends. We were waiting patiently for her and our wait was over after almost 15 minutes when we saw her entering the parking space.

At first there was composure on her face but as soon as she reached the place where she parked her vehicle and upon not finding her vehicle her face turned pale, she turned her head in every possible direction to find her missing vehicle. It hardly took 10 seconds for her to begin crying. That was the first time when I saw her crying and I felt guilty of being the offender.

Her friend was helping her to keep her calm and joined her finding her vehicle, we had our eyes on them but they took 5 minutes to notice us sitting there on her scooty, we were pretending to be unaware of the fact that the vehicle which we have chosen to sit belonged to them. While she was searching her vehicle, we manged to click her few photographs from a distance, but they ended up being blurred but even those pictures were a lifelong treasure for me.

There was a big relief on her face seeing her vehicle and she rushed towards us, we continued to act unaware but before she could reach us a boy called them from behind, he was the cousin of her friend who accompanied her in finding the vehicle. Her friend had called him to help them find her vehicle.

But for our bad luck he had somehow seen us doing the shifting mischief and now he brought these details before Pratiksha which made her face turn red.

She walked past us with a stone face and there was fury in her eyes as if she would spill the volcano of her umbrage on us but she chose silence over her anger. She silently took her vehicle and left and with this left my dream to capture her image. I was very much let down by my own self as I had never thought of bothering her but did despite of knowing the fact that, perhaps that was the last time we were seeing each other. God knows what destiny was beholding for us.

AFTER YOU ALWAYS

Board examination centres were allotted, I was more eager to know her centre than mine. Although there was no possibility of our centres being the same, I was still clinging to the hope of some miracle happening. Which ultimately did not happen but the arrangement was not that bad. Although we were not about to share the same centre but still our centres were within a radius of half a kilometre which was a good omen for a sycophant like me.

My studies were in tantamount with the effort I was making to befriend her, coz I could not let my father's aspirations down. I read day and night solved almost all test papers and a night before I was confident to do well in my exams. I wanted to make her mine but not at the cost of my family's aspirations. I had that in my mind that this attraction might be infatuation and this could not direct my future and thus I switched my focus more towards my studies than daydreaming about her.

After finishing up my exams I used to visit her centre thinking that I may catch her sight. For the first couple of days, I got nothing but sheer disappointment, I could see almost all the familiar faces but hers. Koshlesh joined me every day at this juncture to ease my search for her. As we had very less time to waste, we halted at that centre for 15 minutes and on getting disappointment left to our respective homes. But luck favoured me on the third day when I got to see her dressed in a white top and grey jeans. With a small backpack on her shoulder her watch dial was too big for her fragile wrists but she pulled it of very elegantly, her lustrous hair was tied in a messy bun. Her face looked less vibrant then always with puffy eyes might be due to lack of sleep.

I have had the knowledge that she was very studious and took even the smallest test very seriously. Now it was actually the board exams her such face was justified. I was waiting right outside the main entrance to find her. The moment she noticed me her smile disappeared may be because of the most recent parking blunder. She continued to walk indifferently but only her mind knew the anxiety. We had our eyes constantly at her when she walked past us.

As soon as she left koshlesh began following her.

"Stop! Why are we going after her? Our intention is not to intimidate her" I said

"I am not trying to intimidate her, we shall follow her from behind just to see where does she reside, so that even after your exams you can become the Romeo wandering outside her house" koshlesh replied.

"This would result in stalking. I don't want to hamper her privacy neither I want us to have a hooligan image in her mind." I suggested

"Nothing will happen you just sit quietly behind me, and let me follow her" koshlesh replied while racing the bike after her.

"let's go back to our route I don't want us to be those eve teasers who harass innocent girls, I have affinity for her but I cannot impose my affection at her. Love our attraction has to come naturally and not by imposing ourselves at her" I said firmly.

Hearing my strong denial koshlesh agreed and we dropped the idea of following her and later went back to our respective homes.

On the way back home koshlesh tried his best to convince me to follow her the following day but all his efforts were damp squib.

We had to appear 5 exams whereas those who belonged to commerce stream had to appear 7 exams that meant we had two days extra to admire Pratiksha. With our exams getting over koshlesh egged me on with several reasons to follow her home and as a result I came under his influence and agreed to his plan.

On the last day of Pratiksha's exam, we reached her school half an hour before the finishing time and took our position right before the gate. We had to cool our heels before she came out. as soon as she came outside, she noticed us but ignored us completely and walked past us. She might be wandering that it was the last day she was bearing our faces, little did she know our intentions were to show her our faces every now and then.

There was a composure on her face as it was the last exam, she dressed with an extra effort that day, wearing an A line dress, her hairs were put in French braid and had a tinted lip gloss on, which made her look radiant as always, she spent extra time in school parking than usual bidding the final adieu to her fellow mates. Most of the students had tears in their eyes while parting their ways back to their home. Some were even celebrating by signing at the back of one another's clothes to cherish these clothes as a piece of reminiscence. I saw her filling scrap books and she also made a beautiful one for herself in which her friends were filling up their details and not only that they were writing few loving sentences for her. This practice was mostly followed by girls and for boys it was a bit too creative thing that hardly anyone took the pain of doing so.

Post this separation ritual she left for her house she was accompanied by one of her friends whom she was to drop possibly, I and koshlesh were ready to take our mission further while I was sitting behind keeping an eye on them koshlesh took the command of riding the vehicle. We were sneakily following them at a safe distance. But because there were couple of schools on the way the crowd of students on the road made this tracking a little more difficult than usual. There were instances when we lost them from our sight and then after looking for them round the corner, we found them.

After going for about 2 kms she took a halt near an apartment to drop her friend. She was left alone on her vehicle as she moved towards her house. By that time, we brought our vehicle in proximity to not lose her site. I had my eyes fixed at her like binoculars as I was very hopeful with this plan.

After riding for further 2 kms she took a right turn towards the platinum apartments we saw her entering inside after nodding her head to the security guard. her this gesture ensured us that it was her residence. Waiting outside the apartment we saw her parking her vehicle in 'D' BLOCK. But her flat no was still unknown to us. I tried following her inside but the security asked me to enter my personal details before getting inside the society. By the time I could fill in the details she was already gone. Also, I did not want myself to get caught so abstained myself peeking every flat of her block.

"Did you get her flat? "Asked koshlesh curiously.

"No not yet may be next time" I replied with a blissful smile on my face.

"Then why are you smiling like an insane" asked koshlesh

"Because I am very happy as I can come to see her anytime, I like". I replied

"You have gone mad in love" grinned koshlesh

"Yes indeed". I blushed.

"You need to be cautious we cannot always come here and stand here like mannequins this may invite further trouble for us as well as for her" suggested koshlesh.

"Yes, you are right this way someone from the society can get annoyed with our presence and they may raise an objection on our presence" I agreed.

"let's befriend this shopkeeper, this way no one can suspect our reason for being here" suggested koshlesh while pointing out at the store near her apartment.

I liked the idea and we then went ahead to get something from the shop in order to establish friendly relationship from the shopkeeper.

God was kind enough that the shopkeeper hailed from my native village and this way within no time we befriended him and now the path was clear for us to stay near her apartment for as long as we wanted.

The following days were bright and colourful for me, post my exams I had nothing to look for, then dreams of having her in my life. Although I was worried about my future plans but those thoughts were not as dominant as this one. As the exams were followed by vacations till the result were announced which resulted in a long deserted time span when I got to realise that she left with her parents on holidays, road next to her apartment was my oasis I spent my lonely hours there thinking about her return at times I was accompanied by vijay and koshlesh but they also went to their respective maternal homes to enjoy the vacations.

After a couple of weeks while I was standing outside her apartment, I saw her coming out along with her father on a bike, I was delighted to know that my exile had finally ended. I was elated to break this news before my friends and when I did their immediate question was "did you find out her house number as well?". My enthusiasm deflated as soon as I heard this question, and I replied in disappointment. My friends cheered me up and assured me that finding it won't be an uphill task. But I was a scared for that matter I did not have that audacity to knock on every door as I did not want my impression to be that stalker which harasses you at the back street.

Although my desperation was increasing day by day, I stood outside the apartment every evening glancing at every balcony thinking that it was hers, as I was so frequent with my visits to her locality, I came in the eyes of the locals I could figure out that the elderly people of the society gave me absurd looks which made me conscious.

I asked koshlesh to join me as standing alone was making me get in the eyes of the people but koshlesh who was pretty sure of his bad performance during the exam chose to not join me and stayed back to read to qualify the exams during the retest. When I asked him to wait till the results were announced his reply was, he already knew he was going to fail in physics as he has not attempted the questions and those which he has attempted aren't enough to get him close to passing marks.

Having received the denial from koshlesh I asked vijay who agreed and he also suggested to call manoj Gohel although he was not in our school, we studied in the same tuition classes not only that all of us shared a good bond and knew everything about my insane love story. When I offered him to join us, he was more than happy to join as they all enjoyed pulling my leg and with this invite, I was welcoming the new opportunities for them to pull my leg.

Manoj was jovial by nature he brought light to the ambience just by his presence, his sense of humour was the best amongst us and made sure that everyone around him always had a smile on their faces by the virtue of his witty replies and the little harmless mischiefs' he did. I was glad he was to join me as I knew he had that courage to peek into a stranger's house without being caught for his intentions, he had this charm in him to talk with anyone and befriend them in no time. He had that quality at which I sucked.

The next day we drove to her apartment on my bike and positioned ourselves at the small bridge over the canal in a way that we had our eyes on maximum number of houses on D BLOCK so that we can eye and find her exact flat number. Manoj was very thrilled to join us, and was churning his brain to get new tactics to help me get the house number. He came up with numerous silly ideas which we rejected as soon as we heard but then he came up with a contrivance.

Manoj said "out of all three of us Pratiksha has never seen me as I was not in your school, this means if I go inside to check she would not even know that you are somebody after this."

The idea seemed to be promising to both of us and thus we decided to give it a green flag. Although I agreed but was still underconfident that what if tables turn for us, and what if manoj lands in trouble.

I was in the middle of these thoughts when manoj shook me to bring me back from my thought gallery,

"You are an ideal daydreamer, within no time you are in your own journey of thoughts, manoj said talking a dig at me. What is her surname? He added

"What do you want to do with her surname, are you trying to match their kundali for the wedding, vijay said winking his eyes"

"No silly I want to know her surname so that I can knock at only those doors with the that surname and not only that I can even check for the surname at the block residents list, in most of the societies now a days are equipped with the name plate against every house number this way I can figure out her house very easily". Replied manoj

Hearing such thoughtful strategy from him we both were taken a back as we have always seen him as someone talking rubbish all the time and such wisdom coming from him over such problem was a miraculous event for us.

"I was wondering why did not I think about it, maybe well even if I did, I would not have had that courage to go upfront directly like manoj had, while I was consumed in my thoughts, I heard vijay giving the reply on my behalf.

"It is Chauhan, you can go and look for the surname Chauhan. Vijay replied

"Okay guys wish me luck mission house hunt is on, I hope I don't return empty hand" manoj said waving at us and heading towards her society.

We kept an eye on him till he disappeared and were waiting for his return, while vijay was busy with his phone my eyes were glued at the premises thinking for his return and constantly praying that everything happens in our favour.

Manoj chose to take stairs so that he can assess each house to know on which floor did she stay.

There were 4 houses on each floor and he checked every nameplate to make sure he did not miss any house.

There were couple of houses locked, only till he reached the third floor there were some signs of home as one nameplate of house number 303 said CHAUHAN'S in order to be sure he then went up to all the remaining floors and fortunately there was only one house with that surname.

He then came back at the house number 303 and rang the bell, a lady in her late thirties dressed in a saree opened the door

Yes, asked the lady with a questionable face.

"Hello mam can I meet girdhari sir?" asked manoj will a genuine expression such that he was really looking for girdhari sir.

"There is no one with that name residing here replied the lady humbly

"Oh, I am sorry to have bothered you. Can you please guide me towards his home if you are aware of it" asked manoj

The lady replied giving a confused expression, I am sorry beta I am not aware of someone with this name living in this block I guess they might be living in some other block but still to ensure she confirmed with the neighbour peeking out of her house.

"Mrs. Mehra do you know someone called girdhari living in our block?

No, I don't think so anyone with this name resides here replied the neighbour.

"I am sorry to bother you for the inconvenience aunty, actually I was given this address and therefore I came here, possibly this might be an outcome of some confusion. Thanks for your cooperation. Replied manoj trying to look inside the house to ensure if it was her house or not.

The lady with at most grace replied its okay beta you can inquire with the guard maybe he can help you find the house.

"Thank you so much aunty, can you please get me a glass of water requested manoj in order to peek further into the house.

The lady was very generous and instantly accepted his request for a glass of water and went inside to grab one.

While she left the door half open manoj got a glance at the living room where a girl was taking tuition on closer look, he identified the girl as he had already seen the picture clicked at the farewell and within no time, he knew she was none other than Pratiksha and he had achieved victory in his mission.

By that time the lady returned with a glass of water which he drank and after expressing his gratitude left.

I saw him returning from the building raising his collar and there was a different swag in his walk as if he was depicting his victory through that walk, his body language said it all that he had found the house.

When he told us the entire incident, we laughed out loud. I thanked him for his help as I would not have had that courage to go and find her house.

Thanks to my fried I had climbed one more step of the ladder for my love.

CALLING TO SAY HELLO!

I was joyous of celebrating this tiny little achievement, although it wasn't any achievement at all but for me to have her address felt like I have received the most precious stone on earth, I never felt this crazy before. I was aware of the fact that certain things could trigger the hate emotion immediately in her heart for me but I was unable to help myself from doing so. There was only a very thin line in me being transformed into a stalker as invading a person's private space amounts to stalking which I was doing but was still naming it as love.

While all this was taking place in my life, I have been simultaneously ignoring one person that was none other than Aditi I often received calls from her but I knew she had a bubble of affection towards me which I surely did not want to inflate; I was already mad after Pratiksha and I did not want Aditi to grow crazy after me.

I was very overwhelmed to have received her address that day, I did not take a second to of receiving the call coming on my mobile without even seeing who the caller was.

"Where the hell have you been? Why were you not answering my phone calls?" asked the caller

It took me fraction of seconds to know who she was, none other than Aditi from whom I was constantly absconding and now she was there encountering me for being disappeared.

"Ohh hi I am extremely sorry I have been snowed under some work and hence could not catch up with you, I am extremely sorry for ghosting you, you can be angry on me for this act of mine but I seek your sincere apology for the same" I replied

"Do not try to act so innocent and brush away all your negligence I do not appreciate this behaviour of yours". replied Aditi

"Sorry dear please forgive me this time" I said

"You dance really well I was never aware of your killer dance moves. I had seen you dance during the cousins wedding but I was never aware that you have such great proficiency in dancing" I added

"You would only know this if you would have time to talk with me, but as usual you are always piled up with work and have no time even for texting" replied Aditi

I further asked for an apology from her.

My words melted her heart and then we were back on our usual talks. After a couple of minutes of talking usual, I asked her something upon hearing which her eyeballs enlarged.

"Are you friends with your seniors in school, I have seen you talking with one girl from class 12 in our school. I asked

"Oh, so you have your eyes on me during school?" she asked in a flirtatious manner

"No, it's not like that I have seen you talking with her and hence asked" I replied

 Yes, I know her she wanted to learn dance moves from me and thus we were talking that day" she replied

"Do you mind me asking if you have her contact number?" I asked

 "Why do you want her number, she is not even from your stream" she asked out of intrigue.

"Actually, I needed her number for some work" I replied hiding my nervousness from her.

"I do not have her number we have had the conversation in the school only" he replied.

"Can you please do the favour to get me her contact number, as the schools have been over now, I do not have any other source to have her number. I spoke.

Hearing this she got really upset and banged the phone; I regretted asking her that question but then I was again back to my fairy land of getting Pratiksha's address.

My chain of thoughts broke when my phone rang and again it was Aditi.

 I wondered why did she call me without thinking much I answered:

"write" she said angrily

"Write what" I asked

"Grab a piece of paper and pen, and write what I say" she replied the anger still continued in her voice.

"7651309870. Happy" she dictated.

"What is this" I asked.

"You are not somebody who suffers memory loss this is what you asked for" her humour is bang on when she is angry.

Yet again she banged up the phone,

For a moment I could not believe my fate as If God was readily sitting to grant me my wishes, one after another.

One the same day I have had her address and now her personal contact number as well. Was that really a dream or the reality seemed like the most beautiful dream but indeed it was the most amazing reality for the day.

My smile was hard to hide and my teeth showed up the whole night it felt like I won the greatest treasure of my life.

It was pretty difficult to absorb the pleasant shock of the day that kept me awake entire night, I was suspicious what if Aditi was playing a prank on me and the contact number was incorrect/ in order to not be fooled I decided to make a call on the given number.

My heartbeats were louder than the phone ring. My curiosity was driving me crazy; I was hopeful that it was really her number but simultaneously I had that in my mind that, Aditi might be tricking me. To know what the fact was I had to make that call. My mind was surmounted with ample thoughts. Although I had rehearsed thousands of times in my head what will be I asking on that call but still my tongue was glued to the surface of my mouth.

A melodious voice from the other end answered the call and greeted "hello"

This word was enough for me to know that it was her number and it was her on the other side. I was so lost in the thoughts that I lost the sense of time and did not respond;

"Hello, who is this? She asked again.

Hiding the nervousness in my voice I responded "hello, may I speak with Ramesh?"

"I am sorry you have dialled wrong number." She responded.

"May I ask you who are you" I asked, believing to not get an answer for this absurd question but still trying my luck.

"I am Pratiksha, and there is no one named Ramesh here, please check the number you have dialled. She replied and disconnected the phone.

That was probably the best conversation I have ever had in my life, my heart was blooming I felt very happy, this was for the first time when I felt grateful to Aditi for having me step further in my life.

Pratiksha and her thoughts were something which I could never get enough of and thanks to Aditi and manoj now I felt even closer to her than before.

After a while I sent her a text message saying "hi"

Few minutes later she replied in a very dignified manner "sir, you are approaching on a wrong number please don't message again on this number."

"Hi, actually I have messaged on the correct number, earlier I was just confirming whether it was really you Pratiksha. I am vinay from your school I guess you recognize me" I replied

My heart was pumping blood at the double rate while I awaited her response which took a while.

After almost 15 minutes the response came which deflated the balloon of happiness in me, although I was expecting to not hear anything good but her response was furious and reflected that she hated me invading her private space.

The message read "who gave you my number, better not to ever message or call me again and if I catch you doing so, I shall take no time in raising an complain against you to my father and not only that I will also take stringent action against you with the help of police. I do not appreciate this behaviour of yours."

I was stunned to read this but at the same time I was also petrified to cause any trouble to Pratiksha and thus I decided to not do anything against her will.

"I am sorry this won't be repeated" I replied and thought not to take the conversation ahead.

I felt really sad that I could not help myself dialling her number from different numbers just to hear her voice. Although I was doing something against her will but I felt that one day she will understand my pure feelings for her and she will understand my genuine love for her.

This disappointment was not enough and to add my misery the results were announced I scored really well beyond my expectations my marks were good enough for me to pursue my dream career. My friends and I have always wanted to go for mechanical engineering and my family was also hopeful for my bright future. But the thought of separating from Pratiksha held me for going with my will, I was reluctant to leave the city and this decision of mine was not supported by anyone not even my friends who exactly knew why I was not willing to pursue engineering.

Vijay moved ahead by saying that I was going to repent on this foolish decision. He worked his bone to convince me that I was not being wise in opting for BSC as it was like digging up my own grave but I was ready for it not at the cost of leaving Pratiksha.

My parents had high hopes with me and they were really pissed off with my sudden change in plan. They were not prepared for this but then they somehow swallowed the disbelief in me and allowed me to go ahead with BSC.

"At first you have started a battle in the house for not allowing you to take science because you wanted to be an engineer and now suddenly you have changed your mind and want to opt BSc. Is this some kind of a joke for you." Said my father.

Vijay, manoj moved ahead to Bhopal and took their admission in one reputed engineering college of Bhopal. But they still had one month for their college to open and thus they gave me company more often to the university where I had applied for taking admission in B.Sc.

DECISION OF REGRET

I was too naïve to take any decisions and the ones which I took in adolescence were soon going to show their after effects, the strongest of them being the disappointment on my father's face. I have dreamt of doing something big enough to make my father proud of me but this was something which he might have never expected out from me but somehow allowed me to go ahead, I then took the admission in M.G. Science college to pursue B.SC.

By repeatedly keeping an eye on Pratiksha's whereabouts I got to know about the college in which she took admission and luckily that college was near my college almost 3 kms apart which gave me an advantage to see her more often after my classes were over. Her college had already opened and there was still one weeks' time in me to open therefore I preferred to stand around her college camouflaging myself in order to avoid being caught vijay accompanied me sometimes as he was busy with his packing for shifting to Bhopal.

One afternoon when I was hiding near a food stall, I overheard a group of students relishing their snacks talk about how they were going to celebrate the friendship day which was round the corner. Usually, these days are mostly popular among the young boys and girls. I was in that phase of my life where all my attention was diverted towards Pratiksha and this being the day to celebrate friendship, I found it as an opportunity to befriend her as talking on the calls and through the messages was a total failure and thus, I thought of trying my luck with the friendship band.

I expressed my earnest desire before vijay and seemed to encourage my idea of taking that day as an opportunity and thus we curated a strategy and for that an evening before we went to the market to buy the best available band. After browsing my eyes all over the stores to find the perfect band I settled with a charming dainty bracelet which was more of a daily wear accessory rather than a simple band, I thought that if she liked it, she would continue to wear it even after the friendship day has passed which will be a souvenir with her and will remind her of my existence.

While I was taking too much time to select vijay was irritated to say that I was not there for valentines shopping but little did he know what I was actually feeling. I wanted to give her the best and that being my first ever gift or memory for her I wanted to ensure that it was worth remembering.

Next morning, I and vijay reached near her society and positioned ourselves about one kilometre away from her residence on her college route. In order to ensure that we could locate her we kept an eye on both the possible routes which she might take to reach her college. I was well acquainted with the usual route which she took and thus we remained standing at that route on the narrow passage so that we can stop her midway, and 15 minutes later I saw her coming on the same route where we were standing.

As she was approaching ahead by heart was racing in corelation with her vehicle speed could hear vijay guiding me to stand in between the road, it was a passage hardly used by people therefore there were no plying vehicles. I stood in the middle of the road, my feet were shaky enough to catch attention, my hands went cold I was holding the bracelet in my hand. She noticed me standing in the middle of the road but instead of stopping she raced her vehicle to cross me in haste, I guess she was equally nervous to see me standing there. She crossed me but vijay was standing behind me to block her road further, she gave him the fiery gaze even vijay was taken aback to see her furious gaze.

She landed her feet on the ground from the vehicle to maintain her balance and then yelled at vijay

"Get out of my way right now"

Her fury was evident as we were the culprits of invading her private space,

This act was the final nail on the coffin, she went badly upset with us and her eye balls began collecting tears which she was trying to control and put up a brave front. Her eyes were dazzling flames of fury. I have always seen her poise and calm and this side of hers was absolutely novel for me.

I indicated vijay to leave her path and to allow her to go. But vijay was reluctant and kept on saying "it's the best opportunity, we will not be getting this golden chance again"

He insisted on me to tie the bracelet on her delicate wrists. I could not bear her seeing so pissed off at us. Every time I tried getting closer to her always ended up being more apart this was heart breaking for me to see her crying.

The constant push from vijay made me do the unthinkable, while she was constantly giving me those tough looks, I softly pulled her hands and tied the bracelet around her arms.

She pulled her arm back in retaliation and murmured something which was inaudible for me, but she deserved an apology from my end for which I did not think a second thought.

"I am sorry for all this but I genuinely want to become your friend and that is it I am not here to expect anything beyond friendship and also, I am sorry to have taken this recourse for becoming friends. I should have tried the usual way but unfortunately, I was not able to gather that courage during the school although I tried a lot but failed miserably every time I tried." I said this apology before her, towards which she did not pay any heed.

Pulling her hand away from mine, her eyes showed a slightest presence of calmness in them but still they had tears deposited which would anytime begin the downfall for which neither I was ready nor I ever wished to become the reason for her pain and sorrow.

She said in a very heavy voice "please allow me to go. if anyone sees us here like this, they will create judgments about me and if by any chance my family gets to know about this, I am going to land in a big trouble…I request you to vacate my way so that I can go."

Upon hearing this we immediately spared her way. and she left but my heart was heavy seeing her cry. In order to check if she was okay and was not crying further during her way to college, we followed her but this time from a distance only to ensure her safety.

This incident made me rethink about my acts and then I thought what I really wanted. Everything I was doing was not a part of me and my personality and this way she was getting to know an altogether different vinay which I never wanted. She should only know who I actually was and not this road side sycophant lover who wanted the girl by all means.

Although I wanted to become the hero in her life my activities were translating me into a villain. Thereby I decided to not follow her any longer and if destiny had anything for us it will take its own course but buy harassing an innocent girl will not make me more masculine.

***

Life went on to become difficult as the days passed, my friends moved to Bhopal as the time approached for their sessions to start. Vijay left trying hard enough to convince me to come along he more often said.

"I am again warning you, this love is going to take you nowhere, focus on your career now this is not the time to become a Romeo instead it's the time to sculpt your life the way you want it"

But these words of wisdom passed my ears without reaching to my brain all I had in my mind was that although we were not together yet but if I left city, I will not even have the access to her wellbeing which was quiet a big bargain for me back then and thus I resisted all the temptations coming through my way.

My obduracy led me to M.G. SCIENCE COLLEGE, I began going to the college although I had no interest in the course which I was pursuing, but all I was doing for Pratiksha but unfortunately thanks to the friendship day incident I stopped following her neither I went to her college nor near her apartment to have a glance her divine face, the only place where I could see her was in my thoughts and my heart, she stayed in my heart 24*7 I slept and woke with her thoughts.

Staying in the city within a radius of 5kms and still not being able to see her proved very difficult for me, the days were hard but the nights were everlasting and where most difficult for me to pass. Motivated by avarice, I dialled her number using different mobiles from my house only to hear her voice but I could not continue to do that as I had committed myself of not troubling her any further.

In order to cure my heart and not do anything which can further aggravate the matter I began a part time job during the night so that I was not left alone with her thoughts and I could surf myself out from the ocean of love which I had created in my head. This was peculiarly the time where I felt the dire need of my friends around but when I looked back there was no one I could share my feelings with. Neither I was having a very close association with my siblings where I could speak my heart out nor I had my friends left in the city.

I killed my time by attending college during the day and during the night time my abode was the showroom of TATA motors. I have always had an inclination towards cars and before I was crazy for Pratiksha the only thing which moved my heart were cars, I loved driving them and this job was the ultimate solution as it brought me closer to my first love cars. This strategy had helped me overcome her thoughts and within a couple of days I started enjoying my nights at the showroom, there were hardly two or three of us at the showroom during the night this pleased me more as I was a night owl and solitude lover, this helped me bring my thoughts in alignment.

I was very happy with my routine and finally I was involved into something which helped me get over her memories. Saturday nights where my favourites as maximum staff was on leave and I get to spend most of the time observing the beautiful luxury cars lined up in the showroom.

On one such Saturday evening I was listening to the radio to kill the time as there was nothing to do, I had already completed my work for the evening I saw a brand-new tata indigo in the colour white, it was a brand-new car brought in the showroom for display the previous day only, its paint was glossy enough for me to see myself in it. Admiring its beauty, I felt an urge of getting inside the car.

It had been a month since I joined this place and thus, I was well acquainted with the placements of everything, at first, I resisted the temptation of getting inside the car but then on giving a second thought at it I thought the following day was Sunday and no staff shall be visiting the office and this thought gave my temptation a spark to go ahead. I then went on to fetch the keys from the drawer and as the drawer opened, I saw a treasure full of keys belonging to different cars. Labels were attached to each key for identification this made easier for me to find the key I was looking for.

Curiosity surmounted me as I approached the car, although I was not getting paid for doing this but my dire urge made me do this with thrill. I got inside the car and this was the first time I was looking at the interiors of this newly launched tata indica and they were absolutely neat and beautiful. The sweet fragrant smell from the car air freshener enhanced the experience of being inside the car even more relaxing. I had tried my hands on cars from different brands but not tata and having seated on the driving seat gave me the goosebumps to ignite the engine.

It had a powerful engine yet the car was silent it, best of engineering was used to make the car, holding the steering wheel I felt very powerful. I turned around and looked back to find no one in the office. I ignited the engine to start the car and slowly took it to the first gear releasing the clutch and hurray I was moving. This adrenaline rush pumped my blood faster to my heart, my heartbeats raced I could hear my heartbeat like the clock ticking. This was the result of the fear being caught, but I went ahead and drove the car into the showroom compound which was large enough to give a short ride.

I took 4 to 5 rounds of the compound which made me supremely happy. I was in that age where all these little things matter a lot and I felt like I have got a topic with which I can flaunt about the insights of my happening job profile which allowed me to drive newly launched cars which were not accessible for most of the people of my age. Back then in those years riding a car was a mammoth task unlike today, I felt very proud of me that I had that skill at a very young age.

I was baffled of being caught on the following Monday but it was not taken into consideration by any staff of the showroom and since then I waited for the Saturday evenings, to have the joy for not only that particular evening but for the whole week that kept me going. Finally, I had something which made me happy and I was out of that depressing zone in which I have slipped myself in.

One Saturday night after riding the car I was in a jubilant mood and was feeling like a king who had recently conquered the most effluent kingdom, without taking a second thought I grabbed my mobile to send a text to Pratiksha, although I had promised myself of not doing so but unfortunately, I could not keep the promise I made to myself, earlier there was no option like delete for everyone, once it was sent, it was received by the recipient.

It has been almost 15 minutes since I sent the message and was badly regretting every following second when I was brought back from my self-humiliation by the notification pop up in my inbox. It was a reply from an unknown number which read:

"Hi I am Pratiksha this is my personal number from now on save this number for further conversations"

For a flash of second, I could not believe my fate, I had to pinch myself to ensure it was not a dream, but I actually received a message from Pratiksha.

Without any further ado I bumped on to begin the conversation with her

"Hi Pratiksha, hope you are doing good" I replied

I eagerly waited for her reply but did not hear from her this time my curiosity was unescapable I waited but during this time of waiting my brain was flooded with different different thoughts, it was like a mixed feeling, the feeling of happiness for hearing from her but simultaneously the anxiety of what would she think of me after that friendship day incident.

Seconds turned into minutes and minutes turned into an hour but I did not receive any response for my message. At first, I thought she might have slept and therefore, I did not receive any response from her. But I responded to her message immediately after receiving her message. This entire process did not take more than 45 seconds, this math made me sceptical that she deliberately ignored my message.

My brain was hammering me with hundreds of thoughts per minute. It was already half past 10 in the night and maybe it was not the appropriate time to call anyone but without any hesitation I dialled her to get a closure about her take.

I could hear my heart beats more than the phone ringing and was desperately waiting for her to answer.

"Hi Pratiksha, how are you? I hope I haven't disturbed you from your sleep?" I said calmly in order to hide my anxiety.

There was silence from the other side for a couple of seconds.

"Hello Pratiksha am I audible" I said on getting no response for my earlier question to begin the conversation.

"Who the hell are you to call Pratiksha at this odd hour of the day" a roaring voice of a male came from the other side of the receiver.

This up roaring voice frightened me, at first, I felt the phone was answered by either her brother or father. Therefore, I held my composure to ask.

"Can I talk to Pratiksha; I am her classmate" I replied to get Pratiksha on line.

"No, you are not, I know you are not her classmate instead you are the on troubling her from quite a few days," he replied.

Hearing this my eyes literally popped out as I believed she would not have disclosed this before her family, then I thought to myself who he was.

"Who are you? I asked.

"I am Mehul Gadhvi, Pratiksha's fiancé, we will be married in a couple of years and with this information I presume you will not be troubling her any further, and if I get to know you did something beyond your limits, the outcome will not be favourable for you." He replied aggressively.

I was shaken to hear this news but I did not want to show it before him that I was broken to hear that news, putting up my bravest front forward I replied.

"Watch for your words and don't try to threaten me as I also have my good contacts which will equally be harmful for you, I would appreciate if you keep your warnings with yourself and as far as this call is concerned let's handle the matter practically like grownups"

He was not ready to hear something like this from me, and therefore he was also taken a back but then he agreed to follow my advice.

We then concluded to not call or message any further. It was the most difficult for me but then I had no other option before me.

I saw my love story ending before it could take its first flight and she was gone, keeping an eye on her whereabouts I never bother to stay updated with what was actually happening in her life.

I was totally devasted, following nights were sleepless I kept on judging myself for the decisions I had taken in the past one year, I saw castle of my dream collapsing right before my eyes. Words of vijay kept on echoing in my head it was like all playing in head in loop, a loop which was difficult for me to escape.

My part time job which once I liked was now haunting me. I had no true friends besides me vijay and manoj had left and although koshlesh was there but he was then dealing with his own set of problems and therefore I could not ask him to linger around me all the time to get me out of this heartbreak.

I had even tried making new friends but failed miserably. My anxiety led me to often explode before my loved ones which further dragged me in introspection that what was I doing with my life then. While people of my age were busy in making their career and building their fortunes I was going through heartbreak and was even hopeless to see myself struggling even to do the daily chores of my life.

When I looked back at myself, I was the pride of my father he believed in me and now I was nothing but a cause of worry for him. I had my heart into absolutely nothing, I did not go to college and for the entire time I was home I was lying in my room not interacting with anyone and not even bothering to know what was going on in the family. My mother tried multiple times to get the reason behind my sadness but her entire attempts failed.

This sort of depression lasted for the entire semester and likewise one year passed. This entire incident made me introspect my decisions and I had no other options than to move on. One evening I was weeping about how my life was going on before vijay, he did not take much time to come up with a suggestion.

"Hey! Stop being a cry-baby, whatever happens, happens for our own good, God might be directing you to a new path in your life, now instead of weeping and living in the past come back to the realities of life. Face your fears and begin thinking how do you want to sculpt your life. I have been hearing this drama of yours from past couple of years I have already warned you before you took that decision of staying back. Now what do you want? for one girl are you going to forget everyone who loves you, who is emotionally attached to you, who wants to see you always happy. By being such a sadist, you are not only suffering yourself but are also ensuring everyone in your family suffers too" vijay said reprimanding me.

No, I screamed this is not what I want, I want everyone to be happy I added.

Then instead of finding your entire happiness in one girl who don't even bother about your existence kindly focus what and who you have with you during your thick and thin times. You have always wanted that your father should be proud of you, is this how you are going to make him proud of you. Vijay said but this time in a swifter tone.

You are right but I am totally lost even if I try, I have no focus with me. I don't want to see her still I take the same route hoping she may also take the same path and our ways match unlike our destiny. I said with a heavy voice, because I have been holding on my tears before vijay.

He gauged the pain in my voice and took no time to deviate from the topic of my depression and slowly slid my attention towards other baseless conversations.

After a few minutes when I was calm enough to hear and absorb his ideas, he then asked something which I was not at expecting.

"Are you still interested in pursuing engineering? If yes then why don't you come here with us. This will solve all the problems you are currently tackling in your life. And trust me you will have a better opportunity for your career. He said in a promising tone.

"Bhopal, engineering, I always wanted that but due to my stupidity I am stuck here thinking that nothing is left in my life. Begging before you to help me find new horizon. This past year has snatched my original personality and has turned me an eccentric, you are absolutely correct I have so much to look upon instead of being selfish which I already had been previously I should consider my loved ones. Their happiness is equally important than mine." I replied wiping of the tears from my cheeks.

"How would I convince my parents, earlier they protested my decision for B.sc and now again I am ready for a new voyage." I added

"don't worry I know your parents are supremely concerned with your happiness and if you convince them with conviction they will surely agree.' Replied vijay

"Yes! Thank you, brother, for shedding the load I have been carrying on my shoulders from the past days. Your words were the exact advice which I needed to hear at this time. It's the first time in days I am feeling so relieved. Thank you again for changing my perspective towards the brighter side." I replied overwhelmingly.

As the call disconnected, I was disconnected with the hardship I have had in the last years. I reconciled every problem in my way, this time I was more driven towards the solutions rather than bragging about the problems my way.

It was a little difficult to win my parents confidence back in me but I successfully managed to do so and was ready to take the new life with full enthusiasm.

BHOPAL

I successfully managed to restore my parent's faith in me and they permitted me to go ahead with my decision, although my past behaviour made them sceptical whether this time I could pull off with my promise or it was just like other promises will not be fulfilled.

After getting the go ahead from the family I reached out to vijay asking him the formalities that needs to be done to take the admission, and what will be the procedure to get a hostel room etc. these were such preparations which were required to be done before shifting unless there was no point if going if was not able to secure the admission.

Vijay was kind enough to take the trouble for me and on the very next day he got all the information of new admissions and the documents required and the availability of seats in the college. He already knew I wanted to take admission in mechanical branch and thus he gathered all the information for securing the admission in the college. Which he passed on to me and I was ready with my bag stacked with all the necessary documents to get the admission.

I took the train next day from Ahmedabad junction and reached Bhopal vijay came to pic me from the railway station and as we drove towards the college, he began introducing me with the popular areas of the city, not only that he had also had the conversation with the college dean for my admission as I had skipped a year after 12th and thus it was little less than usual for the admission and thus deans' approval was required.

We have been given the appointment with the dean at 11am and thus at first, we reached his PG and after the refreshments we headed towards the college. Our meeting with the dean sir was nothing but usual where he asked the reason for one year drop to which I Had to give the lame excuse of finance, as the real reason was not worthy enough to be revealed;

Fulfilling all the basic requirements paying the initial semester fees I was ready to rock the streets of Bhopal. But there was still something undone and that was nothing but the arrangement to stay as Vijay's PG already had full occupancy therefore, we resorted to the facility provided by the college, the college itself had the hostel where the students could take admission for some fees. And luckily there were certain rooms having the occupancy. We were shown the rooms, which I quite disliked but then I did not have any other option than to finalize as I had my train the same evening and I had to leave for Ahmedabad finalizing everything.

Vijay suggested me to take the admission in the hostel for time being and once I was shifted here, we could together hunt for a PG with better amenities. I liked his suggestion and did as he said. The entire day went in all the hustle but thanks to vijay I had now a new way carved right before me to travel and do something I had always dreamt of. I already began liking the vibe of the city, it had so many colleges and many more students who were career oriented and this was the horizon which I had to be in, as I wanted my career to now take a kickstart. Career is not only when you begin earning, your academics lays the foundation for your career, this was something which I realised at a little later stage in life but I was glad that eventually I did realise this wisdom.

I was ready to be back to Ahmedabad but this time for only 45 days till the colleges began their sessions. Although the city was haunting me with her memories but this time I had a new perception towards my life, and I was not ready to lose the grip over my life unlike the last time. I mostly spent the days in the house with my family, purposely with my younger brother helping him with his studies as

I realised for the following four years, I would be staying away from them and I had to cherish whatever the time was left in my hand.

I was delightfully surprised to know that my friend koshlesh who flunked in the boards has also taken his admission in the same college of Bhopal and the same course as mine. His decision was more influenced by mine as I had told him earlier and asked him to join me but back then he had to convince his family for the same. Once I took the admission his father was earlier a little sceptical to send him alone and now was ready to send him. He then along with his father went on to Bhopal to secure his admission.

Vijay helped them as he helped me with everything and also made him to select the same hostel as mine this way, we both could share the same space which will help us get acquainted with the city a little easily.

The following days left in our hands were full of planning and getting our bags ready for the next voyage of our lives. Although the hostels were providing all the mattress and bedsheets but my mother instinctively wanted me to carry my own bedsheet and blanket for hygiene purpose. I didn't want much baggage but who has won before a mother. She made sure I was all the protective clothes for all weathers, this was the first time I was settling to a different destination without the family.

This time was overwhelming for me as in the past year I had not really taken the pain to know what was going on in my family neither I talked to them but everyone in my family was so concerned for me, my father took me for shopping for new clothes of my choice. When I was ready to settle for 3 pairs of jeans, he forced me to buy three more so that I could have variety of clothes in my wardrobe. He went on ahead to buy me new things which I may need.

My mom went ahead by making different sorts of pickles for me, on being asked the reason for making them she replied "what if you dislike the hostel food at least you can have breads with these different types of sweet and sour pickles. She even made some dry snacks which will last for a couple of weeks, I felt if given enough space my mom would fit herself in the luggage to be there with me.

I felt guilty of not behaving properly with my family and not loving as much as they did. this entire time gave me a different perspective towards the life and now I only wanted to ensure that my family was proud of me and get myself career oriented. My only motive to shift to Bhopal was to return as a successful engineering whose parents are proud to have a son like him.

Days passed like the snap and now it was time for us to leave.

It was 9th September I and koshlesh had our reservations together. Our families came to the railway station for biding us the farewell. I could see tears in my mother's eyes which she was bravely holding but that dam of emotions broke when the warning siren played, it was an indication that the train would leave the next minute.

As the train slowly moved, I boarded it taking the blessings from my parents with the moving train my mother walked by giving the last-minute instructions:

"Eat well!"

"Sleep on time"

"Study hard"

"Stay away from nonsense drama and non-sense people"

"Do worship everyday"

"Do call me every evening"

"I will miss you"

"Take care beta! Have a safe journey"

"Call me first thing when you reach Bhopal"

She followed the train till she lost her breath of continuously speaking and walking after the moving train. The platform was almost over, I stood next to the gate till I could see them and then went inside on my seat to settle myself. Separation from the family was a little painful but I promised to get a fruitful outcome of this pain.

Koshlesh went on his berth to sleep after having a conversation about how the new beginning will be for both of us, I was again left alone with my thoughts, in the last few days of hustle my thoughts about Pratiksha were restricted but that night, again her thoughts popped up, this time the thoughts were indifferent apart from one thought which was, as I left Ahmedabad, I was leaving all the memories enclosed in my mind behind. Her engagement was a painful truth which I had to come in consensus with. It brought closure to my imaginative love story as she would never be mine, and with that I was bringing peace with me anxiety and the realities of life.

Slept with this thought to wake up in the lovely mountains and scenic beauty of Bhopal, we reached early morning to Bhopal junction. Taking the deep breath with pure oxygen from the nature I was ready to take the new life waiting for me on the other side leaving behind the past.

Heading towards the hostel we found the route mesmerising. The road was both side covered with greenery and mountains, the mountains were Lucious green followed by dense forests, our hostel was located in Kolar area of Bhopal, this area was peculiarly in the outskirts of the city, surrounded by the greenery this area had the best flora fauna I had ever seen. I had always lived in Ahmedabad yet, this scenic beauty was such I had only seen during the vacations or in the movies, the air was less polluted and people spoke Hindi as their primary language than Gujarati which was widely spoken in Ahmedabad.

Admiring the route, we reached the hostel although the hostel looked absolutely fine from the outside, a lot of trouble was waiting for us in the inside. The hostel rooms were congested and the sunshine or natural daylight was hard to find. We were allotted a room which had 2 beds and hardly any space to walk in the room had a tiny window which not even fulfilled its purpose, to ensure that we do not bang ourselves to the furniture's we had to keep the lights turned on always.

This scenario turned our ecstasy into fidgety in no time we decided not to stay in the room but it was next to impossible to find the new accommodation on the same day. Therefore, we decided not to unpack our luggage till we do not find the new accommodation. And to make that happen the responsibility was yet again transferred on the shoulder of vijay who knew the city better than us.

Vijay was also willing to change his PG as he had some issues with the land lord, this request gave him the enroute to find the solution which was going to help us all. He then came up with the idea of taking a flat on rent which is not very far away and had the basic requirements fulfilled for us, house hunting is not a difficult task in Bhopal as there are plenty of houses available on rent reason being there are several colleges which means a lot more students come from different cities, and just like any tourist place has ample hotels these places with surplus educational institutes have surplus to let properties.

And voila he found the house the very next day in piplani nagar sector C it was a 2bhk flat on rent which could be shared between 4 people comfortably and we were already 3 convinced to change the accommodation when we offered the 4th left space to manoj her readily agreed to our proposal and joined us.

Before we could shift, we had to stay for 3 nights into the hostel which were almost unbearable for us reason being the congestion and above that the hostelites were a little less welcoming. We wanted the change as soon as possible. We took a sigh of relief on shifting to the new flat. The new place seemed to be a paradise when compared to the hostel room. It was enough spacious with better light and wind passage. And within a couple of hours our luggage which was already minimal was unpacked.

This flat was partially furnished which had separated cupboards and the modular kitchen and as this room was made with the intention to let it had 4 separate single beds 2 in each room. I and koshlesh as we were in the same semester shared the same room and vijay and manoj shared the other for the same reason. For food we settled to hire a house help who helped us with cleaning and prepare for us home cooked food. Sharing the entire expenses gave us equal shares which did not make a hole in our pocket. Next following days were filled up with the adjustments needed to make ourselves comfortable and aligned with the new place.

This new environment threw new challenges right before us the moment we entered in there and did not give me the time to ponder about the past but this hustle was only to last a few days once we gelled in the atmosphere the memories of the past were back again to wave me hello.

OLD FRIENDSHIP, NEW BONDING

Hefty phone roaming charges were burning a hole into our pockets as we need to make frequent calls either to our family or our friends, therefore we brought new Sim cards that helped me to keep myself connected with the family, this helped a little in releasing the homesickness which I had been experiencing lately.

I never thought it would be that to live away from the family. To ensure that everyone close to me had my new contact number, I broadcasted my number to all my contacts it had hardly been 5 minutes of sharing the contact I received a call, it was none other than Aditi.

"Hello! How are you?" asked Aditi.

"I am good" I replied.

"Why did you change your number?" asked Aditi curiously.

"Actually, I have shifted to Bhopal for my further studies, and thus bought the new number to avoid roaming" I replied.

"What! Are you serious" Aditi exclaimed.

"Yes, dear why would I lie to you" I replied with confident voice.

"You shifted to Bhopal, and you did not bother to inform me about it? "Asked Aditi with anger in her voice.

"I am sorry but till last moment I wasn't sure of whether I will get admission, and as I did, I gathered my luggage and came to Bhopal" I replied.

"You always have an excuse ready at the tip of your tongue." Replied Aditi in a taunting tone.

"No genuinely it wasn't certain if I would get the admission or not and therefore, I did not tell you and later on when the admission was done, to be honest I forgot to inform you in the anxiety" I replied in order to restore her assurance in me.

"Now you are saying the truth, that you forgot, you don't treat me as important as your other friends" replied Aditi keeping her taunting tone intact.

"I am sorry yaar how long will you be cursing me for having done this to you" I replied.

One sorry was enough to melt down her anger over me.

"it's okay now I won't say anything," she replied "which course are you studying there" she added.

"Mechanical engineering" I replied with pride.

"Oh hoooo…. Soon we are going to have Mr. engineer with us" she replied in a witty manner.

Her humour was the best, at one moment she was angry and immediately on the other she had this different witty side of her. And the best part about her was that she could change her mood in a friction of second. This scenario was absolutely adverse for me. If I had my mood pissed off despite of trying, I could not get back to normal as easily as she could.

"I am very happy to hear that you are doing good in your life, I wish you all the luck and success." She replied do let me know if ever you want any help from my end she added.

We continued or conversation for few more minutes before we ended the call. This call made me introspect my behaviour towards her from the beginning. She has always been that friend who asked nothing but friendship from me which I haven't been fulfilling until then. I thought to myself that I should not take her for granted this way and give her the same amount of care and respect which she had for me.

After that day we talked often on calls and our conversations were full of laughter smiles and feeling good about our friendship. These calls although filled a part of the emptiness which was created in my heart due to the separation from the family and Pratiksha but it was not enough for me to get over completely.

I liked the bond that had been created between me and Aditi, I would not call it love it was pure friendship from my end but I always felt she treated me more than a friend which bothered me little as I could not return her the same feeling which I already possessed for Pratiksha.

Although I was physically present in Bhopal my heart was lingering around her apartment waiting for a positive reply from her end. I prayed every night that her engagement with Mehul should not last and she should get single again so that I could be with her.

I made frequent visits to Ahmedabad only to see her but that wasn't the solution I was looking for. I had to pay the price for these visits too my score in the first semester was below average. This news added to the list of things to be depressed about. The number of days I was present in Ahmedabad outside Pratiksha's house was more than the number of days I was present in my college during my first semester.

I was pathetically performing in my academics which not only bothered my parents but also my friends and teachers, as days back I claimed to have all my attention towards my studies I have made huge promises in the past before my parents and friends about how seriously I was going to take this course but the ground reality was absolutely inverse of what I had promised. The rosy picture which I drew in my mind about being in the new environment and taking up the new course was not at all rosy instead it was like a bed of thorns which I was trying to escape all around the semester.

I somehow managed myself to not fail the semester but only obtained exact marks to be qualified as pass category, it was a matter of same for a person like me who earlier was amongst those who obtained the highest grades in the class and now the situation was oi was begging before the professors to help me with their sympathy and grant me enough marks to pass the exam. Instead of reading I killed my time by talking with Aditi chatting with her about all unimportant topics. These conversations helped me ease my anxiety but they were not at all helping me get out of Pratiksha's reminiscences.

The second semester was a level up tormenting for me, thanks to my absent mind I could not grasp the things taught in the college and to top that up this time there was a subject called engineering drawing which proved out to be the most challenging subject for me. I always sucked at art and craft that was the reason why I always absconded myself from anything related to drawing and this subject brought back my age-old fear to life. The trauma of making drawing frightened me and this was not enough, this subject was taken by the dean of our college who was very strict in nature.

He kept a close watch on each and every one of us this made attending the lecture most horrifying, he had his eyes specially on the ow performing students, his thinking was if he personally kept a close watch at the students and their performances and specially on those whose performance was not up to the mark in the first semester and I was amongst the lucky ones who had been successfully got into the eyes of the college dean and obviously for the wrong reasons.

Day by day as the lectures passed the subject got more difficult for me, was already in a state where it was very difficult for me to understand the easiest things and this was drawing with rules which bounced over my head all the time, I tried understanding it. Before giving up I tried taking help from my classmates who were really good at it and also, I tried learning it all by myself but nothing really helped. These failed attempts made my decision concrete of heading back to Ahmedabad my looser spirit made me believe that I was not the one who is suited to be called as an engineer.

Before I could arrive to this conclusion, I had a debate with myself I tried harder to convince myself that I could do it and giving up was never a solution. I saw even poor performers than me in school were doing good with this but I really was waiting for either my life to end or this study. I was aimlessly attending the lectures without understanding even a single word what was being taught in the class. Nothing excited me everything was monotonous the nature which I admired on shifting no longer pleased me. I found solace only in solitude and went quiet. I did not talk with anyone. Struggling with my own thoughts made me so drained that I did not had energy to take up any other task.

Every night before sleeping I thought to myself that the next day my approach towards life would be absolutely different, I won't be ruining my day and will focus on my study, but this plan only remained in my head and never turned into a reality, the following night I would be again making the same plan but never bothering to implement the same.

One fine morning when I was tired of trying and failing in regaining my focus I decided to quit, I knew this decision was again going to bring back the tsunami of questions at me of why I decided to quit something I had taken up because it was not the first time I was quitting, similarly I had quit the B.SC and now engineering. But I was hopelessly depressed back than and could not think anything but quitting. If I had discussed about this with anyone, they would surely ask me not to do so and therefore I decided to keep this news to myself until I left.

I was firm at my decision and began planning for the same secretly but the only hurdle my way was my marksheet of 12th std and other related documents like leaving certificate were with the college administration. It was a statutory condition to deposit the documents with the college and at the final year we will be given back our documents.

At first of leaving without taking them but then I had to think for some backup, if I was not studying there and what if in future, I decide to join for some other course these documents were important in every facet of my upcoming life, therefore to get them back I had to devise a plan accordingly. After giving it a thought, I was ready with my script in my mind, I had to ensure that my reason seemed to be genuine and nobody gets a hint of my next move.

Next morning, I went straight to the administration office as soon as I saw the clerk at the inquiry desk. I asked him about the procedure how can I get my documents back. He then directed me to the head clerk's office who took care of these queries.

Me: may I come in sir

Clerk: yes!

Me: sir I want to request you to provide me with my documents I need them for some bank documentation.

Clerk: why do you want them please elaborate.

Me: sir I am applying for an educational loan and therefore the bank is asking for those documents.

Clerk: why do you want the loan.

Me: sir my family's financial condition is not very good lately and therefore to finance my education I have been looking to get some educational loan. I have had the basic procedure done and the bank is further asking for these documents for further verification and clearance of the loan as soon as possible.

Clerk: okay I can give you these documents for now but as soon as your loan gets passed you will need to submit these documents back as it is the protocol of the college to have the documents with the college records till you complete your degree from here.

Me: okay sir I will do that as soon as I get my documents verified with the bank.

My trick worked and the clerk did not even for one second had a disbelief at me. He was contented with my excuse and without making further enquiries he let me have the documents.

I was very happy holding my documents back as I knew they were my ticket of no return. I was leaving by nothing then which will bring me back here.

I spent the entire day like usual without any change in expression. My frequent visits have made my friends so accustomed of me going that they least bothered to ask me why was I going and when will I return.

I had a very limited luggage with me in Bhopal which I packed stealthily in order to getting in the eyes of anyone, I wanted no one to know, if anyone did, they would surely try to stop me from taking this brave and stupid step, but I was adamant with my decision to quit and was in no mood to change the same and therefore I wated for the perfect time to leave without getting in the eyes of anyone.

One fine Sunday I got this mind-blowing opportunity when all my roommates planned to go for the movie and I took this wonderful opportunity to get my final belongings which I could not take otherwise in their presence, I took the idol of goddess Sharda which was kept on my study table, I used to worship them daily and had no plan of leaving the idol there. After asking for the courage for this bold step I took the idol from the table and packed it safely with other luggage and left fir the station.

Every evening there was one train plying from Bhopal junction to Ahmedabad, I left the hostel during the noon only and therefore had ample of time to spend at the railway station. I purchased the ticket from the station's ticket counter and waited at the railway station.

I went ahead to buy some magazine to kill my time, but all through the way I was creating scenarios in my head of how will I be facing my parents, how will I break this news before them, how would they react to my absurdity. These thoughts made me think twice before boarding the train but there was hardly which could turn the decision for the day.

In order to ensure that there was no one holding me back I switched of my mobile phone to ensure none of my friend could reach me to know where had I been, the train arrived my steps became a little heavier this time while boarding on the thought that possibly I shall never be returning to that city ever.

With a heavier heart this time I bid adieu to the beautiful city which gave me very beautiful memories to carry away for the lifetime. The train raced its paced to its destination but not faster than my heart which was racing at the double speed on the thought of my parent's reaction towards my decision.

I had no courage to face my parents and therefore I needed some more time to prepare myself but the train was in no mercy, it dropped me Ahmedabad on time, I spent next hour at the station thinking where should I go in order to avoid the bombard which was going to take place as soon as I broke the news.

QUESTIONABLE MOVE

I went ahead this time not to my house instead to my cousin's place who was of my age and knew me better as we shared good bond together. When I told the entire chaos that was hampering my cognitive thinking, he was stunned to know everything as before this he was hardly aware of anything, but this time it was him because had I expressed myself before my friends, they were not going to understand me, not because they could not but because they were so done to hear my cries in last couple of years. Also, I needed some other perspective to my situation and thought of seeking it from my cousin.

At first, he was startled on hearing my story but then without taking any second thought, he allowed me to finish my sobbing before he could add his take on the situation before me. His only concern was I came back uninformed and to top it off I had my mobile phone switched off from last 16 hours, he understood the gravity of the situation where my friends at the PG might be searching me and not only that they might have conveyed the news to my parents who would be more worried about my location. This perspective was one such which I had least taken into consideration but was a very grave point.

I haven't thought from this angle before, I was so engrossed into my own despair that I forgot to think about the people associated with me, I began feeling ashamed of my impulsive behaviour and also was ashamed of the fact that before doing anything I should have pondered about the after effects of my act which I probably failed to do. Resultantly as soon as I switched in my mobile the phone flooded with notifications of messages from my friends at the PG, one such message from vijay read:

"Where have you gone with all your belongings, are you safe you aren't reachable on the mobile, we all are worried for you here. If you were about to leave you should have informed at least one of us, ever since we came back from the movie, we are constantly trying to reach you. We even tried contacting your parents thinking that you might have informed them, but there were equally surprised as us. What made you to take this rubbish step of eloping. Please where ever you are please telling me you are fine we are all here worried about you stupid you have kept us all at the edge of our feet. Call me when you read this message.

This message was followed by several other message from my other friends who were trying to reach me. Reading them I realised the level of blunder that I had recently created. After reading this message I messaged vijay instead of calling him as he might have gone to the college.

"I am in Ahmedabad and I am absolutely fine, sorry to bother you last night, I will call you by the evening once you return from college" I wrote a message to vijay. And also asked him to inform all the other roommates too.

This guilt trip was not over yet I had my family to face who already had the news of me being missing and I was so pissed with myself that how could I take any step without any contemplation of the same this was absolutely a terrible situation, where I was looking for a hide away from one such terrible situation, I landed myself in a more gross terrifying situation with no practical reason to offer.

My cousin offered me some black coffee which I badly wanted back then to get my sense back to think in alignment.

"So, what would you do now" he slipped this question before me while having his coffee.

"I don't know, perhaps I will have to clear all mess that has been created by me" I replied sighing in despair.

"Yes indeed, and how are you going to handle the situation this time, because previously you acted in very foolish way which has led you here therefore, I want you to take the bull by its horns this time and without finding ways to escape the reality face it and get over whatever is bothering you." He advised.

This conversation was something which I needed the most, it gave me new horizon and the ability to think clearly, the clouds of self-doubt seemed to wipe away. I was then ready to take the bull by its horn it was the time to confront my parents.

My cousin joined me to my parent's place, he wanted to make peace between me and my parents as we were expecting a sudden burst of anger from my parent's end, but their reaction was inverse of what we have framed in our heads. My mother had tears in her eyes and my father took a sigh of relief on seeing me fine. This was not something I had prepared myself for. The news of me being unreachable and missing had left them stunned and all that they wanted was me to be in affine state and when they saw me standing before them fine, they felt like their wish was answered.

At first there was no discussion they gave me the time to relax, my mother comforted me there was a relief on her face of having me lying under her lap. This entire atmosphere at hope helped me in calming my anxiety which I had been holding for quite long. I had been cooking thoughts in my head of this situation but this was not really in my head all I thought were the adverse things but the reality came out to be beyond my imagination. I had never this side of my parents before, they were hurt but they were not revealing this in their actions instead they chose to calm me before we could come to some conclusion.

The next morning my dad came to me and slowly he slipped into the topic of me quitting my college,

"Son, I don't really know what is bothering you, but one thing I very well know is you are a fighter, I have always raised you like one. But this attitude of yours of quitting and leaving things undone is not appropriate it has been hurting me badly because I have certain expectations from you. I never ever wish that you take any insensitive step before thinking about the after effects of the same. I have had the faith upon you. Now you have been legally an adult person but you will always be my child whom I can reprimand but instead of reprimanding I am here to share my feelings with you.

You have now grown taller than me and also are taking advanced education than me therefore I believe you know certain things which I may have never read but I have learnt from the harsh experiences that life has thrown upon me, because I could not read as much as you are privileged, my father could only afford to give us basic education for college we had no funds and therefore had to opt for a job. But I do not wish for you to have the same fate and therefore I have been working threw my bones to give you and your siblings to have the best possible education therefore you need not see the hardships that I had faced in the past.

I don't want to impose anything on you but I just want to remind you that it was you who came before me to allow you to pursue this degree. Nobody forced you for this it was your own decision to go for this course and now running away from it is also your call but I just want to remind you of the time when you begged before me to allow you to go there so that you can get the admission. If you have got some other plans, you can share that too. But if I can honestly give you an advice out of my own life experience, I would say you have this golden opportunity before you in the form of this degree it can really make your future son, after all you will be getting a professional degree out of this course and todays time education had a major role to play.

All I could do is advice you out of my own experience rest I leave the decision on you, nobody will say anything if you decide to stay and leave your degree, but everyone will be glad to see you completing the degree. Stay calm think about it twice and then take a call, with absolutely no stress of what will anyone say. You father is there with you, I am proud of you my son I only want my son to be happy and nothing else"

Dad left after calmly saying this but his words had a huge impact on me, his advice made me think about the situation of other side of the situation and I realised how foolish I was to abscond away without thinking about the results of my actions. For the next two days I was into my own thoughts thinking about the pros and cons of my decision. I was firm to take a decision but this time I had to be adamant onto what I decide, there was no turning back then. After a lot of contemplation and the words of my father echoed in my ears had helped to take the right decision.

I was ready to be back again but this time my only intent was to read hard and make my father proud of me I had already done enough to have him feel insulted before others but now no more, the news of me fleeing away from Bhopal spread like wild fire and every relative tried approaching my father to take a dig, although they called themselves as well-wishers but they were the ones celebrating on seeing things upside down.

When I talked about my decision to my family, they were more than happy, but before celebrating this my father reiterated his words, I am proud of you my son, I want you to be happy in life with whatever you do I do not want to burden you with my expectations, I don't want you to take any decision in haste a then regret later, be wise to choose what is right for you. I have taught you this thing over the years in the past to select that is best for you and don't compromise your happiness for the world. If your gut intuition is allowing you only then go ahead otherwise take a step back, you can always start a fresh.

These words worked like a magic on my brain, it felt like my brain was rewired to a better and efficient engineering. My perspective towards the life really changed I got to see a whole new opportunistic world before me and the best thing this entire chaos has taught me was about my father. Till then I had this vague image of my father who was a bit strict and connected to his roots in an old-fashioned way. But that was the biggest misconception that I had been carrying in my brain over these years, rather my father was the coolest updated man I had ever known. He understood the agility of my brain ad did what was needed the most.

Thanks to the emotional intelligence my father used on me, I was charged enough to win the battle this time, I promised myself that I had to get the previous studious vinay back and this cry-baby had to leave now I had created enough hassle before my parents but not any further I got my ticket booked and packed my stuff to be back again and I was back to the city which I left expecting not returning to the same.

This time I had a different focus which had brought me here, but before I could settle myself, I owed an apology before my friends because they were also the part of the panic which I left them in, they accepted my apology and welcomed me warmly with a condition of not repeating this mistake. I was happy that everything was back in place but most importantly my sanity was back and I was happiest to have that back. A sense of calm surmounted me and I had got the desired vision towards the life.

Meanwhile time was passing and this whole ambiguity of my brain led me to the second semester examinations which I obviously underperformed because neither I attended the classed with whole heart nor do I prepare for the same. But this was going to be the last time when my grades were so low. I was ready to take the bull by its horns and then began learning and reading with my full attention such that my grades empowered me not discouraged me.

But for making that happen I had to struggle a lot more, my focus was very bad at that point of time and my mind wandered more often but my determination was firm this time I wasn't ready to let go this opportunity to get good grades and thereby I worked hard enough to get the desired outcome

I was already very much ashamed of myself for being so foolish that I had run away but now me came back laser focused and highly motivated to get ahead in life and make my father proud of me.

I changed my schedule and brought balance in my life by opting for regular classes and regular learning sessions that helped me in getting the desired efficiency in my learning and overall performances.

FOCUSING ON THE POSITIVES

Life has never been this good before in a while. I was having the best time of my life, I was over my fantasies of my dreamy love and also was away from all the ambiguity that had surmounted me, I was enjoying my college life thoroughly and never missed a day of my college, I was even present on the days in the college when students conducted mass bunks. After returning from college when my other friends went outside to enjoy, I preferred to stay back to read. At first vijay was sceptical to leave me as one such day when I was left alone, I flew away, but later with the passage of time he was okay leaving me.

I was working laboriously to get myself in the top scorers every morning I reminded myself of the promise I did before my father and to myself, I no longer anted myself to be the quitter instead I manifested myself as the top scorer in the class and for that I worked to my bone and slept every night with content that I had not wasted the day rather utilised it in making my dream come true. As and when the time passed, I began feeling more with my command on the subjects, one such subject strength of material became my favourite, even on days when I felt lethargic to get myself to study, I solved questions from that subject which eventually helped me in regaining my energy and focus. In the next few days my hard work began paying off till then those professors who saw me as an average to weak student changed their lenses to see me as a brighter one, the one who was actually present in the class to learn new things rather than attending the lecture for the sake of attendance. With each passing day I became more and more confident.

One night while I was engrossed in my daily studies a notification made me hold my mobile it was a text message from an unknown number, back than I had no such facility to get the number checked as who it was. Curiosity engulfed me as I kept stressing my brain about who the sender would be, to ease the anxiety build up I replied with hello to the sender.

Minutes later the revelation was done with another reply it was Aditi again, she always kept a check on me even though I always forget to pin her but she never failed, I would ghost her but she never did that to me. To my surprise I was very happy to hear from her I felt immensely happy that she messaged me I expressed my happiness before her to which she replied. "You have to say this every time but you never mean what you say it's me always messaging you asking you, you do not bother to take the pain to call me once in a blue moon".

Reading this message, I did not wait for another second to call her, that call duration lasted for about 15-18 minutes longest in the history of our friendship when I had interacted her over a phone call. Her voice had the charm and the happiness was evident throughout the conversation I had smile from ear to ear during that call as if it released dopamine in my brain, I felt very satisfied and happy that I had her as a part of my life. We ended our conversation with a promise that we would continue to do the conversations like these more often, it was like a blow of fresh air and I had never thought that I could ever connect with Aditi that well, but this one phone call changed everything, I began believing that we could make up very good friends and then decided to never again ghost Aditi, I fell for her genuine efforts of trying to be with me over these years, not that I began liking her but I liked to have her as a friend and guide with me in my journey. We talked for hours either through messages or through voice calls. Morning messages became a ritual but I did not allow this friendship to derail me from my focus and read with the same perseverance.

She kept on insisting that we would meet when I returned to Ahmedabad. At first, I thought of concealing the news of my return as I wanted to avoid these encounters to prevent both us for falling for each other, I had the strongest intuition that she had feelings for me and the frequent meetings may take us in the direction which I was not ready to plunge in.

I worked diligently for my exams and as per the normal drill exams were followed by a long vacation, for this entire semester I was in Bhopal reading with focus and worked really hard unlike the previous semesters therefore I felt the dire urge to visit my family and to meet my father to thank him further again as he gave me the opportunity which I was not ready to give myself. I got my tickets booked along with my friends as everyone of us were longing to see our families and thus we came back together for the vacations, I decided not to break this news before Aditi and give her a surprise to see how will she take this surprise.

Next morning on reaching Ahmedabad we headed to our respective homes, my family was happy to see me this time being more confident than ever after an hour or so having my breakfast I dressed up to surprise Aditi as per my plan, and for that I took the bike from my younger brother and then headed to her apartment. I sent her a text like usual good morning, she never failed to reply to my texts in minutes of it getting delivered, this gave me immense pleasure that I was a priority for her but equally I was ashamed of not returning her the same vibe, but I was here to compensated for all the wrongs which I had done earlier.

"Hey what are you doing? can you spare two minutes of your time to come out, there is a surprise for you waiting outside your house." I sent her this text message and waited for her response. By the time my eyes were glued to the main door of her house. As I had positioned myself to be easily visible, I had framed a story to give if I was spotted by any other member from her family.

After a minute I saw her coming out from her house and her immediate reaction was not to be missed, her eyes popped out and her happiness on seeing me was evident she could not hold herself standing as her feet went trembling with excitement, she sat down for a while to gather herself.

I sent her again a message asking "can we meet?"

"Give me some time to get ready I will update you the time and place in some time, I request you to go now if papa sees you here, he will surely bombard you with questions you aren't ready to answer," she replied instantly.

I went back to my home as I knew she would at least take an hour to get ready, 15 minutes later I received a text from her "lets catch up at 10:30 at IIM bus stand and from there we will decide further where to go"

I reached prior to the decided time and thus began hopping the hawkers stores near the bus stand, I made sure I was near the stop so that she can easily spot me. Minutes later I saw her getting down from a bus, her happiness was evident from her eyes, she greeted me with a gigantic smile and sparkling eyes, I felt immense pleasure in knowing that someone other than my family could be so happy to see me.

We greeted each other by shaking hands and then I asked

"Where shall we go now?"

"Anywhere as you like" she replied while making herself comfortable on my bike.

We decided to go to a nearby café but it was early morning and the café had just opened so the staff was busy in cleaning and setting the café for the day they asked us to wait for 30 minutes before they could start their service, I wasn't ready to stand outside the café and therefore we drove to the nearest park which was not very far from the café near iscon mega mall.

We sat there had some soulful conversation; she expressed her happiness of seeing me.

"I can tell you how happy I am to be here with you, I have always manifested for our friendship and finally the universe had heard my prayer I am really glad that you made this plan of meeting," she elaborated her emotions.

I was too naïve to understand her true emotions behind those words, I thanked her for bearing my tantrums and my not so welcoming attitude.

We sat there for a while talking about our lives and about our interests apart from studies, I was not a pro at talking and expressing myself but she did not give up on me she kept asking me questions to fill her in with the information she wanted about me,

While we were still in the middle of our conversations he spotted a temple near the park, it was a temple of goddess kali, I had always worshipped the goddess and being a true spiritual believer, I never miss a chance of bowing down before the lord, on being asked by her if I would like to join her inside the temple, I readily agreed.

We then inside the temple for seeking blessings from the lordship, I was out of the temple in 5 minutes but she took nearly double the time. This intrigued me and I could not resist asking her why it took er so long.

"I can't tell you that, what we pray with God stays with God. Its personal and I can't share that with you." She replied.

I was surprised at the conviction she said the entire thing I was astound that she had so much faith in God.

It had already been an hour for us sitting there thus we decide to move to the café thinking that the service would now be open. But by then I was quite hungry and was in no mood to eat breads and pizzas therefore I asked her if we could switch to some restaurant where we could get something to eat to which she agreed and we settled for another restaurant nearby serving some authentic Punjabi meal combos.

She was kind enough to ask me what would I like to eat but since I wasn't sure of what she prefers in her meal I let her decide the order, she placed an order for a chole bhature combo which came along with a Gulab jamun. I was okay with her choice as I liked eating them. While waiting for the order she had a pie of complaints against me which she began putting before me,

I have asked this before and today also I am going to ask this in person, why did not you tell me that you were shifting to Bhopal she asked with a choked throat and eyes filled with tears ready to drip down any second, this scene placed me at a little discomfort as I was not very good at convincing girls and calm them down, also we were at a public place and I did not want all the eyeballs of people present around the restaurant to be glued at our table.

I rushed to grab some tissues lying at the tissue stand on the table and fetched her 2-3 plies to wipe down her tears and comforted her with warm strokes of my palm around her back. Hardly had I been able to stop her crying our food was served, I was really thankful for the quick service by the restaurant which helped me to ease her out and divert her attention towards the food, before we could dive into splurging our tastebuds into the meal, I told her certain things to comfort her.

"I am sorry for my past negligence I was not sure that we were such good friends earlier where I need to tell you everything happening in my life but now, I have learnt my lesson and I assure you that mistake shall not be repeated. Let's not turn this magnificent day into a cry day instead let's make good memories with the food before us, if you can stop crying can we just eat these delicious bhatures, my mouth is watering I can't wait more.

"Ouch! Its piping hot I said while digging a hole into the swollen bhatura, it is a bread made with all-purpose flour rolled into a circle like chapati and fried in hot oil.

Aditi could not see me struggling to have a bite of the dish and asked me to back of my hands, she carefully then tore a bite size piece of bhatura and dipped it in the chole topping it up with some onions which came along with the bhatura and then before offering it to me she carefully blowed air to the bite to ensure it was cooled before I could have it.

I was overwhelmed to see how careful she was that I may not have any struggle and for that she ensured that till the dish was not subtle hot she made all the bites ready for me, this was something which I had been experiencing for the very first time. Although during childhood our parents feed us the similar way but receiving this level of warmth from a friend and that too a female friend was way too uncommon for me.

After spending the delightful time together for the first time I felt that the day should not end I was actually enjoying her company, but then we had to return and I asked her to take along to home but she resisted and said it would be better if she went by bus to which I agreed and dropped her to the bus station asking her to drop me a text on reaching home safely.

On reaching she sent me a heartfelt message which read: "vinay I had the best time with you today thank you for making this day so memorable for me, I would never forget this day all my life."

Getting this overwhelming response from her end melted my heart and the conviction I had for her years ago changed all together,

"I too had a great time with you, maybe we can share such memorable days more often, "I replied.

Life was on track I was doing well with my studies; my parents were also happy and I had the group of best people as my friends. This was the first time ever since I shifted to Bhopal that I was actually enjoying my vacations in Ahmedabad without bothering about something and this was also the first time when I was not honking around Pratiksha's residence. I was finally relieved from my anxiety which provided me the immense relief.

FOUND A FRIEND IN HER

One day I and koshlesh had some work together and therefore we had been to the iscon mall area, that area reminded me the wonderful time I spent with Aditi. We were done with our work and were ready to head back home when I saw the time it was 12:30, a night before when I was chatting with Aditi that she had her exams the other day from 10 am in the morning at sahjanand college. This information clicked a thought in me of why not surprising her by paying a visit to her college.

"Koshlesh bro lets go to sahjanand college" I requested.

"Why?" asked koshlesh.

"Today is Aditi's exam and it would be over by 1pm lets go and surprise her" I replied.

"Aditi! Are you serious? Exclaimed koshlesh.

"Yes, my perception about her has changed now and we have been bonding really well lately, I defended myself.

"Its surprising brother once there was a time when you even hated to hear her name and now look at you how much have you changed "replied koshlesh amusingly.

'My perception has changed now, she isn't someone who once I thought she was, she genuinely cares for me and this has made me realised that I have been very hard upon her in the past but now I do not want to carry over the mistakes of my past." I replied.

"If you are done with your interrogation, can we move we have to reach there before 1." I added.

"Okay let's go" replied koshlesh while igniting the engine.

"Wait take a halt at this stationery shop please, I need to buy a pen for her as a present to wish her luck for her exams." I said to koshlesh.

"Ohh God, you have changed so much this time, do you have any feelings for her or what? Asked koshlesh.

"No not at all, but I am guilty for my past attitude towards her and hence I want to make up for it. I justified.

I quickly purchased a pen for her and then we rushed to the college.

We positioned ourselves right outside the main gate of the college giving us the view of the staircases so that whenever she comes out, she could spot us. Couple of minutes later the bell rang and slowly the students began coming down, in seconds the entire premises which was vacant a minute ago was filled with the chatter of the students.

We had our eyes on everyone so that we could not miss Aditi coming out, and thus we focused on every face walking down.

There she was walking down the stairs and within seconds she spotted us, she was walking down one of her friends whom she asks for excuse and ran towards me,

"What a pleasant surprise. Are you here to see someone? Asked Aditi.

"yes" I replied.

"Who? "She asked.

"You," I replied with a smile.

Hearing this her cheeks turned pink and she smiled from ear to ear as this was something unexpected for her and she really liked our presence there.

There was huge crowd of students getting out of the college, the constant honking of vehicles made it difficult to hear one another, getting annoyed by this,

"If you are done with greeting one another can we go to some other place where we can peacefully hear ourselves and grab a quick snack because I am starving", said koshlesh in an annoyed voice.

"let's go to a stall near IIM serving the best vadapav in Ahmedabad it's not far away from here" suggested Aditi.

We then headed to the place Aditi came along with one of her friends on her active and led us to the stall.

After grabbing the quick snack with little conversations alongside we decided to head back home as Aditi had an exam to appear the following day and therefore, she could not afford to spare more time than that. Neither I wanted to spoil her time but before we could part our ways, I presented her the pen which I purchased earlier to give her as a token of best wishes for her following exams.

"Is this for me "she asked with a surprise

"No, it's for your teacher, of course it is for you, I brought this for you to appear your exams. my best wishes are with you. I replied.

She accepted it with a wide smile and left for her home thanking me for the pen.

So did we, we returned our home and I received a message from Aditi later that evening.

'I am really fortunate to have a friend like you, your gesture to come to, my college and giving me the pen was really heart touching I am overwhelmed by your action thank you so much for your support, it means a lot to me." I was really happy to hear that from her.

Since she was busy with her studies we hardly talked and days were nearing when my vacations where about to end and thus I decided to spend the last few days at my sisters place along with my nephew since he was very dear to me, I wanted to spend the time left with him, during those days I was so engrossed that I hardly texted Aditi.

A night before I was about to leave, I came back to my home for packing, it had been around 10 pm while I was gathering my stuff to pack, I received a call prom Aditi.

"Hello! How are you" I asked after answering the call.

"fine" she replied.

"What are you doing" she added.

"Nothing, much just getting my things sorted to pack as I have a train tomorrow evening to catch, my vacations are over, it's time to get back to Bhopal." I replied

"What? You are going? when were you about to inform me about this, she asked in a surprised tone.

"I would of course you before leaving inform you, but to be honest I am not very good with goodbyes and therefore was hesitant to break this news before you." I spoke.

"At what time is your train?" she asked

"8:30 pm tomorrow so I shall be leaving the house somewhere around 6" I replied calculatedly.

"Pick me at the university bus stop at sharp tomorrow 10 am" she said.

"Oh, hello madam, do you have cotton stuffed in your ears or what, I am leaving tomorrow for Bhopal, have so many pending works before me to do, and you are making an outing plan" I reiterated.

"I heard you the first time, but I want you to set aside all your plans and spend the day with me, and don't worry I shall free you before the evening" she commanded.

"This isn't right yar, I would not be convenient yar this sudden change of plans, you know I am not someone who welcomes change so easily," I replied.

After debating for 15 minutes, she convinced me to agree to her demand.

She was someone who never give up unless she achieved what she wanted. This fact was learned by me that evening when she adamantly continued the telephonic conversation till, she heard a yes for her demand.

I was a little surprise over the fact that she demanded it as her right over me but I loved the fact that she had the purest feelings for me. How can one deny such a welcoming heart although I was not in love but the bond, we shared was very pure and I really felt thankful to the god for having found a gem of a person like her.

As per the decided schedule I was ready to receive her at 10 am at the university, but to reach there I had to go through a lot of pre planning, I had to stay up till 1 the previous night just to pack all my luggage to not miss out any important belonging as I was leaving for Bhopal, but if this extra effort made her happy I was ready to take on this, as I felt she became the inseparable part of my life whom I didn't want to lose at any cost.

I was standing at the bus stop at the time given by her, she had left a message on my mobile "hi. good morning, sorry the bus came late and therefore I will be late by 15minutes please wait for me, I am sorry".

She was so gullible that even though it wasn't her fault of being late but still she was so honest at heart.

I patiently waited for her till she arrived. She was wearing a bright coloured breezy maxi dress at first, I was very confused that why did she chose to show up this dressed up for this casual meeting but for me it was casual but for her it wasn't the same.

She instantly hopped at the back seat of my bike without greeting a hello and asked me to start the bike.

"But where should we go, I was thinking to go to the nearest café and some time there. What's your take in this?", I asked

"I am directing you we are not going to any café; simply follow my instructions we are going to a different place today "she replied.

"Alright, but where?" I asked curiously

"You will get to know once we reach there, keep on driving we have a long way to go" she replied.

"Long way, have you gone nuts I had told you already I have a train to catch this evening and also my packing is pending, if we go to a distant place how am I going to make it for my train." I yelled

"Stop overacting I also know you gave a train to catch, I am not absconding you that you are being so offensive", now without further arguments lets go, I know you would love the place once we reach." She commanded

For the next 15 minutes she kept on giving her directions and I followed her obediently like a good boy. But was trying to figure out where was she taking me but I could not.

"Take inside this building and park the vehicle. We have arrived at our location" she instructed.

I was brought to a surprise because it was science city the place specially designed for science geeks where we get to explore the science and the planetary movements and not only that it also had a compilation of various scientific experiments, where one can obtain great knowledge about different rules of physics and chemistry. I was amazed at the fact that she brought me here.

"I always knew you wanted to come here therefore I planned this day out at this location." She explained.

"How do you know me so well? I asked.

She blushed at my question as we purchased the entry tickets and got inside.

The place exceeded my expectation, it was huge with different sections belonging to different branches of science, at one section the molecular composition was described and on the other there was a planetarium, there was also a separate section for aeronautics I felt immense pleasure in exploring tis place as I had never been here before but has heard about this place, and was in my bucket list to visit.

I was literally speechless exploring this place, for somebody like me who had so inclination towards these experiments it was nothing but a treasure cave, during this entire visit I was a kid again and sighed the similar expressions of surprise on seeing everything around.

My eyes swelled up when I saw a building given the spherical shape of earth and it was painted like earth to get the resemblance. While I was busy exploring the place Aditi was constantly busy in registering my memories in her phone which had a camera, she was capturing my picture allowing me to enjoy the place thoroughly.

After about 2 hours our feet were soaring with the constant walk, we decide to take a halt at the canteen to grab a quick bite. But before I could order anything she popped out the tiffin she had been carrying in her bag.

"I knew you would get hungry and thus I brought you some pasta which I made myself, I hope you like it." Said Aditi.

"Can I get you anything else" she added.

"No no, I am good if you need you can get something for yourself," I replied.

"The pasta is really good, I can't believe that you made it, it had the perfect amount of seasoning and sauce making it taste so delicious' I said in amusement.

"Obviously I made it, I really make good food, come home I will make a proper 3 course meal for you, then you can believe on my cooking skills.' She replied irritatingly.

"Why are you not eating, I will eat the entire bowl if you kept on staring at me instead of eating" I said.

"of course, you can, I am glad that you liked the food" she replied with a smile.

While I was splurging my tastebuds with the tangy pasta, she said something unexpected which chocked the pasta in my throat.

"Do you like me vinay?" she asked with a blank face

I guess she already knew what would I say but was still asking to check upon.

"Why suddenly this question Aditi out of the blue?" I asked

"Not, suddenly I wanted to ask this long ago but never had the courage, look I already know your answer is a big no but I wanted to confess my feelings before you because keeping them to myself is a daunting task for me" she said.

"I am absolutely okay with whatever your answer is but I was not able to hold this any longer and thus asked," she justified.

"Look Aditi you have become a very dear friend to me but right now after a lot of hardship I had hardly been able to focus on my studies and therefore I am abstaining from anything that diverts my attention. I hope you understand. But I can't offer you anything beyond what we share today." I replied.

"I already knew this, please promise me this conversation will not change anything between us and we will still be those friends like before" she said.

"Yes of course" I reaffirmed.

 Although I had promised her nothing would change but a constant thought kept hammering which did not allowed usual conversations for the rest of the time, we were together.

I dropped her to the bus stop and returned home to pack my stuff and left for the station before time.

Koshlesh had his reservation with me so we met at the railway station and left again for Bhopal to be back to our routine.

While on a train I kept on thinking about the memories which I was leaving behind with Aditi. but this time I was not ready to dwell into the memories and ruin my studies and thus became more practical to keep my emotions at bay to let my concentration drive me.

GIFT

Life came back to the monotonous schedule where I went to college, gym, library and on weekends along with friends. While each one of us had been back from our homes all of us brought home cooked dry snacks to curb our munching cravings thinking that they would last at least for couple of weeks but they could hardly last for 3 days. And this was not the one-time story, it happened every time no matter how much more quantity did, we bring with us. Leaving us at the mercy of tiffin service which was hardly satisfying our tastebuds. During some weekends we cooked our own food together.

Bhopal became a home away from home, we stayed together, cooked together, and if anyone of us was sick all others took charge of helping the sick in getting better. Those days were such where I found the best people in my life. Even if we try time cannot buy those memories which were being created back then.

The recent addition to the monotony was chatting with Aditi. Although I had been alerted with the confession she has made before me at science city but I was sure that I had made my point very clear before and thus she would understand it and that won't let our friendship get affected with it. Life was the best back then I had my grades good and not only that I had the best support from my family and friends which ensured that I did not lose my focus.

Not only did I devour into the books but also we friends often made outing plans and I also joined for some of them, one such appalling incident which is going to stay fresh in the memory lane was when I koshlesh, vijay and Rajeev made a plan for the movie ishaqzaade on Saturday evening, as the next day was a holiday we booked a late night show, but the only problem we had was we only had one bike and to adjust 4 of us on it was adaunting task thus to reach the theatre two of us went on a bike and the other two took an auto, the only intent to take the bike along was what if we could not find an auto way back home, the bike would act up for our rescue.

The show ended around 1:30am, and when we began looking for auto we could not find any, which left us with no other option than to go on the bike, I pulled up the task of riding the vehicle, but there were spooky stories famous about the route which we had to take, and each one of us was petrified to encounter anything suspicious on our way back home, the route looked hideous because of the darkness caused by the luscious green trees and the mountains surrounding the route, the sound of the barking dogs made the silence even more daunting.

While heading towards the road we were chased by a dog and as we were 4 on one bike it was difficult for us to keep our feet guarded by the dog bite and maintain the bike balance while we were trying to escape the dog we came across a narrow passage, I asked 2 of my friends to get down in order to get through that narrow passage but none of them was ready, somehow we managed to get to the house, but took an oath that we are not going ever again for a late night show. Till today that memory sends chills to my body, it was altogether an experience which we never wanted to reoccur.

Such incidents became an unforgettable memory of my life which I open heartedly shared with Aditi we had daily conversations together and every day she had one constant question to ask

"When are you coming to Ahmedabad?"

She always knew the answer would not be specific rather ambiguous but she never missed asking the same.

One evening when we were having our casual conversation she suddenly came up with a demand.

"I need a present from you, so whenever you come back to Ahmedabad be sure to get me something special" she said.

"What kind of a present, your birthday is nowhere near, why would you need a present?" I asked

"Why you being my dear friend, you stay in a different city, you should bring something for me from there as a token of memory from Bhopal" she justified her demand.

"Why are you trying to indulge me into this, you very well know that I am not someone who aces in doing these sweet gestures and above that I am terrible at shopping for women" I replied.

"How do you know that you are terrible have you ever purchased anything for any girl or either your sister?"

"never" I replied.

"Then do the honours this time, and I need something as a gift and no discussion over this' she replied putting an end to the timeless debate we were into."

She often repeated her demand during our daily conversations which has seeded a thought in my brain to get her something before I go to Ahmedabad during the Diwali vacations.

One evening when I along with my friends went to D.B. mall for some shopping while going across shoppers stop, I saw a kurti on display it was in the colour magenta pink with golden embroidery the kurta looked elegant and the immediate reaction that came to my mind was it would look nice on Aditi, as she was constantly asking me to get her something I went to get that dress.

"Ohhooo…. shopping for Kurti for whom?" asked vijay who came along with me that evening.

"Nothing for Aditi, she has been demanding a gift from long time" I replied.

He didn't say much but gave me a witty smirk which could have a lot of hidden meanings but I least bothered about them.

There was still time for Diwali to come but I had securely packed that in my luggage bag to not miss taking it on my trip back home.

Two months later it was time for me to get back to Ahmedabad for the Diwali vacations, on reaching I spent my day with my family and the next day made a plan to meet Aditi.

This time we chose to go to Gandhinagar and for that I had to pick her from the bus stop I had carried a backpack along with me that day in order to hide the present which I had purchased for her earlier. The moment she saw me with the back pack she began interrogation.

"Why are you carrying a bag today?" she asked.

"I had some documents that needed to be verified and therefore I am carrying them in this bag" I replied, by making a reliable excuse before her to believe.

"Shall we go?" I added

"Yes, sure you said we will go to Gandhinagar but where in Gandhinagar" she asked "it's quite far you will get tired" she added with an expression of empathy over her face.

"We are going for a long drive I haven't decided the destination yet all I have decided is the route next we will see where will this new route take us," I replied.

"And you don't worry I am habitual of riding of vehicles for a long distance therefore it won't be a trouble" I replied.

We were having a great time during our ride; the road was surrounded with trees and that was something which I always liked and therefore I enjoyed a lot.

We reached a garden at Gandhinagar and by that time I was also tired of riding and therefore we decided to take a halt at that garden. Greenery has always made me happy and therefore whenever I got any chance of going to any garden, I never missed that.

the green grass lured me to lie down and since my back was tired, I choose to lie down on the ground on the semidry grass which felt therapeutic,

while I was busy in enjoying the grass Aditi took to my bag lying beside me and started peeking what was inside.

"What are you doing?" I asked trying to take my bag.

"I want to look what's inside your bag" she replied taking her hands back such that I could not catch them.

"You know that its ethically incorrect to look into anyone's bag without their permission" I said.

"This rule does not imply to close friends, if you want you can go through my bag anytime" she replied.

"Wait a minute there is a present, okay this is what you have been hiding from me since morning. For whom does this parcel belong" she asked with a quirky face.

Before I could even respond she read the name written on the present it hers only. Her hawkish nature won her this reveal had I been quick I could have taken it back from her. But at last, the gift belonged to her and it reached it reached its right place.

"Ohh god you girl have no patience at all, this is not how I wanted to surprise you, but you ruined it all" I replied with an irritated face.

"Now take it this is for you; I have been hiding it since morning" I added.

She immediately had the brightest smile on her face as if she had received something which she had been longing to have. She hurriedly tried opening the package but very carefully such that even the wrapper was also not torn.

"The present is inside not the wrapper that you are so gently pulling it away" I said.

"I even would preserve this wrapper for life coz this is very precious to me as it has been given by you" she replied folding the paper carefully.

"What if I give you some junk would you be preserving it too? "I asked.

"of course, anything coming from your end is my treasure which I would surely preserve" she replied with confident eyes.

Voila it was a kurti inside the box.

"Oh my god, so thoughtful of you to have brought this wonderful kurti, I loved the fabric, its design. It's beautiful. I will be wearing this on Diwali." She replied with the twinkle in her eyes.

"Thank you so much for bringing this precious present for me, I loved it! For this wonderful present I would like to reward you with this apple" she added and then she took out the apple from her giant tote bag.

We sat there for a while enjoying the view of the garden and also the apple after almost relaxing for an hour, we returned our home. But before I could drop her, she asked something which I was reluctant to grant her.

"I want you to come to my house this Diwali. I would really be happy if you can please come for some time" she pleaded with the most innocent face on earth.

"You know I am not very good at meeting new people, please don't force me for this, I request you" I replied with an agitated face.

"This request is for once and for all times, I won't ever ask you again to come to my house. Please I request you," she pleaded.

"Alright don't spoil your mood, as you wish if you are willing you can come anytime you want to and if not, it will be okay, do not stress and spoil your mood" she added.

"I am very happy today and I do not want to end this day on a heavier note you let's just presume nothing happened and go back to the normal as we were before this topic of conversation" she said in order to bring the escalated topic to neutral.

She was a peacemaker the moment she realised things could heat up she was ready to pacify the matter then and their itself in order to maintain the calm and tranquillity.

Days went by I celebrated the festival with my family and a day before I was about to leave, I thought of going to Aditi's home as she had warmly invited to her house.

On reaching there I was warmly welcomed by her mother and her elder sister who were present at that time. They served me with lite snacks and a cup of coffee.

Her mother began asking the usual questions about my studies and my plans after the completion of my studies. Her questions although were usual but the wat she kept looking at me and then shifting her focus at Aditi who was standing next to me, made me a little uncomfortable.

Aditi on the other hand was constantly blushing throughout the time, this was a little absurd for me yet it alarmed me to leave the site as soon as possible, because I never knew what thoughts were they cooking up in their brains.

Having finished my cup of coffee I accelerated to leave the house but they kept on insisting me top hold to have lunch with them which somehow, I managed to turn down.

Aditi was flabbergasted on the fact that her mother liked me she on the message said.

"Mummy likes you, thank you for coming this really means a lot to me that you came she sent this message.

Although I was not very happy with the consequential thoughts, I had about this meeting but seeing her so happy melted my frustration.

I was not paying much attention to these events as I was on my career building mission and I had to put back my armour because immediately after reaching Bhopal pre university tests awaited us.

Whatever was happening between me and Aditi although there was nothing wrong but something was strange that was piling up on me and making it difficult for me to see it as merely friendship. This highly impacted my concentration.

A night before my exams I received a call from Aditi, which she began with her usual conversation I tried to end the call by saying I have an exam to appear tomorrow morning let's just talk once I am done with my exams.

I don't know what was wrong with her that evening or whether she was at her PMS she had terrible mood swings that evening the moment I tried disconnecting the call she began the most ridiculous talks of all time.

"Do you know vinay, my mother really liked you, I am really happy that we have our elder's consent with us" she said.

"Consent for what? I asked.

"Consent for our marriage, I really like you, I wish to marry you and not only that I have even shortlisted the names of our future babies" she replied.

"What nonsense are you talking about. Stop thinking this instead focus on your studies, only that will help you achieve whatever you want with life" I replied.

"You are everything I want with my life and nothing else, you know I don't want to force you for anything, I even know that you have never seen me that way but I have always looked up to you in that similar fashion of my husband." She replied.

"Are you out of your mind, what nonsense are you talking. You very well know that I am not okay with these kinds of talks. I have told you several times that I look up to you as a friend and nothing more than that then why are you trying to engulf me in the direction, I am not ready for. Stop contemplating this belief. And for now, allow me to read I have heard enough from you." I reprimanded her.

"I am sorry I did not mean to hurt you by any means, I am sorry if you found my talks absurd" she replied.

We disconnected this call on a notion where she was relieved from her baggage of thoughts and I had a pile on my shoulder of her expectations which I wasn't ready to fulfil.

Her words echoed in my brain not letting me concentrate I was up till 2:00 am but I haven't read a single word from my book, simply pondered on the conversation which we did. neither was I able to read but by the time I could realise that I had little time to prepare it time had already lapsed from my clutches.

Koshlesh came to wake me up for my exam as it was time to leave for college. I was enraged with Aditi because of her I could not read and now I was fuming with anger but had no other option than to turn up to college to at least appear for the exam.

On returning home I was still mad at Aditi but her conventional method of caring was now irritating me, when I saw my phone with a message from her asking about my exam it felt like she was being sarcastic of the conversation which we had last night.

I chose to switch of my phone rather than landing in an argument with her. And in that process, I kept my phone switched off till next evening.

In order to have a news about me she contacted koshlesh, asking where was I, when koshlesh informed me about this I turned on my phone.

83 messages one after another buzzed my mobile most of which read "turn on your phone if you do not want to talk to me, I will not call you but at least be accessible for your family, they might be worried this way."

I did not read all of the messages and deleted them all at once, my temperament was such if I have my temper high it won't ease off. It took seconds to get me high but to let me loose it won't settle in days.

She tried calling me again but I was not ready to have any conversation with her therefore I disconnected her call.

Minutes later there was a long message from her end.

"I know you are mad at me but I won't apologise as I haven't said anything to hurt you instead, I opened my heart before you, but only thing I would say is that you are mad at me and only me then why are you troubling everybody else. This way by turning off your mobile you are not allowing access to you even by your family members, what if they have something to share with you. It can prove out to be fatal if you keep yourself invisible to everyone who loves you. If you want to avoid me then avoid me and only me your relationship with everyone should not be affected by it. I promise I will not call or text you till your exams are over. Now keep your mobile on and don't let anything else ruin your hard work and perseverance."

I was impressed by her conditioning where she knew what needs to be done at that peculiar moment to let the flame of anger defuse. This way I could concentrate on my reading and could perform the way I was willing to.

For the next 15 days we were totally cut off from our conversations which I missed but then thought of reviving them once the exams were done.

BOOMERANG

Koshlesh was not feeling comfortable in the rented flat in which we were living and therefore he decided to change his flat, he was so desperate that he did not wait for the exams to end but shifted immediately as soon as he found a place apt according to him. None of us objected on his decision to move out, but I was surely going to miss presence in the house. We met often in the college before and after exams, his new pg. was 2kms away from our flat and thus we even gathered for group studies quite often.

It was New Year's Eve and the next day was a holiday therefore all of our friends decided to gather at koshlesh place to celebrate new year, we were a group of 5 friends who gathered there for dinner. As we all were having a great time spending the evening with delicious food from the nearest food stall and some coke to enjoy the food, with some melodious music that added the jazz to the evening.

Koshlesh asked something which took me back in the nostalgic lane.

"Hey tomorrow is new year are you still sending Pratiksha new year's greetings every year" asked koshlesh.

"No, she has been engaged and has strictly asked me to abstain from texting or calling her" I replied within no time my voice changed from being too normal to a choked throat with grief.

I still had the same feelings for her, no matter how hard I tried forgetting her but even the slightest thought about her was enough to take me back into the memory lane where I manifested to be a part of her life.

"But if you have always sent her the greetings than why not this time" asked koshlesh.

"Because she said no and I don't want to do anything what she disliked, I don't want her to hate me for being a creep" I replied sighing in hopelessly.

"Give me her contact details, I shall send her this time on your behalf, let's hope that this time she welcomes your attempt to befriend her" replied koshlesh.

"Why are you into digging up old graves, let it be I have convinced myself that she could never be mine in this lifetime, maybe I would be lucky enough to get her in the next life time" I replied like a defeated warrior who has lost his armour in the battlefield.

"Oh god you so depressed, it's just a matter of a text message, stop having high hopes. I will send her the message from my mobile if she replies good enough, even if no replies come no worries nothing will change" koshlesh replied trying to explain me his practical explanation.

Although I was hesitant koshlesh himself took the number from my mobile and saved it into his mobile.

After returning home I began having collywobbles and the thought what if she replies positively, this thought began engulfing me creating hopes of the scenarios which were never going to be true but still my silly mind was ready to believe them to be true.

This desperation was killing me inside but I had that in my mind what I was assuming would never really happen.

I kept on saying to myself. "I had somehow controlled my emotions this time, and was adamant to not send her any message but this one conversation with koshlesh has grown an overnight tree of expectations in my head"

I patiently waited for receiving an update from koshlesh but there was no such news from his end which escalated my jitters, I knew the fact that koshlesh had recently shifted to a new place and for that reason he had a pile of arrangements waiting to be done, therefore I abstained from calling him, believing that if he receives any response, he would surely share that with me.

Clock kept on tickling hour after hour with every notification over my phone I reached to it thinking it was koshlesh but it was not him. I finally decided to call him by the evening.

"Hey! Have you sent her the message?" I asked "did she responded" I asked with high hopes.

"Ohhh! I am so sorry dear I have had a lot on my plate for the day and in that I absolutely forgot about texting her" replied koshlesh.

I was heartbroken on hearing this, all the scenarios that I had created during the day went into dust and met their fate although I was grumpy but did not say anything to koshlesh as he was nowhere at fault although he had ignited the belief in me that I could still have her back into my life.

"it's okay no problem, I was curious to know and therefore call you" I replied in order to avoid any distress between me and koshlesh.

"Wait I am texting her right away and shall get back to you if there is any response" replied koshlesh sensing the disappointment on my vocal tone.

"Now don't bother there is no need as such, earlier also I was not going to make her any texts, and its already evening, new year is about to end what's the point, she isn't going to respond anyway, why to gather false expectations" I replied.

"You just shut up and sit quietly, if I have committed you to text her your behalf then I will surely do that without bothering about its outcome be it negative or positive" replied koshlesh apprehensively.

I was spooked at what if she used disparaging words against koshlesh thinking it was me, it did not my friend who was intending to help me to face any resentment from her end because of me and therefore I resisted on the idea of texting her, but koshlesh was adamant to go with his instincts he believed he could play the cupid in bringing us together which I was sure was never going to happen.

When it was next to impossible for me to stop koshlesh, then I even stopped attempting at doing so thinking that there was no chance of getting a response and even if he gets one it isn't going to be a positive one instead it will be filled with warnings and curse so rather let his bubble of myth break all by itself.

Meanwhile I was struggling with my thoughts soon after the conversation with koshlesh, I received a call from koshlesh.

"Why did you fill me in with all the negative information about her brother! She was so happy to hear from you" said koshlesh in an energetic voice.

My eyes rolled out; I could not believe what I have heard. "What are you saying! Did you used the wrong number or what?" I replied.

"I am not here to pull your leg I am genuinely saying what happened just now" replied koshlesh.

"don't twist it into the tale of words tell me what exactly happened word by word" I said seeking clarity.

"Alright! As per our discussion I sent her a message wishing greetings for new year.

A couple of minutes later I received a reply asking who I was, the moment I introduced myself as vinay, she had her a very pleasant response,

"I had been waiting for your message since morning as I knew you would never fail to message me specially on this day, other people may disappoint or back stab but you were as genuine as always"

"what" I interrupted.

"Was that really her" I added.

"of course! She had asked me to call her at 8:30 pm I will add you on the conference call you can hear yourself to believe that whatever I am saying is 100% fact and not cooked up." Replied koshlesh.

"Koshlesh, I have goosebumps over my body I can't even imagine that what you are saying is true, I will have to pinch myself to believe it to be true," I said.

"You will believe it after hearing the call, I won't invite you over as we have an exam tomorrow but will surely add you through the conference call, what do you want would you be leading the conversation or should I talk on your behalf." Asked koshlesh.

"I would fumble to talk please you talk now as its difficult for me to accept the fact that she is willing to talk with me, please I request you to talk for now" I pleaded and one more request can you please record the conversation I want to hear her voice over and over again.

"Okay no need to request, you are my buddy It's my duty to do this for you" replied koshlesh.

This entire span of one hour kept sending chills to my spine on the thought that she was actually willing to hear from me.

At 8:30 sharp koshlesh added me first to the conference call and asked to keep myself mute to only hear the conversation and not being heard.

"Hello! Hi Pratiksha how are you" said koshlesh.

"Hello! Is that really you vinay, your voice sounds different" she replied.

I was overwhelmed at the fact that she recognised my voice over the fake calls which I gave her in the past.

"Ohh its due to the chilly weather, I have a bad throat infection from last couple of days." Replied koshlesh.

He was a pro at cooking up immediate stories to coverup, I was startled at how smooth his brain functions to never let anyone know he was lying.

"Ohh take care and have your medicines on time to relieve your infection" she replied.

"Yes, thank you! are you not upset with me over the message I sent you" asked koshlesh swiftly.

"No, to be honest I had been waiting for your text since morning. You have been someone over these past years who has never failed to message me especially on new year's. I wanted to text you earlier but unfortunately, I had lost your number and ever since then I had been waiting for this day to have your number back" she replied in her melodious voice.

I went into trance hearing this from her end it felt like I have achieved everything I have wanted with life.

"Okay, right now I have to be somewhere can we please continue our talk later. Maybe tomorrow if you don't mind. She asked"

"Yeah, sure replied koshlesh, good night it was pleasure talking with you after so long" replied koshlesh.

"Same here" she replied as they disconnected the call.

I recalled koshlesh "thank you so much dear I could not believe my ears what I heard was true. Have you recorded the call?" I asked.

"Yes, I did, now let's study we have an exam to appear tomorrow and I haven't prepared anything during the day because I was setting up my new flat according to my requirements." Replied koshlesh.

"Yeah, sure let's meet tomorrow, thanks once again brother this means a lot" I thanked koshlesh again before I could disconnect the call.

The voice kept on playing in my ears as it felt like I was still in a dream, but it was real. It felt like all my prayers from the past have been answered all together.

I could hardly gather my excitement to read and to sleep, I woke up before time to reach college so that I could get the recording, stayed at the parking till the warning bell rang and the clerk pushed me inside my class but till then there were no signs of koshlesh arrival thus I had to wait for 3 more hours to get closer to my dream.

These 3 hours were the most difficult to pass although I had the question paper before me to keep me engaged.

I finished the paper 30 minutes before its given time but it was all fruitless as koshlesh would get out only after the entire time was over. Thus, I waited in the canteen for him to get out.

I glued my sight over the door of the cafeteria the wait finally ended with the final bell, I still had to wait for another 5 minutes for him to get there in the canteen, he was enjoying this whole situation of curiosity he took this as an opportunity where he could ask me to fulfil any of his demand which I was sure shot ready to abide by.

"Why are you walking too slow" I asked irritably

"Because I am in a mood to walk at a snail pace today, do you have a problem with it" smirked koshlesh.

"Please yar just hand over the recording to me than you can continue with your snail pace" I requested.

"Not too soon brother, everything has its price if you want something from me you will have to barter something for it" replied koshlesh teasing me.

"Tell me what do you want, I will give you anything you like." I replied trying to snatch his phone which he was flaunting before me.

"This barter remains pending anytime in future I can claim my reward from you. But for now, I am starving, and I need a treat" replied koshlesh.

"Okay done! You can order whatever you like, the bill is on me. Now please if your majesty allows can I get to hear the recording" I pleaded.

koshlesh was enjoying my desperation and left no room to pull my leg, but I was equally thankful to him, had he not sent the message I would have never been able to get this experience this thrill, as I had already lost all my hopes.

I heard the conversation which koshlesh had already elaborated before me but her voice made it magical for me. I immediately transferred that audio in my phone via Bluetooth and kept on listening to it on a loop. I had my earphones on and was carefree who walked past me I was so much drowned into listening to her voice that those 3 minutes of telephonic conversation became the most played audio on my phone within hours of receiving it.

I could not thank koshlesh enough for giving me this magical potion which raised my dopamine levels every time I heard her voice saying I was waiting for your text since morning.

This routine was followed for the next 8 days as they talked every evening where koshlesh tried his best portraying my best image before Aditi, not that he was making stories about me but he was elucidating all the qualities which apparently every girl wants in a boy, I was very happy to hear the conversations every time, he asked a couple of times for me to now start doing the conversations but I was sure I would fumble before her and I did not want my impression to be stained in her mind and therefore I requested him to take the lead unless I was confident about it.

I was really grateful to koshlesh that he made sure he recorded every conversation they had together I was overwhelmed on the fact that Pratiksha was willing to know more about me.

When she got to know that I was in Bhopal pursing my mechanical engineering her immediate reaction was that "I always thought you were here in Ahmedabad, well it's good that you are pursuing a professional course" she said.

Kar made sure that she had insights about me and my behaviour which could cast a good imprint on her mind about me as a person. Koshlesh had that expertise in him thanks to his warm behaviour that he could easily charm people with his witty sense of humour, I being an introvert lacked in this skill, maybe that was the reason why I always hesitated to take the lead in my hands of talking with her.

When my exams ended on the same night, I received a text message from Aditi which kind of shackled my castle of hopes: "hey! If you are done with giving your attention towards your examinations, can we resume talking like we did"

This message made my heart feel the agony which I had levied upon Aditi during those days when she was nowhere at fault. It was my fault that I could not specifically convey before her that I had no feelings, I felt like digging up a hole to burry myself in it for the disappointment I had levied upon her, I wanted to tell her right away that she should now let loose of all her hopes of the flames which she had always wanted because now Pratiksha was back in my life but could not say anything before her either.

To postpone this encounter with the truth to a later date I simply replied with a yes and felt miserable for doing so, regardless of the fact that I did not feel for her, I always enjoyed her company and I felt fortunate to have found a friend like her who was so warm and loving, I was not brave enough to have our friendship at stake and therefore chose silence and left everything upon time and came back to the normalcy.

On one hand koshlesh was chatting with Pratiksha making sure she had the best impression about me before we could meet on the other hand, I managed talking with Aditi making sure I do not give rise to any hopes in her mind.

While all this was happening in the background there were other things happening in our college too, as exams had ended most of our friends began heading to their homes to spend some time with their families, one such dearest friend was Pratik.

"Hey I am going to my home in Maharashtra tonight, my train is at 11 pm. Please let me know if there are any updates in college," said Pratik.

It was already 9pm when he made this call but I felt an urge to see off him at the railway station as there were still 2 hours left from the train's departure time. I asked koshlesh to join me as it was usually the time when he chats with Pratiksha this way, I thought I could ask him to reply my way.

Koshlesh agreed to this offer and we rushed towards the railways station where Pratik was already waiting for his train, while we were having a little chit chat together koshlesh mobile buzzed with a message from Pratiksha. It was something I was longing for. Delighted to see the twinkle in my eyes on the message koshlesh extended his mobile towards me saying "if you want you can chat with her, Pratiksha should also get a chance to talk to the real vinay instead of this fake one" I was overwhelmed with koshlesh statement and took the mobile to reply. At first, I was a little nervous but somehow, I suppressed my anxiety to have a one-on-one conversation with her for the very first time. We began talking the usual way as I well acquainted with the pattern how koshlesh used to chat with her therefore I followed the drill in order to catch no suspicion from her end.

I became too engrossed with the constant exchange of messages that I forgot to keep the track of time,

"So, it's time for me to board the train now, I shall take your leave but please keep me in the loop for any new developments in the college or if any important circular is presented in the college" said Pratik tapping on my back to get my attention.

I felt little guilty of not being attentive towards him, for the time being I kept the mobile in my pocket and focused on seeing off Pratik watching him board his train, as soon as he boarded his train the train slowly began moving and within a couple of minutes the train was out of our sight.

Koshlesh observed how deeply I enjoyed the wholesome conversation I was having with Pratiksha, he proposed before an undeniable offer.

"Why don't you come along for a sleepover at my PG" offered koshlesh

It was an irresistible offer it felt like it was something I had been secretly praying and my prayed had been answered. It took no time to take the offer and jumped on the bike to reach his pg. I asked him to drive to not miss a single message without a prompt reply.

After comfortably talking for almost an hour I took the courage to ask her something, a thought which was stuck in my head like a rock and which needed to be cleared to know whether I was someone who really mattered in her life or was I just a pawn for her to pass her time.

"If you don't mind, may I ask you something personal" I asked

"Go ahead?" a reply came from her end immediately.

I knew well in my head that the question I was about to ask might not welcomed by her, but for me to get rid of the ambiguity was more important. Therefore, I tried my best to decorate the question enough to not sound rude and up straight.

"Please don't get me wrong but the last time when I talked to you year ago, you said you were engaged to Mehul and were soon going to get married with him? And not only that you also asked me to never show up again. Your sudden change of behaviour is raising these questions in my mind." I nervously asked.

My heart pumped twice its usual speed and I was desperately waiting for her reply. After 5 minutes my anxiety began spiking up. 20 minutes passed by since I asked her that question, at once I thought she got upset with my question and may be that is the reason why she hasn't responded.

To pacify the matter which had already caught fire in my brain I began the work of extinguisher and to elevate the situation to a better place I sent her another message saying

"I am sorry if this is something you do not want to discuss let's just talk about something else and I promise I shall never come back on this topic ever again"

For the next 10 minutes this text also did not receive any response which kind of elevated my anxiety and I blamed myself for asking her this personal question at the nascent stage of our communication, although I wanted clarity but that did not mean that the clarity costed me all the bonding which we have had till that date.

While I was encircled with these tormenting thoughts the mobile buzzed and with that buzz, I took a sigh of relief partially as the message was from Pratiksha it was a lengthy message which read:

" yes Mehul and I were seeing each other, we both liked one another and were confidant of one another, I liked him enough that my family knew about him and were okay if we plan to see our future together, not only that Mehul himself introduced me to his parents and they greeted me with warmth every time I visited their place, I was on cloud nine to be so lucky in love that I had nothing to struggle, because in our country love marriages and not yet supported by the families but our families welcomed our decisions. Their only condition was that before leaping on to our next step in our relationship we should secure our respective careers which was equally important. Therefore, we both began working hard on our academics to get the desired job. Mehul always wanted to pursue his higher studies from Canada and had been working upon getting his students visa approved. And he was fortunate enough to get the visa, he took no time in flying to Canada to chase his dreams. At first, I was reluctant to see him go but for his growth and for our growth as a couple it was important for him to leave.

Tables turned around when he reached Canada, first few days were normal we could hardly talk because of the different time zones. But as the days passed, I stopped hearing from him even when I tried communicating with him through messages nothing was answered which bothered me a little for few weeks, I tried communicating him before I visited his parents' house to take updates about him. And to my surprise his mother's behaviour was exactly opposite of how she treated me earlier, she was rude and was definitely not happy to see me, she asked me to leave immediately and warned me to never show my face ever again to them. This shock was enough to shake my world upside down but to add upon it, the same evening I received a call from Mehul he tried intimidating me to stop calling him and the relationship was over from his end, he added that he had found someone better than me and wanted to breakup, which he already did from his end. This tremor was enough to shake the world underneath my feet and to add upon it he even handed over the phone to his girlfriend who talked shit about me from her mouth. This entire conversation flipped my world upside down. I even took recourse to self-harming but that aggravated my pain instead of reducing it.

It took me months to get out of this shock, honestly, I am not over it yet, but this was the time when I realised your importance. I wanted to share this incident to someone without the fear of being judged and I knew you are someone who has always wanted to be my friend. And during this tragic time, I genuinely needed a friend who really cared for my emotions.

Earlier also I wanted to share this with you but I was scared what if I could lose a friend like you, therefore I did not tell you this beforehand. I am sorry.

This entire message left me in tears as she was someone whom I worshipped and seeing her in such a miserable state was very difficult for me, I wanted her again to be that gregarious girl who was confident and we loved her life. I promised myself that I will try to be her best friend first before I could expect anything more from her and at that point of time, she was in a desperate need of a true friend upon whom she could trust and I wanted to be that friend for her for life.

"I am sorry I wasn't aware of this trauma that you have been through, but I am glad that you did not marry that asshole as he did not deserve a soulful person like you, maybe God has some better plans for you in life instead. From today onwards you not be shedding anymore tears over that moron and I promise I will never ask you anything which revives your scared memories." I replied to bring balance to our conversation which has turned complex.

"Can we please talk tomorrow; I want to sleep now" she replied

"Yes! Its already late, good night take care" I said, although I wanted to console her but I could not supersede her will and therefore agreed.

"Good night bye" she replied.

Although we both said good night but none of us had a good night sleep, I blamed myself for reviving her dark memories.

ARE WE MEETING?

As exams were already over the only place, I had to be was at koshlesh apartment to have maximum reach to his phone to talk with her and know her even better, but I was equally bothered of how I was going to give her my personal number. I and koshlesh were on a mission to device an excuse which actually looked genuine, as I was planning to go to Ahmedabad and koshlesh had some work therefore he was choosing to stay back. This way if I would go without exchanging my number how would I continue to chat with her.

I was partially confident that during this trip to Ahmedabad I will surely be meeting her and I wanted myself to look best on our first meeting to leave a lasting impression on her. For this I took help of my two pillars koshlesh and vijay to help me hunt the perfect outfit for my first ever date with her. We went to the mall looking for the apparel during this time of shopping also I was in conversation with her through text messages.

"Can you please do me a favour? Since you are in the mall shopping you would be awake, I have a headache and therefore I am going to sleep can you please wake me up at 4 pm. I really have to go somewhere important" she said in her text

"Sure, I will" I replied and told koshlesh about her request. I was happy that now she had started trusting me, and shared even the tiniest bits of her life.

Wandering in the mall in search of clothes time flew by and it was 4pm, when koshlesh reminded me to call her, but I declined his idea.

"Why are you not calling her, this way she might get upset with you" said koshlesh with a confusing look.

"I am deliberately not calling her to see how will she react, will she get mad at me or will she forgive me" I replied.

"I can't understand you at times, you are crazy to get close to her and now when she is allowing you, you are taking a step back to see her reaction." Replied koshlesh in a helpless tone.

"Why make scenarios in head let's wait and watch how she reacts and how well does this hunk handles the situation he has been trying to create" advised vijay.

We continued with our shopping when I received the message at 5pm from her

"So, what kept you so engrossed that you forgot to call me"

"Oh, I am so sorry dear it completely slipped from my mind, I seek a sincere apology for this, I lost the track of my time while being in the mall, which lead to this negligence." I replied with innocence.

"it's okay! But you will have to bear the consequences of your negligence and as a penalty you will have to give me a chocolate" she replied.

I fell more for her cute demand; this opened a door for me that now we had reached to a place where we could talk in a flirtatious manner. I took this as an opportunity and said:

"I will surely bring a chocolate for you, tell me which chocolate would you like to have?"

"That I leave up on you, I like chocolates any one will do" she replied.

"So, when can I expect to have my chocolate?" she added.

I was glad that we were on the same page and she was responding to my witty replies with the same frequency.

"If you want, I can present myself before you right away" I replied

"Ahhaaaa! I would be gladder to see you, I haven't seen you from years, come as soon as possible" she said.

Her words filled me in with more enthusiasm and not only that I was now even more thrilled to see her.

When I told my friends about this, they were equally excited as me.

"Everything is sorted with your outfit but I would suggest you to add a watch as an accessory to complete your entire look" suggested vijay.

"Now I will only wear a watch on my wrist when Pratiksha gifts me one, till then this wrist shall remain bare watch" holding my head high I uttered these words filled with confidence.

"don't you think he has gone crazy" asked vijay to koshlesh.

"Indeed, he is" replied koshlesh.

"Okay listen I have a brilliant idea to cook up before her to sound genuine for your number changed" koshlesh rolled his eyes while telling us the idea.

"let's switch off my mobile phone, and keep it off till tomorrow afternoon, later you send a message from your number saying you lost your phone in the mall yesterday and this is your new number I will keep my mobile off for one more day to ensure that she may not dial it" what's your take on this idea asked koshlesh

"Eureka! This plan is absolutely flawless." I replied

I could not be more grateful to koshlesh for being the most supportive person who was ready to do anything to make my relation work. He was a sweetheart.

I did exactly as how I was told. And the plan went as per our expectations, she believed my story without any doubt and now I was ready to board the next train to Ahmedabad. Nothing was now bothering me to meet her for the first time when I could actually see her in person.

I had seen her up-close in the past but always was scared as I was doing it against her will but now, she was equally willing to meet me, I could not thank God enough for twisting his magical wand and make things happen. I had always manifested that day in my head and now it was actually happening.

I was on a heavenly journey, I did not know what was I going to say before her, how will I greet her where will we meet all these thoughts got me collywobbles but this was the first time, I disliked the train journey feeling the train was taking too much time to reach Ahmedabad.

Since Pratiksha had my number now, I kept chatting with her throughout the journey knowing more about her. As I wanted to put my best foot forward to create the lasting impression in her heart and to help her erase all the dark memories of the past.

Her keenness to meet me was evident and I was happy to see her as excited as I was. From the time I boarded my train she pinged me with questions asking if I had my food and was, I carrying water along. These little questions were soothing my heart believing she had begun feeling for me. I could not thank koshlesh more because he had been the reason why I was getting that experience.

"Text me when you reach Ahmedabad, I just want to be included in your journey" she said and if possible, can we meet by the evening? She added.

I was overwhelmed to read this message I was waiting for this day to come ever since I saw her for the very first time in school.

"let's catch up in the evening at 5 at the place convenient to you?" I replied.

We then decide to meet at the café. After enjoying the lunch at my home with my family. I began preparing in my head for meeting Pratiksha.

I wore one of the shirts which I purchased recently and left at 4 to reach on time, also I had to buy the chocolate which she had asked me to bring. So, I went to the shop having the best chocolates and bought some premium chocolates for her.

I reached the café before time and chose the quite corner of the café in order to have some privacy while I meet her, I was already underconfident as to how will I approach her.

She was running late so she sent me a text, "hey I am sorry I am running a little late, please bear with me I will be reaching there in the next 20 minutes".

I really liked her gesture of informing me.

I was sitting in a way that I could keep a watch on the road from the see through mirror. After waiting for a while, I saw a girl in a black kurti parking a scooty her face was covered with a scarf and therefore I could not make it whether it was her or anybody else.

The moment she removed her scarf I saw her walking towards the café.

"isn't she got prettier, look at her dewy cheeks which are glowing like dew drops and her eyes oh my god was she really coming to meet me. She looked like the goddess walking down the aisle. She has gracefully turned into a woman of my dreams" I said to myself.

I waved at her to grab her attention. And she came and sat at the table with a smile.

"Hello! How are you" she said

"I am fine and now feeling the best sharing this table with you." I replied.

"What happened to your voice, having a bad throat" she asked.

"No nothing as such" I replied.

"You sound different?" she sceptically replied.

"Ohhhhh! That may be because the phone which I had lost had a technical problem with its microphone which resulted in malfunctioning of the voice, this is my real voice, you might not have taken notice to it during the school days else you may not suspect it" I projected myself without fumbling to sound confident.

She frowned her brows reflecting that she did not agree to what I said but was least bothered to shoot a counter question at me and therefore took the excuse with a pinch of salt.

I took a sigh of relief when I did not receive a counter question over this. The only thing that bothered me was also smoothly removed.

But at the back of my mind, I had prepared myself that if she was not convinced with my excuse, I won't hide the truth any longer I shall put before her the entire episode of koshlesh and his involvement in bringing us together. But thankfully this wasn't needed any longer.

I was looking at her with astonishment as I had played this situation in my head for more than a thousand of time but still was at lack of belief that what I had imagined has turned into my reality, I was actually sharing a table with her. Good gracious may God protect us from all the evil eyes in the world.

"What happened why are you staring at me like this, is there anything wrong with my face? she asked blocking my thoughts.

"No not at all, it's just that I can't believe that we are sharing this table, I have always wanted to be your companion, and as my long-lost desire had come true, I am overwhelmed with emotions." I replied with utmost honesty, as I wanted to reflect my unfiltered emotions before her.

Her cheeks turned pink as she blushed hearing this and after this her glow enhanced making her more magnetic.

We had of cappuccino and had the most wholesome conversation, since she was running out of time as she had to be somewhere therefore, we had to pause our date and promised to take it further the next time.

I saw her leaving the café, she left but the trail of her aura was still there, I found myself quivering to help myself I again went back to the table and this time sat on the chair she was sitting, which lingered with her scent, the café was full with the aroma of coffee beans but the only fragrance caught me up was the sweet fragrance she was wearing.

After sitting for a while, I left, I was joyous of having shared the time with her and was driving with the melody of her voice playing on a loop into my ears which was interrupted with the continuous honking behind my vehicle, the constant buzzing annoyed my pleasing journey and thus I stopped my vehicle to look around who was intentionally honking at me.

It was somebody whom I was least expecting and which shook me so bad that for a second, I was about to lose my balance on the vehicle. She was Aditi, I did not let her know through our chats that I was in Ahmedabad as I was not looking for divided attention, she was heartbroken to see me which was evident from her face that she was expecting me to tell her before I arrived Ahmedabad. Guilt encapsulated my eyes and I had nothing to justify before her.

"You are in Ahmedabad and you did not bother to inform me about this.?" She said with a stunned expression. Frowning her brows waiting for a lame excuse from my end.

"I came today only, and as usual I wanted to surprise you and therefore prevented myself from spilling the beans." I justified

"Surprise when! It was time for you to leave then?" she replied not accepting my excuse.

"You ruined my plan! We were not supposed to meet her" I said in a promising tone.

"No there wasn't any plan you are fooling me; I have realised this from your past behaviour the way you are trying to cut down our communication channels. At first you gave an excuse for your exams and later you have an excuse ready with you to cut the conversation short. What do you think I am so lame to understand the drastic change that has been coming in your behaviour from past one or two months." She replied in a heartbroken voice.

She worked hard upon controlling her tears from overflowing her eyes.

I felt miserable for having made her feel so let down but I was unable to convey my justification before her. As I did not want her to know about Pratiksha and therefore, I stood before her with my head down in regret.

She released her bottled feelings before me, and it was obvious she has had considered me to be his closest friend and on the other part I had been ignoring her on my convenience, which was indeed shameful.

She waited a minute for me to reply but I could not say anything above sorry. She left wiping off her tears.

I was too happy earlier on my first date and minutes ago something like that happened which scared my happiness in fraction of seconds.

On reaching home I tried calling Aditi to make peace with her, I believed she was there with me on the time when I needed the emotional support and therefore, I could not let her stay angry at me for a long period of time, she wasn't ready to take my calls and therefore I sent her a text message seeking an apology:

"Hey I am sorry! I am guilty of letting you down I haven't informed you about my visit to Ahmedabad I was at fault for this but I did that to surprise you as I have not behaved well with you in the past, I wanted to mend my mistakes by surprising you but the trick worked against me and ultimately lead you to become more disappointed. I am sorry dear for all the mistakes I have committed so far please forgive me".

"You should be sorry for hurting my sentiments, I am highly disappointed with your childish behaviour, and to make things like before you will have to take me out for lunch only then I can think about forgiving you." She replied

I took a sigh of relief reading this, but I was still stuck with the thought what if Pratiksha gets to know about this, she might misunderstand which may impact my budding friendship with her, God I needed serious help I did not know how to deal with this double pressure.

While I was dwindling with my thoughts Pratiksha messaged me about how she felt with me:

"Hey I am sorry I had to head back early today, but it was really nice meeting you. I have exams from tomorrow and I haven't prepared anything. So, excuse me if I fail to respond to your calls and messages. We can get back to our normal conversations once my exams are over."

This message was a saviour as it indicated that Pratiksha was going to be busy with her exams and thus, I could meet Aditi with ease. This relived the baggage of guilt I had been carrying on my shoulders.

Once I got the details of her exam time and place, I then decide to meet Aditi on the time when she had her exams this way, I could ensure that I could not miss any calls from Pratiksha if at all she decides to make one.

Next morning, I sent Aditi a text of meeting and this time unlike the previous times I decide to the nearest café around my house, I did not give her the room to raise any objection against this as I gave her the excuse of a ceremony in my family for which I had to be present.

She unwilling accepted my request for meeting, she was not very sure of my changed behaviour but she did take a notice of it, we had a very brief meeting over a coffee where we shared the usual tit bits of our life. Her expressions said it all how pissed she was at me, but I wanted her to stop feeling about me the way she did lest that would further lead to complications and heartbreak. I wanted to slide through this complexity without hurting her sentiments.

By the end of our coffee, she was composed and partially I was successful at making peace with her. Unlike the old times this day we only spent nearly an hour together and then headed back home with a smile on our faces.

I felt a big boulder off my shoulders as I was feeling a constant guilt of hurting her feelings. And I cherish the friendship bond we share together. This ensured that I was not losing my friend at the cost of my dream girl.

I could predict that my attitude of not taking the bull by its horns was certainly going to create chaos in near future but I was reluctant to let go any of the ends, leaving the problem unattended I focused on the temporary balance which I had successfully created between the two. Believing that time will take its recourse and decide the outcomes of my procrastinations.

THE PROPOSAL

I was very excited to meet koshlesh as he was returning to Ahmedabad, I had a tough time in balancing Aditi and Pratiksha simultaneously, I was pretty sure that if he was around, he would have definitely helped me in finding an equilibrium. I went ahead of time to reach the station in order to receive him.

"Ohhh my great warrior on a mission, how are you doing these days, look how pink have your cheeks turned" said koshlesh while dropping his bag down from the train.

Hearing his compliment, I couldn't say much but rested my hand on my forehead thinking there were people around and his comment has driven the unwanted attention towards me.

Koshlesh was so jolly by nature that he could enlighten the entire dull room just by one sentence from his wit.

By the time we were leaving the railway station I receive a good morning text from Pratiksha.

I replied her without wasting a single minute. Koshlesh observing my happiness over my face while I was replying her said:

"I am really happy for you yar, I am glad that I took the step of messaging her, thankfully that has helped you in achieving this blissful glow in your eyes.

"I have come to the railway station to receive my friend koshlesh, he has come from Bhopal." I replied over the question of Pratiksha asking what was I doing.

"Ohh that is great! I was about to ask you can we meet today? But if you have to be with koshlesh than its okay, as it was my last exam today, I was planning to spend little time together," said she.

"Not an issue, I can be with koshlesh even in Bhopal but with you it's this little time I have" I replied prioritising her over koshlesh, even this was suggested by koshlesh that I ned to show her I was prioritising her over anything else.

"Well, if koshlesh doesn't mind please ask him to join us, this way will also get to meet him and not only that all three of us can her good time together" she replied.

I was overwhelmed at the fact that she was someone who wanted to know more about me and my friends and I was overjoyed to hear this. When I told koshlesh about this idea he began blowing his own trumpet saying what will I do between you two, you guys are going on a date why to carry a third wheel on your date.

You are not the third wheel instead you are the steering wheel which has helped me in steering this relation till here. I said insisting him on joining me.

After a few attempts he was convinced to join us.

We decided to catch up at 3pm outside her college as this was the time her exam was over.

At first, I went to koshlesh house to pick him, I was dressed in the best possible manner to ensure she has a better impression of me. I chose to wear one of the apparels I had purchased from Bhopal, I ensured that I smell good because I had that gut feeling that we may share a drive together and this way I wanted a lasting fragrance.

Look the hero is around for a date, commented koshlesh. If you are going to be dressed superhot then will she even notice me, he added.

That isn't needed either. I winked at him.

"So has the day come" he asked with intrigue.

"What day" I replied being clueless of his question.

"don't tell me you are not briefing your feelings before her" he said.

"don't you think it would be too early to take this step" I replied

"No not at all" he replied, you need to clear yourself before things get any further, she, must know what and how do you feel about her and since when" he added.

This way both of you can be in alignment otherwise you would be in your dream land and she can give you the reality check by introducing you to his other interest" he justified.

"But don't you think it would be too soon, it has been just 15 days since we began talking and immediately dropping a bomb about my feelings wouldn't that be unfair for our friendship to get itself rooted. I replied.

"If you keep on delaying this you will continue to dwindle between her and Aditi and once one side its clear you can make things clear between all three of you demarking your priorities." He explained.

I was still wondering about the probable after effects of this impulsive decision koshlesh was imposing on me. But on the other hand, I somewhere knew I had to stand on my grounds and that could not be possible before making things clear.

"let's go now it's already 2 we have to reach there before 3pm I do not want her to wait. We will decide on this matter during our way." I wanted koshlesh to excuse me from executing this plan and therefore we left the house.

"Take the maninagar route" said koshlesh.

"why" I asked.

"Just do as I say, I will tell you the rest later" replied koshlesh.

Getting down at his desired place koshlesh went inside a narrow passage and 5 minutes later I saw him bringing a small bunch of roses and a goody box of exquisite chocolates.

"Why have you brought all of this" I asked.

"don't act this dumb, I brought this for you, you can't propose a girl with empty hands and therefore I brought this for you, if I do not insist you will never ever express before her your feelings and therefore today, I will make sure you speak your heart before her." Replied koshlesh.

Hearing his intentions made me nervous. I was not mentally prepared to hear no. and above that I was sucker at expressing myself before others and this was like a surprise test where I had to put my heart out before Pratiksha without any prior preparations and without even knowing how she thought about me.

"don't panic, if she says yes Valentine's Day is round the corner make her feel the luckiest girl in town, and if at all she says no don't lose hope she won't break friendship with you" koshlesh said consoling me.

"How can you be so sure, what if she asks me to never show her my face" I responded.

"let's go I can help you with your anxiety but I can only assure you that things are going to work in your favour, this is what my instincts are denoting." Replied koshlesh.

Your instincts better be right otherwise I am going to break down badly" I replied.

We reached late by 5 minutes saw Pratiksha standing on her scooty outside the gate. And as usual she looked marvellous in her Sunkissed glowy skin.

After formally introducing her with koshlesh we stood there for a couple of more minutes, but my mind was already encapsulated with the thoughts fed by koshlesh as I was in no position to think anything beyond that.

"So, where are we going" said koshlesh breaking the ice.

I made an eye contact with her asking her consent "where would you like to go"

"I can spare 3-4 hours so we can hang out accordingly" she replied.

"Well than let's go for a long drive that would be fun" said koshlesh.

"Okay then if you agree let's go to science city, I had been there once it's quite and nice place and it's at a distance from here so it will serve the purpose of long drive too" I suggested.

She nodded in agreement, till this time mostly our eyes were doing the maximum talking.

"Pratiksha if you don't mind, koshlesh can drive your scooty and you can join me on my bike for a ride" I hesitantly suggested before Pratiksha.

"Why I will ride on my, if koshlesh wants he can join me on my scooty." She replied humorously.

My eyes bulged on her reaction but I could not do anything and said "as you like"

I was very disappointed with this, but still decided to keep my expressions unchanged.

"Okay, I will join you, but if you allow can I drive" asked koshlesh.

I was a bit surprised on his promptness to go with her but before I could say anything koshlesh took her keys and drove past us.

She wasn't prepared for this, his action left us in dilemma why he sped away, but after getting ahead of us he said, "now you two come on bike"

I was absolutely astound at his wit. he created the situation where Pratiksha had no other option but to sit on my bike.

At first, she was a little upset, but taking his act with a pinch of salt she sat on my bike resting her arm on my shoulder.

The moment she touched my shoulders I had goosebumps a shiver ran through my spine sending collywobbles to my stomach. I was difficult to elaborate that feeling through words, maybe everyone falling in love experiences such physical signs only than one can decide he or she is the one.

We took the ring road route which was quite surrounded by trees and as it was an odd hour the traffic was light, koshlesh was leading us and I was riding keeping her engaged with some chit chat about her exams, also trying to figure out her mood whether it was apt time to propose her or not.

After riding for about 6 kms koshlesh took a stop and indicated us to stop over. On reaching closer to him he pointed at the flat tyre of Pratiksha's vehicle.

"Ohh no! Tyre puncture, now where we can find a repair shop here.?" she said dramatically.

"don't worry! I am taking your bike vinay and shall come back soon with a mechanic who can help us with this, till then you two spend some time waiting across the service road, look down there are some trees you can stand under there shade" said koshlesh pointing at the trees.

"Try to put your heart out before, there can be no perfect time then this," whispered koshlesh in my ears.

As he left, we went on the service road and there was hardly any vehicle plying from there which gave us the privacy I have been looking for.

Taking a deep breath, I dared to hold her hand swiftly, at first, she tried pulling her hand away but later surrendered herself as I was not ready to loosen the grip.

I pulled out the roses from my bag and said clearing, my throat:

"honestly I am very nervous right now, I haven't done this before but if I don't say this today, I don't know when will I be able to gain the courage the next time, Pratiksha I love you, not from toady but from more than 5 years, the very first day when I saw you in the school ever since that the I have been playing this scene in my head, you might be feeling that at this nascent stage of our friendship I am saying this to you. But I have countlessly said this to you in my head.

I know I had done a lot of mistakes in the past and have troubled you too, but that was all because of these genuine feelings I have for you. But one thing I have realised over these years, the feeling that I had years back for you has only got stronger and I have never experienced something like that for anybody else.

I am not forcing you to give me your response right now, I want you to like me as I do and for that you will have to know me more, and I am ready to wait. And even if you decline my proposal that won't affect my love for you, I always want you to be happy and for that I need to know about your choice. It's okay take your time but only one request even if you do not accept this, please don't break your friendship with me. I cherish you, you mean the world to me, I had already stayed away from you quite long, now I won't be able to take the separation from you.

I am not very good at expressing myself, neither I am the most romantic person on earth but one thing I certain and that is, I will do anything to get that smile on your face and the shine into your eyes. I LOVE YOU PRATIKSHA" please accept these flowers and chocolates.

She stood in silence but her eyes were chaotic with thoughts, they were reflecting several emotions through them and it was difficult to make out what was she thinking about. She slowly grabbed the flowers and smiled and opted for silence.

I was desperate to hear anything from her but the silence was killing me, I saw koshlesh coming along with the mechanic and therefore I neutralised my expressions.

"We will have to take the vehicle to the garage", said the mechanic

"I am going with the mechanic, you guys can come walking its nearby only, 500 meters from here by the time I get the vehicle repaired" suggested koshlesh and left along with the mechanic.

We walked in silence, with thousands of thoughts echoing in my brain. She walking holding those roses carefully in her hands, but I was unable to make out what was really going on in her mind. The only thing I was relieved about was she has not raised any objection against, but I still hoping her silence meant positive rather than being negative.

Pratiksha lost he balance while walking on the road and about to collapse before that I held her waist and prevented her from falling, she was so fragile that I feared if I used excessive force to grab her, she might get some injuries. She looked at me thankfully for saving her, her eyes were so talkative, even if she wasn't using words her eyes were so loud to express her emotions.

I was about the release my hand over her waist when she held my hand and wrapped it across her waist and folded herself in my arms, she really hugged me. I could feel her warmth over my body her natural fragrance engulfed my sensory nerves, and I found myself hugging her for the first time in the middle of the deserted road.

bringing lips closer to my ears she whispered, "I LIKE YOU TOO VINAY, I REALLY DO. after Mehul's incident I had never thought I would say this to anyone this soon but I have seen the honesty in your eyes when you are there with me, you have made me realised that one bad accident does not define that life cannot be good, you have helped me restoring my faith in love and following the emotions of your heart. I am sorry for ignoring you in the past. Had I noticed you earlier I need not go through that heartbreak.

Being around you makes me feel alive and its gives me butterflies to my stomach the moment you touch me, I want us to be together. I am sorry too if I had hurt you in the past, but now I want my future to be in your company.

While she was saying all of this there were tears in her eye and so were in mine. Caressing her forehead, I wiped the tears overflowing through her eyes, a swiftly gave her a peck on her forehead.

"We are in the middle of highway" she blushed and moved away from me.

I grabbed her hand and began walking holding her around her waist. When we reached the garage koshlesh was surprised to see us hand in hand.

He gave me a curious look lifting his brows to which I responded with a smiling nod, he understood she said yes.

"rab ne bana di jodi" he began singing this song giving us a teasing smile. We both blushed hearing this.

By this time the tyre was repaired and as we were leaving, she willingly sat on my bike grabbing my waist tightly. I loved the way she pulled herself closer to me so that there was no gap between us this intimacy was contagious. I held her hand while driving the vehicle and we enjoyed the drive.

We were inseparable at the science city as well, we walked hand in hand and shared the ice-cream, it was a very delightful experience, for which koshlesh was to be thanked.

We reached our homes, I thanked koshlesh for his persuasion he was the one because of whom this story could start and if he had not pushed me today, I would not be able to have the happiness in my life.

"I am really thankful to you vinay for becoming a part of my life and accepting my past. I am glad that you are in my life now, I wish to be yours forever" said Pratiksha through a text message.

I was overwhelmed to have her as my official girlfriend, I had been manifesting this day for over 5 years now and finally it had come to reality. Could not be more grateful to the almighty for fulfilling my earnest desire.

VALENTINES DAY

The festival to celebrate love was round the corner, koshlesh being a cinephile was pumping air in me about how should I make this day memorable for Pratiksha, I being a neophyte was unable to catch the similar frequency as was with koshlesh, he derived his inspiration mostly from the movies and romantic shows and wanted me to frame alike situation but I to make that happen I had to do a lot of research to gather ideas on making things happen. I browsed through internet and made a plan accordingly.

On Valentine's eve I and Pratiksha were chatting and I made an excuse of feeling sleepy and ended our conversation, but I wanted her to stay awake till midnight and for ensuring that I asked koshlesh to involve her in chatting this way I could give her the panned surprise at midnight. Koshlesh did the needful and kept chatting with her.

When the clock struck 12, I called her, she was surprised to receive my call:

"You are still awake? What happened is everything fine why did you call at this hour?" she asked.

"Everything is fine I just called you for something important, please reach to your living room balcony" I requested.

"Balcony! But why" she asked.

"don't interrogate just do as I say it's very crucial" I replied giving the whole scene as a serious tone.

By this time, she was worried why was I asking her to do all of that.

"Okay I am here, now what!" she replied but with some worry in her voice.

"Turn towards your left" I said.

"Is this really the time of this game vinay!" she replied while turning around.

There on the opposite side of the road I was standing with the flash light on in one hand and fluorescent balloons on the other which were glowing in the darkness of night.

"Can you see me; I asked waving the flash light.

"Is that you" she asked with a surprise.

"Yes sweetheart! How can I sleep without wishing my darling on Valentine's Day.

Happy Valentine's Day dear, I love you" I said in a dulcet voice.

She smirked and replied "I thought you slept unknowingly that it was valentines, I never expected you would come over to surprise me"

"Before meeting you all these days served as normal day for me, but this time it was different, I have you in my life and I want you to experience all the flavours of love, and cherish every small moment together" I replied.

Overwhelmed by this gesture her voice cracked as she was about to cry, she said "thank you so much for this wonderful surprise, I never thought I could experience being so special."

"Hold on! Today is not the day to cry, it's time to release these balloons up in the sky which are going to demarcate our love to this world, as I am releasing these balloons, I am manifesting our relationship forever before the universe."

"Thank you so much, you eternalize this evening for me, its high time now you should return to your home, we can continue our chat once you reach" she suggested.

Once I was back home, I found an emotional message from her which read:

"Thank so much vinay, your efforts meant a lot for me, from the bad experiences of the past I have never thought I would be so fortunate to have found someone like you who can make me forget all the trauma from the past with an ease. I love the surprise and those glowing balloons were the show stopper for me, happy Valentine's Day."

"I love you" I replied.

We talked for few more minutes on deciding where we will meet in the morning.

Next morning, I was super thrilled as I had planned another couple of surprises for her and therefore reached the place decided before time, although now we were together for quite some time but still, I got anxious every time I went to meet her.

That day when I saw her walking towards me in that scarlet-coloured top with blue denims she looked ravishing, like always I found her magnificent, I always thanked God for fulfilling my wish that she became a part of my reality.

"So, where are we going today" she asked while sitting on my bike.

"Be ready today is going to be indelible, I promise" I said while starting the vehicle.

We reached to a picturesque café. The café was TGB this was my first time when I was visiting that café thanks to koshlesh who suggested me to take her there it was an idyllic place to be with her, the food was lip-smacking and the ambience was apt to take unlimited photographs which we did.

I also presented her the flowers and chocolates which I had brought for her, she was very happy on receiving them.

While we were indulged in our conversations, the manager of the café came up with an important announcement.

"Hello young couples! It's your day to celebrate today. And to honour that we have made some special arrangements for you all, on the first floor we have arranged some live music for all the young couples, and not only that there is a small competition sponsored by lifestyle also is going to commence soon the winner of which can get a chance to win gift vouchers worth rupees 5000 which you can avail at lifestyles stores near you, so ladies and gentlemen pull up your socks and be ready to hit the dance floor"

Dance and shopping were something Pratiksha loved; she could not stop herself to ask me to go upstairs.

On moving on to the next floor its was magically decorated with red heart shaped balloons giving it the perfect valentines vibe, the warm lights and soft music was loved by all the couples around. The latest chartbuster songs of that time were being played one after another.

"let's go, on the dance floor please, I can't wait to dance with you" she said enthusiastically.

You will have to help me out with this, I know nothing about dancing but if this makes you happy, I am ready to come along" I replied.

"don't worry I will teach you" she said while pulling on the dance floor.

It was hardly 10 minutes of learning the basic dance steps when the DJ stopped the music to announce the games:

"Hello my dear love birds! Let's spice things up a little with the most promising contest between couples which Is sure to enhance your chemistry… it's time for the paper dance.

For those who do not know the rules let me make them clear for you, each couple will be given a piece of paper and you have to dance on it, every time the music stops you have to fold the paper in half and you have to ensure both of you are on the paper, if any of the partner gets out of the paper they are disqualified. So, roll up your sleeves and buckle your shoes it's time for the game to begin. Winners will be given gift vouchers so play with full spirit."

On knowing the rules, I was flattered as this competition was going to give me the chance of getting closer to her, which I could not miss. I was thanking my stars that I brought her there.

Once the game started, there were total 5 couple including us who were participating in the game, each one of us at first started with the ease and none was disqualified, but in the 2nd and 3rd round as the game intensified 3 couples were out and only two of us were left.

In this round the DJ played the number one hit of Arijit sing "tum hi ho" this song was the most relatable song to our story because she was the world to me. And thanks to this paper folding game, we were almost hugging each other and dancing, I could feel her warmth. I wished this song would never end. We shared a romantic moment together and we were deeply into one another. Had the song been played for few more minutes I would have surely kissed her, but the applause from the people around distracted us.

When we were asked to fold the paper one more time, there was not enough space where we both could stand and thus, I was given the golden opportunity to hold her in my arms, to which she was hesitant at first and later allowed me to lift her. This was the best feeling I had ever experienced. To hold her up-close I could feel her breath. We moved by gazing at each other this time the song was "kehte hain khuda ne iss Jahan me sabhi ke lie, kisi na kisi ko hai banaya har kisi k lie" and she was the one, this song was the true depiction of my emotions for her.

Before the song could end the other couple lost their balance and we were declared as the winner of the competition and as an accolade we were given the gift vouchers.

She was smiling from ear to ear receiving the voucher, who doesn't love free shopping.

I was so happy to see her smiling, I then pulled out the actual present that I had brought for her.

"What is there still anything left for the surprise, vinay you have already filled my day with exuberance" she said seeing me pulling out something from my bag.

"Yes, my love this day has to be the best day of your life, I held her hand and placed the gift on her palm asking her to open it.

She curiously opened the pack, rings! She exclaimed.

"Yes, these are couple rings one for you and the other one for me, these are not ordinary rings, just like us being hundreds of kilometres apart our hearts were attracted so are these rings the moment they are brought closer they get attracted to one another. I want to gift you this as a token of our love, so every time we get close these rings help us to get even closer." I spoke.

"May I" I said while asking for her hand.

She had tears in her eyes by then. I don't deserve this much love; I have let you down in the past and you on the other hand are doing so much for me" she said.

Don't you know, excessive crying is deleterious for the glowing skin. I said wiping her tears.

No let them flow, I have to make up for it, ever since we are together you always bring something or the other to pamper me this time, I also have something for you. She sobbed.

"What? You brought something for me" I reassured.

"yes" she said giving me the box.

I was not expecting anything in return but her gesture proved that we were aligned and were feeling the same for one another.

On opening the box, I found out it was a beautiful wristwatch from titan, it was a leather strap with silver round dial and intricate detailing, I was very delighted to receive the beautiful time piece.

This gift reminded me of the promise that I made before vijay, when I told her about that she was happy that she gave a thoughtful gift, I asked her to tie the watch on my hand, which she did and surprisingly she even kissed my hand once the watch was tied.

I could have not thought for something better gift than this. When we both held our hands tightly our rings with magnets came together.

Just like these rings I want our relation to remain stronger, Pratiksha, I love you, I hope you feel the same for me. I spoke.

"I love you too vinay please be with me forever, I am thankful to God that I have someone like you in my life, I want you to know one thing our love is beyond little arguments and problems. Promise me any external problems or circumstances won't affect our relation." She spoke.

I was very happy and grateful to God and koshlesh to make this love story possible.

INTERNSHIP PERIOD

We were profoundly in love for one another and with each passing day we were knowing something or the other about our lives, as Pratiksha has already talked about her past, I felt insecure of not telling her about Aditi and therefore put the facts before her. She was having no objections over my friendship with Aditi which once I thought she would have.

Everything was going great, I even went to meet Aditi a few times, now the vacations were about to end I was returning to Bhopal, but this time I was returning as a committed person, we talked daily but the initial days were challenging because I was so used to be with her that her absence was bothering me.

Studies were equally important and demand our undivided attention, therefore as the exams approached, we had to minimize the time we spent on the phone, this made Pratiksha a little insecure as she had been in a relationship where the distance made them apart and therefore, I had to take special care about this, if not that caused problems between us. We too had arguments and difference opinions like all the other couples which we resolved as early as possible, I personally believed that the more we keep dragging an argument the more we are losing our precious time of the relationship.

We won this test of time by being apart yet together, a new announcement in the college filled me in with zeal:

All the students had to undergo a 3 months internship training under a factory to be qualified to appear for the exams and during that time colleges would remain closed all the students had to compulsorily undergo the training and secure the certificate, the best part about it was the students were allowed to get the training at any place of their choice, the dean allowed us to go to our hometowns for this 3-month tenure as well. This announcement was enough to bring the smile on our faces, as each one of us could go to our homes for the next 3 months and for me the happiness doubled as it would give me the opportunity to be with Pratiksha.

Koshlesh had a relative who owned a factory and he asked his uncle for both of us and thanks to him he was ready for giving us the certificate of internship and unlike others uncle was generous and did not bind us with respect to time, thanks to these flexible hours I could have enough time to meet Pratiksha. It was not that I compromised with the learning, I did that too but the moment I got chance I went ahead to meet her.

I even informed Aditi, she being my good friend deserved to know and also, I did not want myself to be caught by her in the city without her knowledge. This time Aditi was different than all times, unlike Pratiksha, I had not informed her about my relation for obvious reasons but she sensed from it somehow, there was hardly any conversation between us, and if hardly we talked, she used scurrilous sentences which made the possible talks impossible.

But that hardly bothered me as I was so involved in my internship and Pratiksha that I did not take the pain to bring peace with Aditi, maybe I was negligent to keep her hurt for so long but at that time of my life my energy was focused only on myself.

One evening I received a call from Aditi;

"Hey if you are free, I can get a minute of your time I want some favour."

"Why are you being so formal Aditi, say what do you want me to do for you" I replied.

"I want to enrol myself for MBA course, if by any chance you have someone in your acquaintance who can help me more about this course" she replied.

"Ohhh! That's wonderful. You want to do MBA its certainly going to help you in your career, and for the acquaintance I do have a friend of mine who is doing MBA, let me call him and check for the necessary help. Just give me some time, I will circle back to you on this" I replied warmly.

I went ahead to gather as much information as I could and then forwarded the same to her.

She than asked me if I could join her to the college suggested by my friend to gather the information about the seat's availability and fee's structure and if everything falls right, then and there only she will take the admission.

We then decide to meet the following day, to go to the college, I had already informed Pratiksha about my plan with which she did not had any problem.

The next day when we went ahead for her admission, she only held conversations to the point, unlike old days neither was she trying to hold any communication with me nor was she trying to make an eye contact. It felt a little discomforting at first but then switching back my attention towards viewing the college I spent the time with her.

She had really helped me with my stay in Bhopal when at first, I was ready to give up on everything she was the one who pacified my anxiety. And this way by being with her I could return the favour.

As per her choice we did the formalities for the admission and without wasting any further moment returned back to home, when I asked her to join me for some snacks, giving a lame excuse she declined my offer. It was an awkward meeting though I did not give two hoots about it and was back to being normal.

On the other hand, my relation with Pratiksha was stepping the ladder one after another, after spending more time after my training I got to realise that she was someone who can get furious easily therefore I always weighed my words before speaking as I did not want my relation to suffer over the silliest possible topic.

Although I was also a less temperamental person but I worked against my nature to prevent differences in my relation. My priorities had been clear since the day she said yes, I kept her above everything else and expected the same in return. But this peculiar habit was caught in her eyes and she always asked me to be as normal as she was no matter if it resulted in endless arguments, this way we could get the insights of our true nature, I agreed to her point but still lacked at emoting myself, she was raw before me unfiltered but I had layered myself with different filters as I wasn't ready to lose her at any cost.

But Pratiksha was adamant and when she could not decode me, she began taking help from koshlesh, she kept on asking him about my trigger points my weaknesses and the things which I hated the most, not to irritate me but silently she was bringing all the necessary changes into her behaviour since she got to know that I disliked certain things.

This did not end here she also tried to know about the foods I preferred eating and tried ordering them every time we went out to eat. At first It did not click me but eventually I realised that she loved me so much that she was trying her best to be with me, also changing her behaviour which I never forced her to do. Koshlesh had been the guiding angel in this process he uniformly helps both of us in this journey.

I still remember one hilarious incident which although was trap for me but gave the best memory of my life.

Pratiksha was on her mission to know my likes and dislikes and at times she deliberately did pick up things which I disliked just to know how would I react, one day when she got to know that I was not a pluviophile like her, she thought of framing in for a prank and koshlesh was enjoying this because in our stays at Bhopal I always asked him if he could get the work done if it rained.

One morning it was a rainy day and because of the rain I had even cancelled out my plan to go to the factory,

"I would rather spend the entire day slouching on the couch than to get out in this weather" I said while informing koshlesh about my plan of not going to the office.

He being a true informed broke this news before Pratiksha and joined hands with her on their plan to get me out in the torrential rains.

Few minutes later I received a call from Pratiksha, seeing her call at 8 am in the morning was a bit awkward as it was her college time during which we hardly had our conversations

"Hey babe! What are you doing" asked Pratiksha.

"Still under my bed" I replied snuggling my blanket.

"If I could please ask for a favour from you" she asked.

"Feel free to say anything my love, your wish is my command" I replied.

"Could you please come to the college right now, I have an important assignment at hand and I really need your help. I know it's raining outside, had this been not so important for me, I would have never asked you to come in this atrocious weather" she requested.

"Ohhh…. If it's important for you I will come don't worry, I will be there in half an hour" I replied preparing myself to go out in the rain

I believed she was in a desperate need and therefore I rushed to her college getting wet.

On reaching her college I could not find her anywhere in the canteen, where she had asked me to join.

I tried calling her repeatedly but her server was unreachable making it unbearable for me to wait as I was completely wet.

But I thought she might had gone for her lecture and therefore decide to wait in the canteen, to calm down my shiver chills I even ordered a soothing cappuccino to help me ease. I repeatedly tried reaching her but her unavailability made my tolerance go hay where, but the thought that she really had some important work for me held me there with my eyes looking for her all around.

I heard a giggling sound from behind which sounded familiar, on turning around I found koshlesh and Pratiksha were talking surreptitiously.

"didn't I tell you, he hates rain, but he really loves you to come in this weather for you." Said koshlesh.

"I am really thankful to god to have found someone like him" but you were saying he will get annoyed if he did not find me, he still seems to be less annoyed. She spoke

"That is because I never thought in my dreams that you will prank me, had I known this before I would have declined to your request." I replied lividly.

"I am sorry sweetheart, I just wanted to see how far can you go for my love" she replied.

"Yeah, I am really peeved about this that you found it apt to trouble me for no reason and now you are coming with this lame excuse for what" I reprimanded her, "fine if you do not have any work from me, I am leaving" I added.

"Sorry, don't spoil your mood we were simply trying to prank you, look how convivial the weather is, lets enjoy the day together since you are here." She replied tickling my palms with slow strokes of her fingers.

I was actually enjoying the extra attention and efforts being made to reconcile me; therefore, I continued the drama of being aggravated.

But could not hold my laughter for long and my strategy was busted out.

"By this time the rainfall had pacified and there were only drizzles, which were very soothing and made the weather, like poets say the most romantic weather.

"Finally, the rain had stopped, now it's the perfect time to leave, let's go and reach our homes before the rain restarts" suggested Pratiksha while gathering her belongings and putting them inside her bag.

Koshlesh nodded at her suggestion and grabbed his bike keys lying on the table.

"You have called me here in haste what do you think will I allow you to go home so early" I replied with a naughty smile.

"What do you mean" replied Pratiksha widening her eyeballs.

"You very well know what I mean" I flirtatiously replied.

Koshlesh understood the assignment and said "you guys carry on with your drive date, I am shooting off now."

I loved it when I need not to give any explanation or briefing to koshlesh and he could even understand my silence.

"Wait koshlesh, where are you going let's all three of us spend some more time in canteen," said Pratiksha.

"Canteen! Who said we are staying in canteen" I said shrugging my shoulders.

"Where will you go then it's raining outside" she objected.

"Wherever the road takes us, and likewise you said, it's a convivial atmosphere let's take the most of it." I replied.

She tried her luck at holding me at my place, but I was not ready to hear anything but yes.

Grabbing her hand, I began walking towards the parking where my vehicle was parked, she tried getting herself released from my grip but failed and at last surrendered.

The showers were soothing and the road the trees and everything looked so clean, the rain had cleared the dust in the air, which made everything pop up, the trees were freshly bathed and looked mesmerising, there were still water loaded dark clouds which speculated the prospective rainfall, but now as I had the most amazing company with me, I was least bothered to get drenched.

Due to the rain the traffic was minimal which was an unusual sight in the city. Once we were out of the usual street ways and were on the main road, the picturesque rainbow was visible, upon seeing it Pratiksha was thrilled and acted like a toddler who has seen the rainbow for the first time in their life. I really liked her this quality that she enjoyed all the small things, the simplicity she has had in her behaviour made her unique.

While driving I swiftly reached out to find her hand to hold. In order to tease me she tried taking it away from my reach but I was adamant to have full pleasure on this ride. I clasped her hand, brought it closer to my face and swiftly rested a kiss on them, she wasn't ready for this but I was. I was firm and bold I guess the rain has released some fresh dopamine in my brain cells which allowed me to do things which I abstained from doing.

"What are you doing in the middle of the road" she objected taking her hand back.

"I am simply enjoying this ride with my girlfriend do you have any problem with this" I said holding her hand again and bringing it forwards.

I then reached out to another hand making her hold me by my wait minimising the gap between us on the bike.

She was amazed at the valour I was presenting.

Slowly she melted in the vibe I was offering her and began enjoying, she did not take her hands back instead tightened the grip leaving no room for air to surpass, this was the first time after that dance during valentines when our bodies were so close, I was having a whale of a time.

As soon as she started enjoying the ride, she began singing songs,

"Ye same, sama hai ych pyaar ka, kisi ke inezaar ka. dil na chura le kahin mera Mausam bahar ka" the melodious masterpiece was sung by the nightingale of india "lata Mangeshkar ji"

She sang the song in the most beautiful manner such that it sounded like the singer was singing.

"You sing really well dear; I never knew about this" I said surprisingly.

"ye, singing is my passion. I had taken singing lessons in the past" she replied

"Wow you are a bundle of surprises, I get to know your new talents every time I meet, first dance and now singing, is there anything else that I am unaware of" I replied

"There may be, you will get to know with the passage with the time" she replied with a wink and continued her singing,

Her voice made the ride even more magical but the weather turned atrocious when it began bucketing down, luckily, we found a garden and stopped our vehicle to go inside the garden and stand under a trees shade.

"Look this is what I was fearing, now we have been stuck in this terrible weather, fully drenched." She began complaining,

I was high on my emotions for her, and the only way to stop her constant chatter was to seal her lips, I don't know from where did I get that courage but then I slowly leant down at her held her face from my palms and kissed her.

She was startled with my move, she lowered her lashes and tickled pick, I was hoping she might not get offended with me over this but her reaction was enough for me to understand that she wasn't against this, but seemingly she found it a little shocking, as she wasn't expecting this.

I had also not framed that in my mind but the thought of kissing her that moment was too quick that I reacted as soon as it reflected my brain without even emphasising the thought and its after effects but I was glad that I did what I did.

Seeing her cheeks turn pink I knew I was doing the right thing, I took a pause and again reached out towards her and this time she lifted her chin up to reach me which made it obvious that I had her consent.

Our lips melted together creating sculpture of a loop, I tasted something fruity. God I was tasting a lipstick or whether it was a lip gloss I am not pretty sure of it, as it was the first kiss of my life, I had never felt something like this before. Her lips were smooth and soft unlike mine they were chapped.

I took temporary pauses to assure whether she was comfortable, slowly we both fell in the melody of the rain drops, our eyes closed we were deeply in that moment of passionate kiss, she wrapped me tightly in her arms and so did I, we lost the track of time and honestly, I don't bother for how long we have been standing there.

The buzzing horn of the vehicles brought us back to the reality as the rain had stopped.

"I think we should leave now" she said without maintaining the eye contact with embarrassment

We both enjoyed this drive and touchwood has been the best day of my life yet.

I couldn't thank God more for the blissful days I had been enjoying lately, this internship proved out to be the best part of the engineering degree, I had the privilege to spend enough time with her which was necessary for our long-distance relation to bloom.

THEY ARE STILL CONNECTED

One day I had been to Pratiksha's college to meet her after not meeting her for almost 5 days, I decided to go to office only after I was done spending some quality time with her, I waited for her to join me as she was in her class attending the lecture and has requested me to wait there for some time.

I was witing for her while having my cold coffee by now thanks to my frequent visits to her college canteen the canteen staff were easily able to identify me, and had a great welcoming smile on their faces as and when they spotted me.

"Sorry, the teacher took extra 5 minutes to leave the class after the bell rang" she replied grabbing my coffee cup to get a sip from the coffee.

"it's okay, slow down a little bit, do you want me to order you something" I asked taking her bag from her hand

"Yes please, I am famished, I will take one vegetable magi and cheesballs." She said sipping another shot from the coffee.

Since it was a self-service café, I went ahead to place the order and make the payments at the cash counter.

"Why is your bag so bulky today, what are you carrying in it, drama costumes or what." I asked looking at the oversized bag

"No not a drama costume, but a dress for sure," she replied checking her mobiles on the calls or messages received during the class.

"Dress! Why do you need an extra pair of dress in the class" I asked

"Now, it's not for me. I have brought this dress of mine as one of my friends was asking it to wear in her fresher's party." She replied

"She will be here anytime soon, to take this dress." She added

"oh! I see, but why is she asking for a dress from you, doesn't she have one of her own" I asked out of curiosity.

"She asked me for this and frankly I did not go in for these details instead said yes for her to take the dress" she replied

Our Maggi and cheese balls have arrived by now, you cannot hold yourself when you have such a scrumptious food waiting in front of you.

"By the Way, you know her" she said, blowing her to the bite of Maggi she had prepared for her self

"Know whom" I replied juggling the hot cheese ball in my hands.

"My friend or should I say your best friend" she replied sarcastically

"My best friend" I asked shrugging my shoulders

"Aditi" she replied grabbing another bite from her Maggi.

The moment I heard the name the cheese ball which I was having dropped from my hand and fell into the plate. I was startled on the fact that how could she and Aditi be good friends, I had always made sure that both these girls were poles apart than how could this happen.

"Why are you so amazed, just like you she is my friend too," she replied casually.

For her it was not even a thing to matter but for me it was like a thunderstorm. I had not revealed before Aditi that I and Pratiksha were dating and I did not want myself to be introduced before her directly by Pratiksha as her boyfriend.

"You haven't taken the pain to bring this information to me before, you very well knew she was my friend and not only that we have some family relations too and still you did not tell me that you both were so good friends that you tend to share clothes with one another" I said furiously

"Why are you making it a big deal, there is nothing to make a mountain of a molehill." She defended

And for your kind information I haven't told her anything about you so please stop over reacting" she added

"Thank you for your mercy that you haven't revealed anything about to her, things can escalate quickly, we are in the nascent stage of our relationship and I do want neither of our families to get involved and therefore keeping our relation limited to us is the only option we have right now with us." I explained

"She can easily circulate the news in the family creating further troubles for us please try to understand and although she is your great friend try not to discuss your love life with her" I added

"Relax I know what I am doing, but she is a very nice girl and a very good friend of mine even before I met you, and just like you I can't let her of for the reason of our relationship" she replied

"If you are done with your anxiety, can I now relish my snack, Maggi wont taste good when cold" she replied

"By what time will she be here?" I asked

"Within half an hour" she replied

"Alright, then I must leave before she arrives as I have no intention to invite any troubles, for neither I want you girls to have your friendship spoilt for any baseless reason" I replied

"I was also about to ask you the same, you can leave once we are done with snacking." She replied

Although I left but the thought of these two girls sharing good bond was not leaving my thoughts, I was scared a bit more know because Aditi may say anything about me to her which she may not like, as I had spent time with Aditi in the past and that peculiar thing was the cause of my worry.

But my overthinking had no outcome and this way the day passed, Pratiksha told me everything about her meeting with Aditi and mentioned that they only talked about her new college and the way she was going to dress herself for the fresher's party and what accessories was she going to pair with the dress.

Two Days later when they were about to meet for taking the dress back Pratiksha this time informed me in advance and therefore, I abstained from meeting her that peculiar day in order to avoid any close encounters by any chance.

BHOPAL HERE SHE COMES

Three months passed with a snap of a finger. After taking the certificate for internship we were ready to return to Bhopal where our semester exams were waiting for us, these three months had been very helpful in making my relation better with Pratiksha and not only that these days had helped in making koshlesh and Pratiksha very good friends, they even talked for hours I felt really grateful to him that thanks to him I had the most beautiful and most warming partner.

Life became monotonous getting back to Bhopal, with regular classes to be attended. Since we were inching closer to our degree coming to an end there were a lot of things happening simultaneously. We had to attend the classes regularly and the weekly tests were conducted the college which demanded my attention more, which ultimately resulted in less conversations between me and Pratiksha.

I changed my pg. and shifted along with koshlesh as his room partner has left and the past three months, I had been so comfortable with him that I thought to staying together was the best option for both of us.

"Ohh god this last month has been so difficult, I hardly got time to talk with you." I said on a telephonic conversation with Pratiksha.

"Yes, but I am glad that you have now some times as all your tests have been conducted and now for the next fifteen days there is nothing lined up for you, so finally we have some time to talk" she replied

"indeed" I replied in agreement.

"So are you ready" she mysteriously asked

"Ready for" I asked

"Ready for a mind boggling surprize" she replied making it sound more dramatic

"Please fill me in" I replied since I was in the moment

"Hold your breath since you are going to hear something unexpected and overwhelming" she said making it sound even more mysterious and dramatic.

"Please year now don't exaggerate and tell me what the news is, I haven't heard something nice since I returned to Bhopal" I replied.

"So, the news is, the following week that is the next Friday on 10th of this month, I am coming to Bhopal" she replied.

"Wait what did you just say. Let me pinch myself" I replied.

"This isn't a prank right" I added.

"Not at all. I am coming to Bhopal for my auditions for singing" she replied.

"You remember last month I had gone to give my audition in the reality show, I had been shortlisted for the mega auditions and they are going to be held in your city so I will be there in your city for the entire weekend." She replied with thrill.

"I can't not believe my ears, and first of all congratulations for clearing the auditions and secondly, I a more exited for you. You will be here" I replied.

"I will show you all the beautiful places that I had described about Bhopal to you once you are here, I can't not believe my dream of taking you to the most loved places of Bhopal is coming true" I replied overwhelmingly.

"Yes, I am also super excited, since I had this misconception that my parents won't allow me to travel to another city but on receiving their consent has made me happier." She replied.

"Will you be accompanied by anyone" I asked hoping the reply comes no.

"Now, this is going to be my first solo travel, at first my mother was willing to join me but then I made an excuse about having a company of my friend from Baroda and thus he agreed for me to travel alone" she replied.

"I lied because had she been along, I would not be able to spend the time with you" she added.

her this gesture to give me the importance gave me collywobbles as I was super excited to welcome her.

"You will have to do me a favour now, you will have to find an apt hotel for my stay" she requested.

"Hotel for what, you can stay here at my pg." I replied.

"Have you gone nuts or what, the moment my mother gets to know about this that I am staying with two bachelor boys she will never ever let me leave home the next time" she replied furiously.

"Bring your thoughts to a halt this isn't happening" she added.

"Alright calm down, I will find an apt place for you, but during the day you will be with me" I commanded.

"undoubtedly" she replied.

I was super thrilled to have her here in Bhopal. When I told koshlesh about this he was equally thrilled to know.

On raising the question of her stay, koshlesh objected.

"Have you gone made, she will be better safe here with us than being with total strangers, as far her parents are concerned, they will only know when we will tell them or allow them to know about this, this thing will be been three of us so how can they even get a gasp of it." I replied.

"But she seems adamant and it is going to be difficult to convince her" I replied.

"You leave that on me, and don't tell her about our plan let her come here first then I will convince her" he replied.

I did what he said, but I wanted her to have a lasting impression of her visit to my pg., as this was the first time she was going to see how do I stay, believing on the thought that girls want to have an organized partner I pulled my socks in transforming the house in a better and organised manner, koshlesh helped me in this work and this way a week before her arrival we sat down on the mission of deep cleaning the house, arranging our closet and organising our books were two main works.

I even went overboard to clean the ceiling fans which never in my life I ever did at my house but for her to notice that I was a tidy man I really worked hard.

Finally, it was the evening when she was boarding her train to Bhopal. It was difficult for me to contain my excitement, I was constantly chatting with her all this while, and was also tracking the train online.

I had already informed her that I would be coming to pick her and therefore she had to stay at the station till I arrived.

As I was keeping a watch of the train running status, I reached the station before the train arrived and stood at the place where the graphics were displaying the coach layout, since I was aware of her coach in which she was sitting I reached there and waited for the train to come.

I saw her standing at the door when the train was still moving, we both were smiling ear to ear seeing one another, this was no less than a dream for us.

"Welcome to Bhopal" I said with a grin.

She blushed as we headed towards the parking.

"So, you have booked a hotel for me, right?" she asked.

"Right now, we are going to hotel, we are going to my pg., where we will be having our breakfast, koshlesh has been waiting for us," I replied in order to avoid the question.

She did not smell anything fishy by then.

On reaching the house she gaped and spoke.

"I never thought your house would look this tidy".

"Why, you are a lucky that your future partner isn't a messy one" replied koshlesh from the kitchen.

she blushed hearing this and began the usual talks with koshlesh.

After about an hour and a half when we were done with our breakfast she said.

"I think I should leave now, vinay if you could please drop me to my hotel."

"Listen Pratiksha, I know you want to stay in a hotel but trust us this is the best place for your stay as your auditorium is 3kms away from this place, and to be honest I am not comfortable at leaving you in the hotel all alone with strangers, its better you stay here with us, you can take my room and I will use the drawing room till then" I said.

"no. I had already asked you to get me a hotel booked, and now you are asking me to stay here. What if my family gets to know about this. I can't stay here" she rejected my offer which was quite expected.

"But who is going to inform your family about your stay at our place? Neither of us" defended koshlesh.

"Listen vinay is right, leaving you all alone with strangers in the hotel isn't wise, when you have your boyfriend around you, wouldn't that be unfair for him that he is getting one chance to host you and you are taking that also away from him" added koshlesh.

His diplomatic skills helped him win every argument; he raised too many convincing points before her that she had to agree in the end.

The day ended with nothing interesting as she was engaged in her rehearsals and therefore, I did not disturb her leaving everything for the next day and went ahead completing my project work with koshlesh.

The following morning my sleep was interrupted with the magical voice coming from my room it was Pratiksha who was already up and rehearsing for her bog day with her EarPods on.

I woke and headed straight to the kitchen to make a cup of tea for her since she was my guest, I had to make sure she was provided with everything she wanted.

"Room service" I said knocking at the door.

"What!" she grinned hearing my adaption of a housekeeper.

"Since you were in a hotel last night therefore, I thought to give you the related services in the hotel" I wittily replied.

"Stop it, I am already very nervous, I don't know what will happen today, I want things to turn out in my favour." She said knuckling her fingers.

"Everything happens for our own good, keep this thing in your mind, you are giving your hundred percent and that's what matters the most apart from it everything is beyond your control, so stop stressing about it. You can only work the outcome will decide the future." I spoke.

"And before this tea becomes iced tea kindly have it, I made it specially for you, taste and tell me how do you like it or not." I added.

"Have this soothing cup of tea and get ready by that time I will get some breakfast for you and then we will leave for your audition" I suggested.

I wanted to make something special for her but I did not have the required culinary skills in me and therefore without experimenting I thought of bringing her the famous breakfast of Bhopal: poha and samosa.

Having done with our breakfast we left for the auditions.

AUDITION: FAIL, DATE: PASS

On reaching the auditorium it was and since it was the mega audition a total of 64 contestants were present and out of these 64 the judges were to select only 12 contestants, making this time the judges were to notice the minor mistakes and take decisions.

All the other contestants were equally nervous as her. Most of them were accompanied by their acquaintances and family and here I was along with her to give her the moral support required during these tough times.

Before she got inside, she talked to her mother through a call to get her blessings.

The acquaintances were asked to stay in the hall area which telecasted the live auditions this way we could see who were they performing. When it was her turn, she turned red from anxiety. I gave her a tight hug and wished her all the best before she could get on the stage.

She bowed before the stage before she stepped on it which reflected how much she respected the art of singing.

"hawa ke jhonke aaj mausamon se rooth gaye" she began singing the song which was from the movie lootera sung by renowned singer monali thakur. Before this I hardly knew about this son or movie as I was not very big fan movies. But since she was involved in it, I loved the melody of this peculiar song.

She performed really well and she had that stage presence in her which connected with the audience. This was something I had never seen in her. She was brave confident and grabbed the audience throughout her performance. I was very happy to see her there on the stage.

The reviews from the judges were also very comforting but one or two technical loopholes were noticed by the judges which honestly did not catch my attention by as an audience view point, she rocked the stage.

The results were to be announced when all the performance took place, while we were waiting for all the performances to end, she was still cracking her knuckles which kind of irritated me but I could feel her how she was battling for that time to pass.

All the contestants were called in a group and the judges were giving their verdict on reanalysing the performances

"You had the stage presence and were fantastic at some areas but at some places you fell short of the sur, and on this level you need more practice to avoid these future mistakes.

But you have the voice of a playback singer so please take my advice to brush your skills to get the desired outcome, as far as the verdict is concerned, for this time we cannot select you but wish to see you in the next season with a better performance" said one of the judges on Pratiksha's performance.

Unfortunately, she could not make it to the top 12 I was deeply saddened hearing this because I did not want her to be hurt and she was having a lot of expectations from this show, not getting selected shattered all her hopes, her face turned pale this time and she held her tears back before she could leave the stage.

I didn't know how to offer her support and calm her,

She made a call to her mother breaking the news of her rejection. We had too many plans of exploring the cities but this news broke all her excitement and all she could say was.

"let's go home" I could not see her like this, ang bringing her back home would mean she would lock herself inside the room weeping,

I could not see her like this and therefore I took her too lake view the best and most relaxing place of Bhopal it was a lake and had the most amazing natural escape where one can find oneself closer to nature against her will.

"Where have we come, I asked you to take me home and you have brought me to this random place" she said annoyingly.

"Since you are upset you find this place random, but this is the best place to get you relieved from your anxiety. "I replied.

"Take me back home I don't want any nature to heal me" she reiterated.

"You need to stop your blather" I said holding her hand and taking her inside through the entry walkway

Earlier she had that vague idea that the place would be similar to kankaria lake which is in Ahmedabad, and therefore she was not willing to go.

The moment she saw the beauty of the place she went numb.

We sat there for a while keeping our feet submerged in the water. Which actually helped her in pacifying her emotions. A trail of endless tears began from her eyes, which I wated to stop but thought of allowing her to get her emotions out otherwise there were going to be toxic for the rest of the day and therefore let her loose and allowed her to be with herself for some time.

"let's go for a boat ride" I asked to bring some change.

"No, I am good, you go" she replied.

"Listen dear, you did your best that's what matter and even if you weren't selected at least you got to know that you still need to work on a specific area to be the perfect one. I am not saying that you are grieving in vain I understand your pain but the only thing you need to understand is we have only hard work in our hands and the outcome is in the hands of God. And believe me God never disappoints anyone, if you couldn't make it this time maybe God has planned something better than this for you" I pacified her.

"I agree to what you are saying but it is getting worse to convince my heart, I had thought so many things prior in advance that if I get selected, I will do this and that and now all those dreams are shattered into pieces before me and that is what is killing me deep inside." She replied in a choking voice.

We took a boat ride it was a paddle boat for two persons. Despite of her refraining to join me I convinced her to come along. We were paddling and slowly she began liking the effort that paddle boat was taking it kind of help her divert her attention.

After riding the boat for few meters away from the shore she again started weeping about her rejection this time I was not ready to allow her to cry again for hours and console her. I found no better idea to stop her.

Since the boat was very small, we were very close to one another. Our feet were actively involved in paddling but the rest of the body was free, I brought my face closer to hers and sealed her lips with mine, while she was still crying. She was amazed at my brave step since we were in the middle of the public place.

"Now no more crying, we have only 24 hours left with us where we can be together, and I don't want to waste any further minute in repenting." I said caressing her and settling her distressed hairs.

"I am sorry, my overwhelming reaction spoiled your plans for the day" she pleaded.

"No, the only objective was to be with you so no plan has been spoiled we are together it's just that we are not on the places where we should have gone otherwise, but this silence nature, boat ride, you and me is a perfect date setting. Couldn't have asked for anything more." I replied caressing her forehead.

She brought herself closer to me and we entered into the lip lock again and this time it lasted long such that we forgot the sense of place and time, we melted into one another and that one action made the day better again.

We came back to the shore to return home; she was calm but was not interested to go anywhere.

Meanwhile I received a call from koshlesh, he was equally upset to know about the result,

"I will not be there with you guys tonight as I am going for a night out at Ankit's place" said koshlesh.

"Why such spontaneous plan" I asked you should stay she will be going tomorrow you can go tomorrow for your night stay" I added

"You are a stupid and will remain one forever. Listen I have a useful gift for you in my cupboard. Take that you might need it" he said abruptly and disconnected the phone even before I could persuade him to stay back.

Koshlesh was very good at breaking the ice unlike me therefore I thought what will I do to enlighten her up in the house.

On reaching home we both were exhausted and therefore both went ahead to get a warm bath to relieve the stress. While she was in the washroom, I went ahead to check what the useful gift was which koshlesh was talking about.

When I opened his cupboard, I saw a pack of condoms with a sticky note attached.

"Your protection guard" with a teasing emoji made on it.

I wasn't thinking about this at all but this naughty thought has been seeded in my brain with this act. Then I thought about the proximity we shared at the boat I felt like I may never know if I could get lucky enough to get my hands on this useful guard.

I then went to another bathroom to take bath, on coming out I saw her sitting on the couch she was wearing her short night dress which made her looked very seductive, I was floored to see her but still did not want to create any mess and therefore diverted my thoughts.

"coffee" I asked to talk with her and spend time with her.

"Yeah sure" she replied, "if you want, I can make that" she added

"No! I hardly know to make tea and coffee please allow me to serve you with it" I replied.

We were having our coffee in the living room on the couch sitting next to one another, when she slowly reached towards my hand and held it.

"Vinay! You are one of the best things that has happened to me in the past one year I don't want to lose you at any cost, I might have failed the audition but spending this time with you is my victory" she said with tears in her eyes.

I felt short of words as she was having the same feelings as I have for her and that was the greatest gift of time I had received.

I went closer to her she smelt fruity maybe because of the shower gel she used. I held her cheek from one hand and used another hand to feel her body from waist to thighs the short she was wearing allowed me to touch her thighs, slowly dwelling into her eyes I leaned towards her neck to give her a love bite, she was ticklish a bit but moaned with pleasure.

We both then juggled with our lips teasing one another with frequent kisses, though the couch was a little discomforting yet it was the most passionate moment I had ever experienced in my life. I felt that this moment should not end but then I had to bring myself together to not cross my line without her consent.

I then took a step back calming my racing breath she kept looking at me silently but her eyes were chaotic they had so much of thoughts in them that it was difficult to address what was she thinking.

I slowly lifted her in my lap as I always had a keen desire to lift her again after the valentine dance but since we always met at public places this desire remained unfulfilled, this day was apt for this wish fulfilment and therefore I lifted her and took her in the bedroom to slowly place her at the bed.

In order to not lose my control, I began to leave the room, when she held my hand.

"Please don't go, I want to feel you" she said seductively.

This blurred all the doubts that I had been having about taking the step further, I than reached to get the gift koshlesh has had for me.

I switched off the lights as the lights coming from the window was enough to spread the minimal light required in the room.

I had never thought I would make love with Pratiksha in Bhopal but life is full of surprises and it was indeed the most pleasant surprise I was experiencing.

I ran my hand which went cold with nervousness around her waist which tickled her, gently reaching towards her hair and untied them leaving them loose as I loved the fragrance of her hairs, I slowly and gently undressed her kissing every exposed part of her body she loved the sensation and kept her eyes closed. Her constant moans encouraged me to grip her harder, I reached her neck and gently kissed her she had been aroused by then she had goosebumps all over her body. She kissed me back over my neck and slowly sucking it with intensity leaving a hickey. I was happy to get the return stamp of our love making.

I went down on her, she moaned with pleasure she quivered when I brushed strokes down on her, I then slowly began to thrust inside her, at first stroke she made a loud cry I went on kissing her and with the following strokes I plunged inside her deep into that maddening clutch, as the strokes became faster our breathes ran faster and we felt the feeling of completeness. This was truly the most satisfying feeling of our lives.

I was spent and laid next to her having the most satisfying sleep cuddling her. I was indeed very happy that we became one that night and this incident changed our chemistry to a different level altogether.

WHY SHE HAD TO RETURN

The other day did not feel like a normal one it felt I have got a new life after that magical night with my lady love, when I opened my eyes, I was a little surprised to not find her besides me, when I looked in the watch it was already 11 am, I have never slept till this hour before, maybe it was the after effects of the labour of last night.

I looked for my t-shirt as I slept without wearing any, and stood up to find Pratiksha. I saw her in the hall sitting having a cup of tea.

"Good morning sweetheart" I said giving a peck on her forehead.

"Good morning, I saw you sleeping peacefully and thought of not disturbing you and therefore came and sat here," she replied.

"You also made yourself a cup of tea, didn't you find any trouble finding the ingredients" I asked.

"Not at all everything was easily accessible" she replied. "Would you like to have tea, should I make one for you" she added.

"I would like a cup of coffee if that is convenient for you. Also let's make something to eat I am famished" I replied holding my stomach.

"Alright, if you can guide me in kitchen I can make excellent omelette for you," she said lifting an egg from the egg tray.

"Well, that's an excellent idea, I will help you with toasting some bread to go with the omelette" I replied.

"You know what after our marriage I will always help you in the household chores, I believe kitchen is not the duty of only girls, your counterpart is equally responsible for sharing your workload" I replied peeling an onion.

"Our marriage, it's not happening soon first we have to get good jobs for ourselves and only than we can think about this step-in life" she replied.

"Obviously, what do you think your parents will allow you to marry a jobless person, certainly no. but I am not here for flings I am damn serious about you. I have made up my mind you and only you are going to become my wife" I replied pulling her towards me holding her waist.

"Alright future husband, lets come back to the present and make this scrumptious breakfast, I can hear rats crawl in my stomach." She replied pushing me away.

We both enjoyed making the breakfast together and cleaning all the mess that we had created in the kitchen, since it was Sunday and the house help was on leave, we had to make sure to keep the house tidy.

"I can't wait to live this life with you in our forever home, your visit to Bhopal has given me immense happiness" I said holding her hand

"Your train is at night we still have the afternoon with us so why not go out for some drive" I said excitedly.

Or if you want, we can stay at home and cherish the moments like last night" I proposed leaning towards her and kissing around her collar bone resting my head there.

"No ways koshlesh may come anytime here it would be better if we go out" she replied rejecting my offer while pushing me back to stand straight.

"Okay now let's take shower and get ready to go for a ride" she added.

"Shower together! I like the idea, let's go." I said lifting my brows in a witty space as I knew she wasn't suggesting a shower together yet I was trying my luck if she would agree to this.

"In your dreams. we will be taking bath but in separate bathrooms your apartment is equipped with two washrooms instead of one so to avoid further delay I was suggesting to get shower." She replied killing the smile I have had on my face over the thought of bathing together.

"Okay fine. You go I will take bath in some time as I have to get the house organised, I don't want koshlesh to see the bed in a mess. Once I am done doing that, I will also go to take shower." I replied while folding the mattress we had used last night.

While I was cleaning the room, I found her purse lying adjacent to the bed, I have always wanted to peep into a girl's bag as I have always wondered why do girls need to carry a huge bag along with them every time they step out of the house.

My curiosity was enough to get me open the bag full of surprises as it had a huge collection of cosmetic items, I had ever come across with most of them where so new to me that I failed to recognize them. This was the very first time I was seeing the mascara wand. I was not aware of what it was and where it was supposed to be applied.

Then there was a separate pouch full of medicines and the medicines were being consumed as the packets where half empty that raised a suspicion in my mind why was she having this huge collection of medicines but to kill that thought I gave an explanation to myself that she might have packet of common medicines as she was travelling for the first time alone and therefore, she might have carried every possible medicine with her. Because my mother had asked me to carry most of the medicines for the first time I was travelling to Bhopal.

But a slight thought of worry kept lingering in my head for what reason she had been carrying more than 15-20 medicines on a two days trip. I decide to put this question before her to get a valid reason once she was out of the washroom.

After cleaning the room back to perfection, I went ahead to get shower. While I was taking shower, I was able to hear some voices coming from the living room and it took me a while to identify that koshlesh had returned and they both were having chit chat.

After coming out I saw koshlesh and Pratiksha talking but her body language was screaming for help as she found herself uncomfortable on reaching closer, I realised that koshlesh was drunk and was smelling of booze, I was actually embarrassed to have her experience this awkward situation.

Distress covered her face and she turned red, batting her eyelids faster she went inside the room and nervously began packing her stuff, I could she her juggling with her clothes but I had to make sure that koshlesh was properly taken to the bed room, as he was intoxicated and was facing trouble in maintaining his balance if left unattended, he would bang himself on the wall or any object coming under his way.

I carefully dragged him to his room resting his arm over my shoulder, I was shocked as he has never drunk this much before, knowing that Pratiksha was at home how could he be so careless to go overboard and consume so much alcohol to lose his senses.

I helped him with his shoes and made him lay on the bed. I also gave him some lemonade to soothe his hangover, he then again went back to sleep after blabbering for few more minutes. Once I was assured that he was comfortable then I headed to see if Pratiksha was fine.

"Hey are you okay" I asked.

"hmm" she replied with a disappointment on her face.

"Listen I am sorry I was absolutely clueless that he would come back this drunk, this is the first time that he has been so drunk believe me, he drinks but responsibly, I am too embarrassed that you had to see him in this state, but trust me don't judge him for this habit, he is a nice human being in general" I said trying to brush image about koshlesh that has recently pictured in her brain.

But my words did not levy any high impact on her and she resorted to her hmm as a reply.

"So, if you are ready let's go" I asked.

"No not really, I guess we should abort our plan of going anywhere." She replied.

"Why what happened we just made a plan earlier and you were equally thrilled about it and now suddenly you are opting out of it". I asked with surprise.

"Koshlesh has come home drunk he needs you right now and also I am also experiencing acute headache so it would be better if I could sleep some more this way it can get better and if not, I have to travel my journey in discomfort" she justified.

I could grasp that she was making an excuse maybe koshlesh had said something which he shouldn't and that has probably killed her mood but she wasn't ready to reveal her true emotions rather she felt more comfortable at layering them with excuses.

"If koshlesh has said something inconvenient to you than I ask forgiveness from his behalf, I have never seen him this drunk and maybe he has something which is leading you to change your mind" I said with puppy eyes.

"No not really, men say stupid things while being drunk I know that, be I would not be wise on our part to leave highly drunk koshlesh alone at home he can set the house on fire if left unattended" she raised a concern.

I hated to admit that but her apprehensions where quite correct the state on which he had returned home was absolutely dwindling and I did not know what next, he could possibly do apart from sleeping.

When she saw me a little convinced, she banged the door on my face saying,

"You keep a watch on him I will take some sleep to soothe my headache"

"But you haven't had lunch yet." Before I could finish up saying the door was closed. I was so embarrassed that I could say nothing much but wait for her to open the door and then ask her for food.

Meanwhile I kept a close watch on koshlesh and saw him doing the weirdest things he has ever done yet, her words resonated in my ears saying he could potentially put the house on fire, which he indeed could.

I killed my time by waiting for both of them to come out but none came out, I did my college work for a while but then I slept on the couch hopelessly.

"Hey! Good morning. Its 6pm lets get dressed to go to the railway station my train is at 8:30pm." She whispered in my ear.

"6 pm what are you saying," I rubbed my eyelids to check whether it was really that time of the evening.

I even checked the whether outside to see if it was really evening.

"How could I sleep for this long; you haven't had anything in lunch and I also failed as a host to serve you your meals on time" I said feeling pity about my hospitality.

"it's okay now, don't curse yourself lets go get ourselves ready and will first have something to eat and then will go to the railway station" she suggested.

In the next 15 minutes we were ready as she was already packing her stuff for how long I was absolutely unaware of.

Koshlesh was is deep sleep, we left the house making the house fire proof in our absence, and locking the door from outside such that no trespasser can get the free entry to our home in our absence.

Taking a pit stop at a food joint we opted for proper meal as it was already onset of the night and both of did not had lunch so our stomachs were growling with hunger. We ate a fulfilling meal and ending with a wholesome Gulab jamun to complete the dinner.

It was 7:45 already, we headed to the station and waited for the train to arrive, it was on time, I had been praying that the train might be delayed for an hour so that I could talk to her more but it was not.

"We settled on the bench at the platform on which her train was scheduled to arrive. Holding her hand, I said:

"Pratiksha, I know you have been dulled because you came here for your career first, regardless of the fact that I was here, your sole intentions where to build your career. I know how much you have begged your family to give you this opportunity, but I want to tell you one thing. don't get dishearten with this setback, rather work upon the flaws pointed by the judges so that you need not make those mistakes in future."

"As far as the time we spent together is concerned it was the most magical time of my life, I don't want you to simply be happy with me for the time spent because I know you had other intentions with this trip but I love and respect you even more than before. I am so proud of you my darling" I added.

Her neck was rested around my shoulder and I felt a teardrop, she was overwhelmed to what I was saying and gulping down the chocked throat she said:

"I am sorry I was unable to take the day and therefore took my time, I know you have had plans with me but thanks for cooperating."

"I indeed had various hopes as my future was at stake with this audition, but by making it to the qualifying round I had already proved my willingness before my parents for my passion, I hope they allow me the next time too if such opportunity knocks in" she added.

"of course, they will" I reaffirmed.

We sat there in each other's company without talking much, we were enjoying the scenes at the chaotic railway station. Although there were hundreds of people around us but all other distractions seemed to be blurred out. we were quite but our hands were not ready to loosen the grip of each other.

The train arrived and it was not there for more than 5 minutes therefore we had to be quick to get her board the train along with her luggage and I also wanted to make sure that her co passengers were decent. No matter how safe the railway transport system is but that peculiar day I was really scared to let her go all by herself in that train, maybe that was because now I had more affection towards her.

After assuring myself of her seat and her co passengers I came out of the train while she remained outside the door of the coach, I bounced back on the train to give her one last good bye hug before she left followed by a sweet peck on her forehead.

I replayed the advices I had been repeatedly giving her since evening, to keep her phone on general mode, do call me if any of the problem arises and keep chatting with me till she was sleepy.

Before I could finish up the train started and I had to loosen the grip of my hand to let her go. It has been the most difficult goodbye for me, since we came into relationship as it was always me who was leaving, this was the first time I was experiencing her leaving me and honestly it was heart wrenching for me, this separation has restored my belief that how badly I wanted her to be a part of my life and now all I wanted was to finish up my study and grab a decent job to have her forever in my life.

I stood there seeing her standing at the door of the train waving goodbye to me with her eyes filled with tears, these two days had really changed the equation of our relationship for better. Till the train was out of sight I remained frozen at my place and later started walking back to my place taking all the beautiful memories of her in my heart.

After returning home I had to confront koshlesh for his behaviour and what went wrong which made him get so high, he was never like that he had never had drunk beyond his limits and he was certainly out of his senses and therefore I was equally worried for him for what reason did he drink so much but that could only be done when he was totally out of his hangover, which seemed quite difficult for that particular evening. When I went ahead to check upon him, he was still sleeping, and when I asked him for diner, he excused himself and preferred to sleep.

I went back to my room where her fragrance was still lingering and I could still feel her warmth around the room on the bed and mattresses where she had been staying, and this gave the feeling of a warm hug from her.

As decided, we kept on chatting till, she was sleepy, on looking around the room I found she had forgotten her stole the one she had been wearing and I was happy to find it there it made her presence felt. I wrapped it around my neck and sniffing to her scent I went to sleep feeling the oneness with her.

UNVELING TRUE COLOURS

Koshlesh has been acting weird lately with me, and so is Pratiksha there has been a presence of a veil around three of us which I am unable to figure out. I had tried my best confronting these two with the idea that something seems to be fishy to me but none had coincided with my thought. But my gut feeling reiterates before me that something isn't right for me.

It has been a week since she left for Ahmedabad and not even a single day, we have had a full-fledged conversation, whenever I try to talk to her she has an excuse of family being around or she has some college work excuse ready with her. Hardly I get to have her attention.

As the matter of koshlesh is concerned he is always on his phone texting but I don't know whom is he into lately. He brushed off my question when I asked him if he was seeing someone. And these days he is very cautious about his mobile phone, the other day when he was in the restroom and his mobile rang, he hurriedly came out to grab his phone as if I do not hold it.

Two of my closest people are acting weird making me wonder what actually could go wrong. I even brought Koshlesh strange behaviour before Vijay but he seemed to be unaffected but I was surely being affected.

 Another 15 days passed with this similar pattern, I therefore could not take how Pratiksha was avoiding me and therefore I decide to go to Ahmedabad to check what was bothering her because by now I had known her this better that there was something which was preventing her to act normal. On the other hand, after several attempts made before koshlesh I could not unfold the mystery behind his switched behaviour, but for me Pratiksha was more important as she was away from me and I had to ensure if everything was okay in her family.

my decision to head to Ahmedabad was so impromptu that I did not even tell koshlesh about it and randomly left one Friday evening after finishing college to return before Monday if everything seemed right.

Not finding me at home koshlesh sent a text.

"Hey its late where are you, are you staying over tonight at somebody's place.?"

I ignored the message not wanting to tell him anything as I was pissed up with him for being so secretive lately.

I went directly to her apartment and stood there making calls to her which she avoided at first but later answered:

"What, I am at home my parents are here I can't talk with you" she whispered.

"Come outside" I said.

"What outside, have you gone nuts or what" she mumbled.

"I am standing outside I want to see you" I replied.

She then came outside along with her phone on her ear,

"what's wrong with you, why have you come here, all of a sudden"

"I want to meet you" I replied. Just tell me when and where can we meet"

"Now I can't come I have to go to my college and I am not free, its better you go from here I will call you once I am free" she replied.

"Okay then I am coming upstairs if you don't have time, I have plenty of it. I won't allow you to avoid me anymore" I said rejecting her plea,

"Okay we will meet after my lecture ends at 2:30 Shambu café" she replied. Now please leave from here."

Fidgeting with my thoughts that what could be the reason of her strange behaviour I knuckled my fingers hoping that there could be no such family pressure on her to end this relationship as I have known her, she is very emotional and if her family gets a small hint of us being together, they may force her to set us apart and that is the last thing I want for our relationship.

She came on the table fiercely dropping her bag on one chair and with a commanding voice she said:

"What is your problem, why did you come to Ahmedabad without any prior intimation and how many times do I need to tell you that it isn't safe to bump around my house, if anybody gets a hint of us being together than I am not sure about you but my life will be finished."

I was taken back by her strange behaviour she has never lashed out me like this before.

While I was still processing her behaviour she was quivering and tears were running down from her eyes. Which made my belief firmer that something wasn't right there.

"Calm down, why are you acting so strange and fuming with anger. I just felt that there was something bothering you, which you weren't disclosing before me and therefore I came here to unveil the actual stress that has encapsulated you, I know there is surely something that you are preventing me to know but I still want to know to ensure that you have your anxiety relieved.

Resting her elbows on the table she dropped her head in her hands she began crying.

"You won't understand, it's difficult for me too to behave so improperly with you, but what unfolds beyond this is even worse and that's why I am preventing you to intervene"

I held her head and said, we can do everything together, please at least tell me what is bothering you and then we can together get rid of your anxiety, what is it, has anyone in your family said, or is there anything else bothering you" I said urgingly.

"I think we should breakup. Our breakup will settle everything" she said.

"What! Are you out of your mind, and for God's sake now tell me what is the matter enough of these riddles now tell me what the matter is" I said assertively.

"This is the last time I am asking you and if not, I am going home today with you to know what the matter is" I added.

"There is nothing wrong at home" she rejected my idea.

"Then where the problem is, enough of these riddles can we get to the point now Pratiksha, I can't take this suspense any longer. I have travelled to Ahmedabad because I was worried about you and even after coming here, I am unable to know what is causing this. Stop crying and speak up what is the matter." I spoke. My patience was talking a toll now.

"You won't be able to take the truth neither will you believe what I am going to say but still I would say since you are here to listen." She replied wiping her tears and gulping down water through her throat.

"I am all ears" I replied with determination.

"Your friend koshlesh the one whom you consider as your brother, he is not how he pretends himself before you. He wishes the worst for you. That day at your pg. while you were in the washroom, he tried molesting me, and since that day he has been constantly torturing me to dump you because he wants to have a relationship with me" she said.

It took me a while to process what did she said, I kept on shaking my head in disbelief.

"Is this a prank what both of you are playing on me" I replied in disbelief.

"No this isn't, I would now reiterate word by word what he said to me although it was something I want to forget. He said seems like you have had a good night but trust me I can provide you more pleasures than him, how about joining hands with me. I regret the day when I called you using vinay name I should have used my own since you were an easy catch. If you wish we can still come together dump vinay and become my girlfriend we will have the best relationship, or else I can give your Bhopal staycation details to your parents that would even be more fun" she said gathering her breaths.

"This was the reason that I was not meeting my eyes with you, I know how much importance does he hold in your life and putting these allegations on him will destroy your friendship and therefore I decided to stay away from you to invite nay further complications". She added.

"But this torture did not end here, he has been constantly texting me vulgar messages and has been sending me obscene images to force me to break up with you so that he can get access to me, if you don't believe me you can check the recent messages he has sent me I have a few of them as these messages are so obscene I had to delete them as and when I receive them so that no one in my family by chance get access to them". She said dropping her head on her hand and weeping.

My hands were trembling when I took her mobile in my hand, there were 5 messages from his number and all of them were vulgar context I never thought this was something in his brain, I had been living with him under the same roof and still I was unable to know his earthed feelings. I was drowned in shame as she got to know him because of me and because of me she had been going through this trauma for the past few weeks.

Slapping my head on my hands I sat there shaking I had my eyes filled with tears as it was a trauma for me koshlesh was someone whom I was least expecting for this betrayal, my entire body was shaking as I had touched some high voltage current and my thinking capacity was taken aback.

I felt choking and it seemed impossible for me to breathe there, she was crying too but I could help her to stop crying.

"Why didn't you tell me this that same day that same time that fucking day, why did you carry this pain in your heart for so long" I asked.

"don't you remember he was drunk. I thought he had said this because of the intoxication and he did not mean it actually and therefore I kept quite that day thinking not to cause tension in your bonding but later on reaching here is interruption continued which caused me to keep myself distant from you because I did not know how to put this before you." She replied sobbing.

"You should not have gone through this all alone, I don't even know what to say. It feels like I have been stabbed on my back" I replied breaking down.

Guilt engulfed me, I could not meet my eyes with her knowing that she had to go through that because of me and koshlesh could do something like this it was more of a shock which would not enable me to trust anyone anymore.

My feet began shaking and despite of several efforts I could not gather the strength to stand up.

We both were left out of works and specially my mouth was choked therefore we left the café without much conversation.

"I am sorry can I get some time to process this I shall call you by the evening, I promise I will get you out of this mess and shall confront koshlesh but one let me get back my senses. To think aptly" I pleaded.

She replied with a nod and we both left. But her words kept replaying in my mind and I was taken aback it was the worst thing that has ever happened to me.

The golden memories of the past with koshlesh kept playing at the back of my mind and then they were thrashed with the current truth of those ugly messages. It completely shattered me into pieces.

Being betrayed by someone you trust so deeply hurts even bad than several bones fractures. I could not help my tears flowing out he not only said bad to Pratiksha but knowing how much I loved her he tried hard enough to break my relationship contradictory to the fact that he was the one reason why I could be with her.

Although it was heart wrenching for me to confront him but I had to end this at any cost and therefore I called Pratiksha in the evening to inform her about my next course of action.

"I want you to allow him his disgusting chat one more day I want to confront him face to face I need to see the hatred he carries for me in his eyes and ask me what did I do wrong with him to face such betrayal from his end.

The day when I reach, I will ask you to call him when he is at home and I want to catch him red handed saying all that crap to you, not that I do not trust you with these messages but I want to catch him saying shit to you. I want to see his hate in his eyes that he has been carrying against me.

Please I need your help in this and that can only be possible if you do as I say. She agreed to my plea and I did one more thing I kept ignoring his calls such that he did not get a hint whether I had come to Ahmedabad or not.

When I reached Bhopal the other day he asked where I was and I made up an excuse of visiting my maternal uncles place in Satna to check on my grandmother's health.

When he asked me why wasn't I answering his calls I made excuse to wrap the fact from him.

Later I went ahead in my room and sent Pratiksha a message to call him so that I can hear his malevolent intentions and confront him.

As planned minutes later Pratiksha called him, I was stealthily keeping a closed eye on him from my room where I pretended to get some rest after the hectic travel.

"Hello sweetheart, it's strange to see that you made me a call, it's always me who calls or texts you, have you changed your mind or what. Are you ready to dump that asshole, if yes that this is going to be the best decision of your life. You are always welcome" he said with the evilest smile on his face.

"Listen I haven't made this call to you for accepting you all I have to say is if you continue to harass me this way, I will tell vinay everything about your evil intentions and you very well know how aggressive can he get, he will break your bones" she warned.

"Ohhh my god, I am trembling from fear, that loser can't touch me even, your vinay isn't a superhero and whatever he portrays himself before you are unreal and fake, I know what he truly is, a rookie yokel." He said, not knowing that I Was standing right behind and hearing everything.

"If you still are opting to stay with him than my offer stands clear I shall inform your parents about your beautiful honeymoon that you have spent in the name of a fucking competition and be ready to take the rollercoaster ride of your denial" he replied.

"What do you want why are you harassing me, we were your friends." She cried.

"I don't want to see you two together, seeing you both as a couple sends chills down my spine, I hate the fact that you could have been mine instead I willingly talked to you on his behalf, it could be us but thanks to my stupidity I had to see you sharing the chemistry with him. It's okay if we both don't match but I will not allow both of your relationship to sustain." He replied.

This was it; I could not hold this anymore and patted his back to confront him.

"Whom are you talking to?" I asked.

His face turned pale he wasn't expecting me there, I could see the fear in his eyes of being caught. I was fuming with anger because I was still hoping that he was my friend and this was all a joke, but it wasn't and having heard him talking to her this way and nit only that seeing all the hate that he has been carrying against me in his eyes made me reflect upon the golden days of friendship we have had.

"Show me who is it" I tried taking the mobile from his hand.

He pushed me against the wall and said "its personal" and rushed to disconnect the call.

"No, it isn't" it's not someone I do not know. Its Pratiksha isn't she" I asked.

His anxiety was conspicuous, he was caught and now he did not have any other way to escape and that's when he began shedding his skin of false emotions and brought his real self out.

"Yes, she was Pratiksha and if you already know the truth so let me make one thing very clear you don't deserve her, ever since I have known you, you have been acting deeply in love but you are nothing but a fool, I regret the time when I introduced myself as you before her, If I haven't done that, she would have been mine." He said aggressively.

"I was okay till it was a long-distance relation but when she came here, I felt pained by the fact that she came for you, she is a nice girl modern my type. I wonder what is that in you that girls fall for you, I am equally good-looking yet that Aditi is after you and now Pratiksha too, I envied you for this, whatever attention that you have been getting from these girls should be mine" he added.

"If this is what you actually think about me then what about that deep friendship that we shared, our friendship was beyond these things" I replied feeling dejected.

"Fuck your friendship. There is nothing I share with you any longer, and it's good that you have got to know the truth I was actually tiered of pretending to be your friend. There is nothing we share in common other than the fact that we both want to have Pratiksha" he said.

I swallowed the lump in my throat and prevented the tear from falling my eyes as I did not want him to know how shattered I was to know his real colours but he began cursing Pratiksha and said something inappropriate about her character I could not help myself from slapping him hard on his face.

But it did not end here, when I slapped him, he came against me and pushed me against the wall blocking my throat with his hand, it initiated a series of blows from both the ends, I punched his abdomen to loosen the grip of his hand over my throat as I was being choked. He slammed my head on the wall causing me an injury on my head.

Years of friendship, loving memories came crashing before my eyes, the head was rammed so bad that I fainted it was a blackout for a couple of seconds, he was so furious at me that he was even ready to cause me harm, I could not cope up from the fact that I always treated him like my brother and he was not someone I thought he would be.

He left the room, and not only that he left the pg. within an hour of our outburst and I was still under the shock of what just happened, it was no less than a heartbreak, or I could say it was worse than any heartbreak I believed I was blessed to share this great bond with my friends but it ended up being a mirage which was no way near the reality.

I needed some time to process all of this the air in the room suddenly became so toxic that it began choking me I felt suffocated, everything was although the same but the entire vibe of the place changed dramatically, the place which was my favourite to spend my day felt like a crematorium where I lost my dearest friend my brother my trust for life.

I was glad that he left because if he chose to stay the close violent encounter that happened between us would often repeat.

Later that evening when I received a call from Pratiksha after making sure that she hasn't received any further threats from koshlesh I requested her to please allow me to have my time I was absolutely shaken and had no clues to bring myself back.

I laid on my back on the bed with my eyes wide open focused on the ceiling fan which was running with a screeching voice and the silence of the house made the noise even more evident, tears kept dripping and I did not even realise when did I fall asleep crying over the reality that has unearthed my emotions so badly.

ANOTHER DITCH

Next morning, I woke up with a bad pain in my neck, it instantly reminded me of the sight when koshlesh tried stifling me up, sleep had hardly made me escape the reality for few hours but the pain brought back the nightmare back to life. The pain was hard to handle and therefore I had to rush to the nearest physician to get myself examined, it was obvious for the doctor to gasp that I had been through a fight but since the doctor was amiable, he prescribed me few medicines for the pain and to normalise the stiffness in the neck he asked me to wear a neck brace for at least 24 hours to get the muscles relax.

I went back home and decided to stay in the house only as I still could not process what happened, I wanted everything to be back to normal as it was earlier but I knew this was such a crevice that was going to stay forever, and although the pill of truth was hard to swallow but eventually, I had to process it and come in consensus with the reality. As I had to talk with Pratiksha to check upon her if she was okay, after taking an update from her I still wanted time for myself and therefore did not talk to her much neither I told her about the injury that I had succumbed.

The mental trauma was more hard hitting than the physical one, I could take pain relieving tablets for the physical pain but this mental pain was excruciating. The entire flashbacks of our happy days were coming in my thoughts and the moment I was appreciating those days I was slapped with the reality of last night the hate which he was carrying in his eyes for me, it was hard to swallow this pill of acceptance that the friendship has broken and now nothing can bring back those wonderful days.

Taking the medication, I went back to sleep as I was under a miserable state, I had no one to talk to neither I could share what just happened between us. I wanted to get my other friends involved in this so that they could help koshlesh to understand his mistake but, then I felt this can frame a negative image about koshlesh in the minds of people therefore I refrained from saying anything to anyone, not even vijay who has been the dearest. I believed sleeping could only kill the time and help me in pulling myself out of my negative thoughts.

The constant ringing mobile forced me to get out of my bed to pick who was being so restless to talk to me as I was not willing to talk with anyone, on flipping the phone towards me I saw it was vijay and there were another 5 missed calls from his number,

The moment of truth has arrived. I knew he got too knew about the incident of last night, exhaling a long breathe and rolling over my eyes in dilemma I answered the phone.

"Where are you man, why were you answering my phone, I have been trying to reach your for almost an hour." Said vijay.

"I am sorry I was sleeping and therefore didn't realise the call" I replied.

"What happened, I heard you and koshlesh had a fight, what is the matter" he asked without wasting and further time on lame conversations.

"He must have told you, then why are you asking me" I replied dejectedly.

"He hasn't told me anything but last night he came to my place with all his luggage and above that he was bleeding too from his nose, I knew something isn't right but he did not utter a single word upon asking." Said vijay.

When I heard him saying this, I took a series of deep breathes thinking that how will I put this whole anecdote before him, as it was something I had been running away to admit this reality.

I somewhere in the back of my mind knew that vijay was tricking me as he was very manipulative to get the information out, he could possibly lie that koshlesh hasn't shared anything with him but the reality might be exactly the opposite.

"I and koshlesh are not in good terms now and therefore he had left the house" I replied taking the lump down my throat.

"Ohh thanks for your wonderful acceptance, but this is something that I know what I want you to tell me is that what happened that led you to this state" he replied agitatedly.

"Vijay I already know that koshlesh has told you what happened what are you instigating me to go through it all over again "I said.

"Because I want to hear your side of story too before making an impression about this particular incident in my mind." He replied demurely.

I was convinced and told him everything that had happened between koshlesh and Pratiksha and how I confronted him and how his dark reality came before me.

While I was repeating this there were times, I had choked because of how difficult it was for me to relieve that horrific incident which tore me apart. Yet somehow, I concluded and waited for his reaction.

"listen brother, all I could grasp from this entire chaos is that you both have fallen for the same girl now instead of fighting over it let the girl decide whom she want to be with, why you both are entering into a wrestling match, you have always liked her from the school time yet you allowed koshlesh to get closer to her now this was very obvious for him to get attracted to her because she is really very attractive no one can prevent himself from wanting her to be a part of their life, so instead of fighting and creating problems for one another, ask Pratiksha whom she wants to date and then go ahead with her consent" he replied.

My eyes literally popped out I could not believe my ears what was I listening, I never thought vijay could be nincompoop yet his advice proved him to be one. It took me a while to gather back my senses to respond to his stupidity.

"Vijay, if such statement came from a person who did not know me well, I would have willingly accepted it, but I am startled to receive such a shitty advice from a person whom I considered my best friend, you and koshlesh where like a family to me, you both even those things about me which even my family is unaware of, and you are advising me to take this casually."

"Were you not aware that I loved her, were you and koshlesh not aware how I have waited for her consent to be my girlfriend, were you not aware that I wanted her to become my wife, were you not aware that she meant the world to me. Tell me were you not aware," I screamed to my loudest pitch, loosing myself breaking down and falling on the ground while I cried and said all of this to vijay.

"Listen, if you love her, koshlesh also does and he also feels the same for her therefore I am asking you to let Pratiksha decide" he replied.

"Decide what. And what love… is blackmailing and intimidating okay with the person you love? it's more like a hook or crook, that she has to be mine or else I will make her life miserable she won't be able to live peacefully" I asked.

"What koshlesh has tried doing is not how you love someone, it's more of a crime that you are harassing a girl to be with you just because you are physically attracted towards her" I added.

"ohhhhh vinay stop being so overdramatic, if koshlesh fell for her even she was also flirtatious with him, I have seen them chatting and I have seen that when koshlesh tried to give her any hints she responded well with those and therefore I can say it cannot be one way, your so called darling Pratiksha is equally responsible to get koshlesh to this stage, and now she is acting innocent before you, at first she staged this entire drama and now after successfully igniting a war between you too she is acting as if she had never said or done anything which can give koshlesh any positive signals for his attraction towards her." He replied with fury.

Didn't know what was wrong those people whom I loved and treated like family became my enemies all of a sudden, they both knew my crazy love for her yet both of them were saying the things I wouldn't want to hear even I, my dream. I could not hear him any longer neither I had the courage to respond and fight with him. I disconnected to his call.

Bringing my knees to my chest and wrapping my arms over them I scrunched like a baby and cried for hours on the floor, I felt stabbed, it wasn't really a matter that two people have affection towards one person what was painful that these two friends of mine who were with me on every tiny step of this relationship they have seen this growing they even helped me to make her mine and now all of a sudden they have become against as if they were never aware of the seriousness that I had for her.

My neck injury worsened and I cried for hours and hours, feeling hopelessly alone this wasn't something I could share with anyone in the family too and therefore I grieved in silence.

I THOUGHT SHE WAS MY FRIEND

It took a lot of courage for me to get back to the normal life but I had to yet I wasn't ready, my final exams were approaching and so were the final campus interviews and all the other practical exams that were bound to follow to get us through the final process of obtaining the degree.

I began disliking going college reason being my best friends with whom I spent my day had now been strangers to me the familiar place also felt alien when we end up a situation like this, yet I was determined to perform well in my exams and thereby was ready to face everything. My only concentration was on performing well in the exams and securing a job in the campus placement.

It did not take much time for our classmates to notice that things were not going well between me and koshlesh we even hated to come across one another, it was obvious and people took notice of it few of them came to me asking about our reason for the conflict but I chose silence instead of defaming him. But the place where I had spent nearly 4 hours had turned alien for me, I was not at all comfortable there as if I had no connections yet there were a few of my friends who talked to me, but our gags which we friends did the laughs and the fun everything was gone.

Then came the announcement of the farewell organised in the college for the final semester students and we were all asked to come for the celebrations where the students were about to perform, previously when we saw the farewell preparations for the senior students, we used to plan that when it would be our farewell, we friends will do this and that and now when the time of the farewell has actually come up, I felt like skipping it. This test of time was taking a toll on my mental health, all I wanted was to lock myself up in a room without anyone.

I had already made up my mind of not attending the farewell but a professor from our class insisted on all the students to join in, and one of my class friends insisted me to come up as he knew the reason, I was not willing to join later I went in the party with a heavy heart.

The party was vivid colourful everyone had a happy face and were enjoying the vibe of good music good performances and lip-smacking food, it took a lot effort out of me to actually stick on a smile over my face and enjoy, I struggled yet battled out the awkwardness prevailing in my head and began enjoying the evening with all other classmates.

I came across koshlesh a couple of time but by then we both had aced the art of ignoring one another as if the other person never existed, I didn't know about him but for me to act this way was more tormenting yet I did it.

I enjoyed the food, other friends were engrossed in dancing and making videos I preferred to sit back and see them having a blast I even made a couple of videos as memory to cherish and take back with us from our engineering days, I wish this chaos would not have happened, then this day would have been different these celebrations would hit differently.

Alas! The college was ending so was the friendship and this was a bit more painful than the college ending but life goes on and we become stronger day by day.

The farewell was splendid the professors were giving their tips and tricks to present ourselves to the outside world we were about to enter and they wished us the best for our careers and life ahead, not only this the teachers grooved on the music along with the students which made the entire celebration even more happening and memorable.

I was feeling abandoned and this feeling was making me feel worse I was losing all my interest in being there in Bhopal yet I had to finish my study to get the desired job and therefore I kept myself stuck to my books all the time and the time while I was away from reading, I was either talking to Pratiksha to get back to our old days or was at the hanuman temple sitting alone seeking strength from the almighty.

One evening when I was done with my reading, I felt the urge to talk to someone as I was feeling very heavy but Pratiksha wasn't my first choice, the talks with Pratiksha were more kind of forced now, earlier we need not think twice on what to say and what not but after this entire scenario we had to think before speaking anything to anyone and yet the conversations were not that wholesome.

My state of mind was not allowing me to think beyond this entire problem and I really needed someone to talk with for a while who could help me forget this problem, I began scrolling my mobile phone and thought of looking at the contacts in my phone.

On scrolling for a minute I came across the number of Aditi, I knew she was upset with me over my relationship with Pratiksha and I had been not that great with her in terms of telling her about my relationship status yet I missed how nicely she treated me, I missed the time of us together I missed the warmth I felt in being with her, I was abandoned by my friends koshlesh and vijay and the vacancy that they left in my life made me feel miserable and forced me to doubt myself that maybe I was the one over reacting, I needed someone to understand my side of the story unlike today where everyone stood against me.

I was dwindling with the idea of whether should I text her or not because I knew somehow that she understood me better than anyone and that was something I was in need of, of someone who understands me, of someone before whom I need not prove my point. Regardless of the fact that she was someone whom I have disappointed I was ready to face the wrath but I wanted her advice over this, I was trying to seek validation from her about this peculiar matter knowing that it won't help me anyway yet I wanted that help.

Talking a few deep breaths before taking any action, I began rubbing my thumb over the screen of my phone after struggling to frame hundreds of reasons in my head that what will I say her why did I send her this message, was she angry with me, what if she ignores my message, etcetera I finally typed a message to her:

"Hi Aditi, how are you?"

Tapping my fingers on the table waiting for the response, my anxiety began and different thoughts began falling in me my head

What would she think about me?

What If she has blocked me?

What if she decides to not respond.

What if she come to argue with me. These all thoughts were although playing in my head but the voice of my head was so loud that I could hear them even in the silence of the night.

20 minutes passed in these 20 minutes I have had multiple reasons being played in my head and by the end of it I had lost all the hope of even receiving nay response from her end. I took off my eyes from the phone screen which I have glued since I had sent the, message losing all the hope, and now I had to convince myself that I had to keep my feelings to myself and this idea of seeking validation to feel a little better was about to go in the drain.

Before I could switch off the lights to call the day off with disappointment my mobile screen popped up with a message from Aditi.

"Hi vinay, I am good, how about you?"

I was so relieved to hear from her, I was even happier that her message did not reflect that she was mad at me, she greeted me with the same warmth as she would greet me earlier and that was something that gave me the feeling of lightness that I haven't lost the only friend I had now, she was still my friend.

If you have ever been this alone like I, was you would really relate to me when you find at least you have someone having your back, it wasn't that Pratiksha was not there but there has been something which I was not comfortable sharing with Pratiksha, I wasn't comfortable sharing with the ideas which koshlesh and vijay were having in their brains because that would even make her feel worse about herself.

"I am fine, where you sleeping, did I disturb you?" I asked formally

"Not at all, I had gone out for a walk after my dinner and had kept my mobile for charging" she replied.

I loved the energy she was having for me; she was so amiable with me that made me feel very happy.

We talked for a few minutes over the SMS and then I asked her If she was free than could I call her.

 It took her no time to grasp that I had to share something with her

"Is there anything you want to share" she asked "is everything okay" she added.

She was truly someone who could even understand my silence but then I recollected that koshlesh was equally understanding and I never was required to say anything to him he even understood the unspoken. This similarity between her and koshlesh made me swell up and the thoughts of even loosing this friendship surmounted, she had enough reasons to not talk with me yet she was talking that kind of felt better.

"Yeah, actually I am going through a very bad phase in my life and I really needed someone to talk with, if you could please spare some of your time that would be a really great help, I won't force you but if you can that can indeed be something I will be forever indebted to you" I requested.

"Ohh, you don't have to plead this much you stupid, relax I will call you after a few minutes just wait till then" she replied with a whole room of energy that made me feel a little better already.

10 minutes later she called me and we began talking for a while we talked about the usual and without discussing anything with her yet I was feeling lighter, her aura made me feel stable and helped ease my anxiety,

She was very good at handling typical situations like these, she already knew I had something heavy to express before her, but she ensured that I was at first free from any guilt that I had been holding against her, that way I would be able to express my heart out without any presumptions.

After talking for a good 10 minutes sharing some good laugh over the wittiest jokes, she makes she slowly slide to the topic which was bothering me.

"Now vinay tell me what is that bothering you, I have noticed in our conversation you don't feel the same, there is something that had shook you from within, so much so that you are experiencing trouble in being yourself" she asked.

Her words came out so straight like an arrow she had hit the right point, I wasn't the same, I was experiencing trouble in taking the conversation further.

I curled my lips before I could say something to her, rolling my eyes over to the ceiling and taking two to three deep breaths I gathered my words to tell her the reason for my distress, the thought of repeating what had happened in the past few days already filled my throat with a lump and I had to swallow the lump before I could make way for the words to come out of my mouth.

"I don't know where to start, I hope you know I and Pratiksha are in a relationship" I said.

She agreed with a yes.

"Our relationship is facing the heat these days, two of my best friends koshlesh and vijay have turned my enemies and things are going out of my hands, I have become all alone, I have absolutely no one here with me with whom I can share my feelings who can understand me." I said by this time my voice had turned heavier and the words were coming out with a lot of difficulty.

She was kind enough to hear me out without interrupting but gradually she asked more and more questions to fill her up with all the information about what exactly happened and what lead us to this situation.

"Listen vinay I am not saying what koshlesh did to you was correct but did you ask him if he had such feelings for her than why did not, he tell you at first, he should have told you about his feelings this way you would not feel cheated as you are feeling now."

" but I would further like to add something which you might dislike and that is, Pratiksha is well aware of the fact that she is beautiful and she uses her beauty to grab attention from all the boys, I am not saying this because I envy her or anything like that but I am saying this because I have too known her, and there are lesser known facts about her which you are unaware of, I won't be surprised if koshlesh comes up with an argument that she wooed him and therefore he fell for her" she added.

Her words tasted bitter; I was not looking forward to hear something like this. I had sought her help to get me out of this mess but she was aggravating this situation by her opinion.

I went cold for few moments on hearing this and her words filled me with anger because hearing anything against Pratiksha was enough for me to cut ties with the person saying this shit.

"I know you would not agree with me on this as it is about your beloved, but if you consider me to be your friend than trust me, you do not stay in Ahmedabad but I do and I have seen her roaming around with other boys too. I have never brought this topic before you because I felt who am I to say about your relationship, nut now that you have come up yourself, I can finally say what I had seen." She spoke.

Her words began disturbing me and I could not help myself but to get the sudden outburst.

"so you have also joined the gang against me and Pratiksha, I don't understand why on earth everyone has begun having problem with my love life. Or this the problem with me that I have made such selfish friends who can't see me happy, they all have problems with me how is this even possible."

"I thought you would understand what I have been going through on losing my best friends but it seems you too want to join the league of the people I had stopped talking" I added.

She tried making her point but I was not ready to listen.

"Listen if roaming with boys makes a girl slut and of a low character so let me remind you of the days when you roamed across the streets with me, does that also make you a slut?" I yelled.

"Vinay watches your words, she warned.

"Ohh so now you are fucking caring about the words when the question was formed for you, and while you were painting a target on my girlfriend did not you think about this enlightenment of watching your words before you speak" I justified.

"I was telling you what I say I was not painting any target against her; I know you love her and won't stand any negative comment about her but I was only putting what I saw before you" she replied.

"Did I ask you to give her any character certificate" I asked.

"Then why the fuck are you giving your opinions about it" I added.

"Ohh stop over reacting, what your friends said about her might be true and that was I trying to make a point. And if not, may God bless you both with your relationship. I thought you were my friend and therefore I was being protective for you, which lead me to say what I saw. But remind you I did not come up to you complaining about your chick, it was you who has come here to discuss your personal life, so stop yelling at me for no reasons" she apprehended.

"Yeah, it was absolutely my mistake and not yours, I came thinking you would understand, sorry my bad" I said with a disgrace.

"You better be sorry, I am not saying what koshlesh did was correct, he absolutely did wrong knowing about your feelings but it was your fault too that you always Wanted him as a third wheel to balance your relationship" she replied.

"And now when you have lost that third wheel in your life you are here before me looking to gain some sympathy and a shoulder to nag about what others did to you isn't it, if I am not wrong, you never needed my presence in your life before this day, and now suddenly you see a friend in me" she added.

Her words were so harsh that it pierced deep into my heart.

"You know what vinay, I understand what koshlesh did to you was absolutely unfair and he should have never done this if he really thought you were his friend but I would still suggest you, don't blindly trust your girlfriend, there can be malice in her intentions too. After all she is also a human being, and like others she might have done or said something which might have passed wrong signals to koshlesh, I am not defending koshlesh but unlike you I am not seeing the thing as black and white, it can be grey too. Which you need to understand" she said with a consoling voice making me doubt Pratiksha.

By this time, I have had enough from her and I was no longer ready to take any other word from her, before she could finish up saying her opinion, I disconnected the phone call followed by switching off my phone as I did not want this matter to alleviate any further.

This phone call disconnected me with one more friend of my life and I was yet again alone on my journey of struggle.

The entire night I cried my heart out, her words kept on echoing in my heart there were times when I began to think the questions which she has raised can possibly be correct but my heart was not ready to accept them and thus nullifying all the doubts against Pratiksha I brushed aside my emotions to focus on the day ahead of me.

CAMPUS 3 SELECTION

I was alone but I had that urge in me to prove everyone who doubted me and my relationship wrong, I paved my way to bring my mental wellbeing in alignment with my aspirations, the first step towards this alignment was to take my life in my control and to get a hold on my aggression.

I was filled with rage when I found out everyone, I trusted some way or the other betrayed me, koshlesh, vijay and now Aditi each one of them knew my sentiments associated with Pratiksha yet they tried to tarnish her image before me, in such a way that it could possibly hamper my future with her.

I spent the next few weeks in solitude building up my self-esteem and practiced my heart out to get the best job in the campus selection as the selection was round the corner, I approached the faculty from our college to guide me to for the upcoming interview. The professors were equally willing to help me out and they extended their utmost support in guiding me on how I could make myself an impressive CV and how to answer the questions asked by the interviewer.

One of my professors has given me the best advice:

"Vinay the interviewers also know that you are a fresher and therefore they are not seeking your expertise what they will be seeking is your confidence to take up any task put forth before you and the willingness to learn if something props before you, therefore all I can suggest is be confident and don't be afraid if you don't know anything just speak up straight that this is something I will learn under your guidance"

I followed every advice which came from the professors my dedication was liked by the professors and their direction really helped me at the time of interview, as directed by them I presented myself in the similar way and gave the interview with confidence.

Upon getting a question which, I was not pretty sure about I promptly replied "this is something I will learn under your guidance", this brought a smile on the face of the interviewer and he was really impressed with me.

"You don't need to wait for the final calls, we are selecting you right here right now," said the interviewer.

"We are delighted to get such fresh young and willing candidate for our company, you have all the qualities which we have been seeking in our employee this makes you the first selected candidate. Congratulations" said the interviewer extending his hand.

It was the first good news which I had heard over the past few months which gave me a reason to be grateful to the god, the moment I heard that I had been selected I thought of jumping and celebrating but I had to hold my calm as I was yet before the interviewers and there were still some technical discussions being done.

The Developers Arcade group of companies was the company that selected me, I was then appointed as the junior engineer at their Pune branch and it was only a post for the training period of 3 months after that I would be appointed as the senior engineer over that post. This phase of 3 months was done to ensure that I was well acquainted with the work and all the machining and processing work.

The biggest flex about this company was that it had its another branch in Ahmedabad and once the training was over the doors of getting transferred to Ahmedabad were open for me, it felt like God had finally began answering my prayers. I was finally having a day without stress and crying and all that mellow drama that had been a constant from the past few days.

I was soaking in this happiness when I was told about my package for that job it further escalated my heartbeats as I was actually underestimating myself for this and had not really hoped that I could be placed for more than 5 lac per annum package.

But the interviewer might have seen something in me which I was not aware yet that they offered me with a package of 7.5 lakh per annum which would be incremented once I become the senior engineer. My feet began shaking with excitement, I felt like this is something which is surely going to bring smile on my parent's face, especially my father. He had really encouraged me while I ran away from here back during the time of 2nd semester.

I simply wanted myself out of that room only to celebrate this news with my friends and family. Only later to realise that the friends I had were no longer there to cheer and celebrate with me. I walked out of the room with a wide smile on my face a few students waiting for their turn congratulated me but there was no one around who would be genuinely happy for me.

I even saw koshlesh on the que trying to ignore my presence in that room, I even caught him staring at me from the corner of his eyes but this expression was something I was not in a mood to see and therefore I left the group discussion room as it was not needed for me to stay there any longer.

I walked out of the college with elongated spine and swollen chest with pride as I had really worked hard to get there. I called my dad,

"Daddy!" I said in a sober voice.

"Yes beta! What happened, did the interview not go well?" he asked

I release a breath in response without uttering a word only to intensify the reaction.

"it's okay! Campus selections are not the only means to get the job, you can try your luck directly by visiting the companies and uploading your resume online, no need to worry you can still get a very good job" he said trying to console me.

My dad has always been very supportive to me throughout this engineering and yet again with his response he was proving that he was my biggest supporter.

overwhelmed with his reaction my throat was full as I was able to imagine how nice and happy, he would feel on actually knowing that I had bagged the highest package available and landed a job in a renowned company.

"Vinay are you there?" asked my dad on not hearing from me.

"Yes dad, I want to share something dad. I got the job In Developers Arcade group of companies. They offered me the post of junior engineer in their Pune branch with an annual package of 7.5 lakhs" I said gulping down the lump in my throat and wiping off my tears of joy.

"What! Seriously no joking." asked my dad

"No dad your encouragement has done all this wonder and I had really got this job" I reaffirmed.

"I am proud of your beta; you have given me the best surprise yet. It was my keen desire to see you succeed and you with your dedication has made it happen, there can't be any blissful day than this" he replied with some heaviness in his voice. It might be because he also got equally emotional as I did.

"don't tell this news to mom I want to give this news to her in person, I could not hold it for longer and thus shared it with you but I wish to see how is she going to react and thus I will only tell her that the result is yet to be announced for the interview, you also please keep this secret intact. I will be visiting you during the weekend and then we shall have a grand celebration" I devised a plan to keep this news as a secret.

"As you wish, but it's a news which needs to be broadcasted and you are asking it to me to keep this as a secret. How will I be able to hold this" dad replied.

"You will have to; weekend is 2 days away keep this news under wraps and thus we will see how everyone is going to react to this news." I spoke.

"Okay, today I can team up with you for any conspiracy as you have given me the opportunity to be a proud father. God bless you; may you achieve great heights in your career and make us proud" replied dad.

"Thank you, dad, see you on Saturday. Till then lips sealed" I giggled.

GHOSTED

Pratiksha had begun behaving absurdly, I tried contacting her multiple times but she did not reply to my calls and the only message I had been receiving from her end is:

"I have my examinations going on can't talk right now, will talk once the exams are over"

There had been her exams in the past yet she never ignored me this way, she at least managed to have a minute talk with me no matter how busy her schedule was. But this time it was evident she was deliberately avoiding my calls and messages.

I had my limits and time was already testing my patience and this time upon getting her cold response I decided to allow her the given space she has been asking for so long. She had been a difficult person; I have always dealt with her with due patience but the circumstances have made me lose all my calm.

I was angry with her for the reason that she had already know I had no one In my friend circle and this was the time when I needed her the most. I broke all my other relations to ensure that my relation with her remains intact and receiving such blank responses from her made me fume with anger that she did not love me as much as I do.

Although these emotions where only the result of the neglect that she has been trying to do yet it was making us apart.

I got so mad at her for her this ignorance that I did not even share with her that I got the job.

And she despite of knowing that I had my interview, she did not bother to ask how my interview went.

I was mad and deeply hurt because I had already been filled with misinformation about her thanks to my so-called friends and her behaviour of not considering me of any value landed me in self-doubt whether those people were correct and maybe she did not love me.

To put an end to this trail of negative thoughts, I filled myself with the happy memories of the past and convinced myself that maybe God wants me to surprise her too upon visiting Ahmedabad I will tell her.

I began thinking about how will everyone react, this anticipation was sending chills in my body. Whenever I thought of their reactions the assumption of this which was about to turn into reality was giving me collywobbles.

I was getting nervous jitters as in the past two days I haven't heard from Pratiksha, one thing bothering me was if koshlesh was still harassing her and she was abstaining to say this before me thinking of not giving me any stress.

But these were only speculations of my brain, but my insecurities were very loud. I kept a close watch on koshlesh during the college hours to see if he retains the similar body language as her was presuming few days ago. But I could not find anything fishy yet my suspicion was growing on things not being well with her.

I was merely 12 hours away to meet my family and see their reaction, although my father was my partner in keeping the secret hidden yet I was scared that he might have spilled the beans before my mother.

But next morning I was taken with a surprise that he was brilliant at keeping the secrets intact which I had least expected from him. When I reached home my mother had a confused face to see me there, she slowly asked,

"Did your interview go well beta"

I choose to nod takin my chin down only to hide the happiness in my voice.

But mothers are mothers they can even sense your micro expressions.

She gently used her thumb placing it on my chin to lift my face to gaze into my eyes as if she could read what I was trying to hide on my face. she dived into my eyes to extract the truth and asked

"You got the job, right?"

I was amazed at her accurate prediction and stood startled thinking that my father revealed before her, I looked at my father confusedly to check if he has but he nodded in denial that he hasn't said anything.

"stop looking at your father, I know it even if you have decided to keep it a secret, I can read you both I have spent my life with your father I know when he is hiding something from me, as far as you are concerned I have given birth to you sweetie, I even know those things about you which you don't even know about yourself, know if you are done can I now get the surprise, for which you have come all the way to Ahmedabad.

Her justification blew my mind and for a second, I felt so tiny to try hiding things from mom she even knows the hidden things because mothers are really the greatest creation of God.

"Mom! I have got the job in Developers Arcade group of companies, they were so impressed me that they have offered me the highest package in the college among all the students, I along with 3 more students only got this good pay scale. It has all been possible because of your and dad's motivation" I said while grabbing her shoulders and making her spin out of excitement.

"Seriously! You aren't making this up, are you?" she reassured before she could possibly react.

She then grabbed me tightly around my waist resting her head around my shoulder, her voice was cracked because of the overwhelming news she said

"I am so happy for you dear; I have always kept your success in my prayers because I wanted you to get what you have wanted with your life and this being just the beginning. I hope you do extremely well professionally to embark further such more achievements in life.

My siblings and neighbours were equally happy and joined us for the mini celebrations, my father bought for me my favourite breakfast and some sweets to cherish the moment of success. After spending some quality time with my family, I thought of making things right with Pratiksha and dressed up to go to her house to see her.

I tried connecting to her through mobile but her network seemed unreachable. Before this day I had never walked up to her house because I was scared to introduce myself to her parents as an unemployed person, but now I had a well-paying job in my hand and therefore this suspicion of being rejected cordoned off from my head and I was ready to get in the eyes of her family and trace my identity in their lives as their future son in law.

I was getting nervous jitters while walking up the stairs to her house, I was trying to make sentences to how was I going to greet them, "hello I am vinay, Pratiksha's friend we were in the same school"

No this could have been said better I said to myself and pondering what next to be added to sound impressive and friendly.

By this time, I was at her doorstep and rang the bell I was so engrossed in myself introductory preparation that I completely ignored the big lock outside the door and rang the doorbell again. It took me a while to realise that the house was locked from outside and there was no one at the house.

I again dialled her number but could not reach her. Presuming they might have gone for shopping I decided to come in the evening, but I got the same lock every time in the evening and then the next morning.

I wasn't in Ahmedabad for a long vacation I was there only for the weekend which passed with a snap and I could not get the chance to meet Pratiksha neither I got to talk to her, I was having mixed feelings because of the last argument we have had although I was not willing to go back yet I had to because I had my final exams coming up before me and therefore, I had to leave.

I repeatedly tried connecting her through text and messaged her to text me back whenever she was back online.

I was pissed at her this time, if she was to go somewhere where there was no network, she might have informed me prior, I would not be bothering as much as I was doing now.

All I could do was patiently wait for her to text me or to call me.

My journey to Ahmedabad was half fulfilled yet half remained dissatisfactory as I wanted to enjoy this news with her as well which was now only an unfulfilled wish. As I would not be able to give her this news face to face now, she would be hearing about my job over a phone call only.

I could not contain my anxiety as where was she, I relentlessly tried connecting her but my every effort went in vain. I struggled to find peaceful sleep in my train, every time I closed my eyes, I had some wrong thought about her disturbing my sleep.

I brushed all these wrongful thoughts aside and began chanting god's name in order to seek asylum for peace before the almighty, which eventually helped me soothe my anxiety.

I checked my phone next morning only to see no new notification, and every time the phone pooped a notification, I hoped it was her, the patience of time was killing the peace in me. I went to college for my lecture, as this was the final term hardly there were students attending the class, but I had no reason to sit behind in the pg. neither I had anyone to spend my day with therefore I went ahead to stay in the college read there for some time and in the free time I went in the library to do some reading for the approaching exams.

By this time, I had good connections with the professors and therefore I went ahead to meet them sharing my happiness and also thanking them for their insightful advice that has really helped me in clearing the interview.

While I was reading in library, I finally got the message from Pratiksha.

"Hey! I am so sorry, I had to come to my village in Rajasthan and due to power cut I could not put my phone on charge, my grandmother passed away this Friday morning and therefore we had to leave in a rush. I was about to tell this to you but thought this can ruin your interview and therefore avoided to tell you, had I known that there would be no connectivity over here I would have told you. It would still take us one more week to come back home therefore I can't say when will I be able to talk to you. I miss you; I love you, and how did your interview go?" she summarised everything in one text.

"Ohh God I was so worried for you; I am sorry to hear for your loss. I even came to your house yesterday only to tell you that I got the job and now we have a good income together, I will tell you all the details once you return, I badly want to hear your voice, I miss you more" I replied.

"Congratulations. I will call you once I return, I wish I would be here to celebrate this with you, nevertheless you enjoy and will talk later." She replied.

Her text was enough to shed tonnes of baggage that I had been carrying from the past 24 hours. And I finally took a sigh of relief.

SAH

It has been nearly 12 days and I had not her voice, ever since we came into the relationship this has been the first time that I had not heard her, although we have had arguments and the days where we could not talk much yet this situation of desperation was making me anxious.

After returning to Bhopal, I was back to run my errands, simultaneously I began gathering my stuff as it was only one more month left for me to leave the city. Once the exams were over, I will go to Ahmedabad once for 15 days and after that I would be stepping into the new hemisphere of life in the new city. Life was still difficult in Bhopal because the memories with my friends kept erupting and as and when they popped up the memory which destroyed also popped which was had to forget and swallow, I tried avoiding the encounters as much as I could and lived in my own bubble.

One evening when I was preparing for my exams as the next day was my exam. my phone rang anticipation of being her call I jumped to receive the call only to realise that it was Aditi who was trying to call. I could have picked the call but the fact that last time when I shared my problem with her, she blamed Pratiksha for her and stood in support of koshlesh paced my heartbeats and I did not myself to lose my calm and say anything which I should not and regret later and therefore I did not answer her call.

She called nearly 3 times followed by a text message:

"Vinay, not answering my calls and avoiding it will not take away your problems, neither talking with me will aggravate your problems. I wanted to share a news with you about my life, I still consider you as my dear friend and therefore I wish to share all the important updates of my life with you. I hope if you are reading this kindly call me back"

I was already pissed with her and was not in a mood to talk or hear her justify her stand, neither I wanted to say anything which can sound rude and therefore I abstained from responding to her, I further knew that she would not stop here, she would further call me after sometime therefore to end that probability I switched off my mobile, as I knew Pratiksha has not returned yet and she would not be calling me and I had no other people calling me.

Over the past 4 months have taught me to be mentally strong and to react only when it is necessary, I abstained from entertaining those conversations which could lead to any sort of argument or mental trauma for me, these incidents only lead to self-introspection and I began blaming myself that maybe I wasn't good enough and therefore I had no loyal friends.

Two days later finally Pratiksha was back and my loneliness substantially reduced as I could now talk with her. There was something that had changed between us, the chemistry which we shared felt missing. I was trying hard enough to ensure that she was happy yet I was feeling a vacuum between us. I asked her several times if there was something bothering her only to hear that nothing was bothering her.

I deliberately did not tell her about the Aditi argument as she considered her to be a very good friend and I knew how it felt to be betrayed by a friend as I was too dealing with it.

Aditi on the other hand went ahead to meet Pratiksha:

She was her good friend and her parents knew her well and therefore she was always welcomed at her house.

"You look so lifeless Pratiksha what has happened to you, you look remarkably different and weak" asked Aditi with a wrinkly forehead.

Yes, I was not really well,

"I am glad that you came, it has only been 15 days since I was out of here yet it feels I had been away for months and I have missed out on a lot of things" said Pratiksha leaving a long sigh.

"Yes indeed! A lot had happened" replied Aditi.

"What do you mean?" Pratiksha asked

"Nothing actually, I am here for a reason but don't know whether should I say it or not" replied Aditi

"Say, why is there a need to be so formal" replied Pratiksha.

"I am getting engaged on the 10th of next month, I have come here to invite you. And I want you to be present there and no excuses allowed.

"it's absolutely okay you don't need to be so formal" replied Pratiksha.

"By the way who is the lucky guy" she asked.

"His name is Satvik and he resides in Ahmedabad and is a doctor by profession. We met 2 months back our parents fixed the engagement and he is really nice. I like talking with him. So far so good, let's see how it goes for both of us" replied Aditi.

"Woah that's great I am really happy for you, congratulations to you both" replied Pratiksha

"If you can than please join me, I would really feel happy if you do join." Replied Aditi

"of course, I will" said Pratiksha in consent taking the invitation card from her hand.

"If you don't mind, can I ask you for one more favour." Asked Aditi hesitantly

"Yeah sure" replied Pratiksha.

"Could you please inform vinay about this engagement, he isn't talking to me lately yet I want him to know about this," said Aditi.

"Why, what happened why are you guy not in talking terms, as far as I know you both were very good friends and vinay often talks about the good bond that you both share." She asked frowning her brows.

"Yes, indeed we were, but recently something had happened that turned the situation upside down and now he no longer wants to see me or hear from me" replied Aditi with tears in her eyes.

"Oh my god, what had happened Aditi, what went wrong. If you find it okay to share that cause of your dispute" asked Pratiksha in pity resting her hand on the shoulder of weeping Aditi.

"You are the reason" replied Aditi.

For a moment Pratiksha was not in a state to understand that how was she behind all this chaos as she has not had any conversation with vinay for the past 15 days and how come she could have created problems between them without any exchange of words.

Not able to grasp what she wanted to convey Pratiksha asked in quandary, "how come I be responsible for something I am not even aware of, and if there is something please say everything whatever you have in your mind so that I can get to know whether I am actually at the bottom of all of this and if not, I will try to erase any sort of misconception cropping up".

"Listen, I don't want you to think I am a person who hates you, but the opinion which I shared about you were not in your favour which led to all this fiasco of the point I was trying to prove before vinay which he did not take as I wanted it to be conveyed." Said Aditi jumbling the words.

"Aditi, if you really want to share something than please be specific, I hardly have enough energy to understand what you are trying to say, I can't figure out your cryptic meanings behind these jumbled phrases." Said Pratiksha in a tone that was a little choked yet bold to take any worst possible scenario.

"Vinay told me everything about what happened in Bhopal, and also what koshlesh did to you after that. Vinay was weeping that night when he called me that he had been stabbed at the back by koshlesh, he very well knew that you guys were seeing each other yet he tried to woo you and also has begun blackmailing you." She said taking multiple pauses.

"I knew you were dating him but I never thought you would go to Bhopal and spend two days with him in his flat in his room, that was quite surprising for me. I am not taking it otherwise but somewhere I still feel that you did wrong walking over your parent's trust would be the last thing I could ever dream of doing. And upon hearing this I was taken with the flow and unknowingly I have said some harsh sentences against you for which I am extremely sorry." Said Aditi also elaborating further allegations that she had put against her before vinay.

"You have always known me Pratiksha, I had always been very vocal about my feelings and this time also when I spoke my heart before vinay, he did not take the meaning as I wanted him to take and that lead to this. I know he is hurt and therefore I need your interception to help ease out this misunderstanding.

Pratiksha's breaths got heavier and heavier as this was something she was trying to forget and yet again it was here in a gigantic form before her.

"The more I am trying to escape this the bigger it is getting. I am not even talking to vinay because I believe it is because of me his most cherished friendship broke but now you too are the victim of this debacle and you too have lost your friend. I never thought I would prove out to be such a lossmaker for him that he had to lose on so many people from his life just to be with me." Said Pratiksha gathering her breath while sobbing.

The talk was stressful enough for her get back her panic attack, her health was at the edge and any news with stress could trigger to make her condition worse, Aditi realised she was not doing well lately but she failed to realise the gravity of the situation, had she known that exposing Pratiksha to any stressful news can cause danger to her health she would have never said anything.

Pratiksha began panting heavier breaths, when her mother entered the room with the cup of coffee and snacks in her hands, she took no time to address the deteriorating health condition of Pratiksha, and immediately laid her down on the bed and began preparing a syringe with a shot of some medicine.

"what's happening to her aunty, she was fine 5 minutes back and now I see you with this injection, what is wrong with her health?" asked Aditi in panic.

"Ohh God, I should not have listened to her and should not have left you both alone. Were you talking about something that can cause her some sort of stress?" asked her mother, running her hand abruptly inside the drawer next to her bedside.

The drawer was filled with medicines of different kinds such that it looked like a mini pharmacy store, but what was the point of so many medicines in a young girl's room. Despite she was sick but that did not mean that she had to survive on all those stacks of medicines.

"What is wrong with her aunty is she suffering from some serious illness" asked Aditi worriedly.

"I would suggest you to leave right now, I have to call the doctor and her father to help me take her to the hospital, every minute counts here and the delay of even a single minute can cost us her life" said her mother with panic in her voice.

"I am fine maa… relax it's just the trigger, I will be fine hand me my medicines they will help me ease out" said Pratiksha in a cracking voice.

Aditi could not contain her tears seeing Pratiksha in a devastating state and began blaming herself for her miserable condition, her feet began trembling she has never seen anyone in such state ever before.

There were several questions in her mind that what had let Pratiksha into this state and she was standing there patiently first to see Pratiksha's health getting better and latter getting answers to her dilemma.

It took nearly 30 minutes for her breathing to stabilize, by this time her father and the doctors have arrived at her house, it was only after high sedation she was brought back to being normal but those medicines made her drowsy and she went into sleep as soon as the medicines began acting upon her.

"Aunty please tell me what has happened to her and what kind of illness is she suffering from why did you get so bothered for her taking any stress. Is there something serious because it really looks like so." Asked Aditi.

"Yes, she has been battling with a life-threatening disease, the doctors have raised their concerns that if not taken proper care for the critical initial days we might lose her forever, she has been suffering from subarachnoid haemorrhage, commonly known as SAH, this has not developed because of a trauma, commonly this is the result of some trauma but her care is very rare that it has happened because of an artery ballooning and rupturing in the space of her head and skull." Replied her mother wiping off her tears.

GONE TOO SOON

I was excited since it was my final exam to this marathon course of engineering and after 4 long years of assignments, exams, practical's, this and that we were inching closer to our destiny of being qualified as a mechanical engineer. The past 4 years were a mixture of a lot of sweet memories with the friends which I wish to cherish forever along with some bad ones which I badly wanted to erase from my memory.

I was supremely excited about this as the past few months had been very difficult for me to pass and therefore, I had already got my tickets booked to go to Ahmedabad since I was living alone lately, I had all my belongings packed well in advance, but I was going to Ahmedabad only for a visit for a couple of days I would return for getting my stuff from the PG and my bike.

My excitement was contagious and to spread it over I called Pratiksha right before my exam.

"Hello! Finally, the day has come which I had been waiting for a long time, I will be boarding the train tonight and tomorrow we will be meeting, I am over the moon."

"Yes, finally your earnest desire to become an engineer is turning into reality, I am very much proud of you, you deserve this happiness, yes indeed we will meet tomorrow" replied Pratiksha faking a smile knowing that this time it would not be easier for her to get out.

"Okay I will have to go the final bell has rung I shall call you once I am done with my exam, see you love you…the days of exile are finally ending I am coming to meet your parents this time, you will be mine forever" I said wittily.

"All the best" replied Pratiksha with a giggle in her voice.

I on the other hand oblivious of this incident kept calling her on her mobile since my exam ended but every time, I called my call remained unanswered, which was not normal yet it did not bother me much because I was meeting her the next day.

I took my bag and boarded the train on time but before falling to sleep I further tried calling her but the result was same, therefore I left a message for her before sleeping.

"Hey where are you why are you not answering my calls, are you trying to play this trick on me? Don't worry I am coming tomorrow morning to meet you, stay tuned, I can't wait for this night to pass, love you, see you tomorrow."

Next morning upon reaching my home and having breakfast with my family I headed towards her house, since I had been calling her and there were no responses from her end that made me quite uneasy.

Upon making repeated calls with no response, I decided to go to her house directly thinking that if I get to meet her family, I will also get myself introduced there.

on reaching her house I saw the door with a lock this had happened the second time earlier when her grandmother passed, I was welcomed with a lock like this, while I was prying around her house, a neighbour came out.

"Whom are you looking for" she asked.

"Pratiksha! She resides here, I am looking for her but there is lock."

"She is in the hospital, yesterday she met with a fatal accident and is in the hospital since then, she also underwent a surgery, may god bless her and she recovers well" replied the lady with pity in her eyes.

The news made my face went ghost white and for a moment I lost my ability to stand and took the support from the adjacent wall.

Gathering me breathe I asked "could you tell me which hospital?"

"City hospital "she replied.

"Thank you" I said barely breathing.

I hurried towards my bike to reach the city hospital, throughout the time I kept on praying to God for her wellbeing, my heart was sinking to the bottom of my stomach it was the most difficult bike ride for me, I somehow reached the hospital with several thoughts rushing my way.

I entered the hospital with my eyes already filled with tears and headed towards the reception desk asking for her room.

The receptionist directed me towards the ICU I ran across the corridor to reach her, I saw her mother sitting with her head resting on her hands with her elbows resting on her knees, she looked lifeless, her eyes were swollen and red, her lips seemed cracked and dry as if she had not had water since then. Her condition looked worrisome.

Her father sitting adjacent to her was also in a broken state, his hairs untidy and his face turned pale.

Looking at them made me realise that she isn't okay because if she was her parents would not have these many lines of worry over their forehead. I slowly walked towards the ICU when her mother saw me, she recognised me because a day ago she had seen my picture with her, which I was unaware of, she slowly pointed towards the ICU and then broke down again.

I took a lot of courage for me to walk down that 10 metre corridors, although no entry was allowed inside the room, we could only see her through the glass window.

She was lying on the bed with the bandages around her head, those hairs which she always flaunted styled in different manner where now shaved off her head and there was a huge bandage wrapping her head like a helmet.

She laid in that room all alone with all those machines, the rooms quietude was punctured by beeping sounds of machines which had possibly kept her alive.

I stood near the window with my nose pressed against the glass and my breath was fogging it, I was in smithereens, this was not something I was prepared for, it was the most devastating thing to ever happen, I stood near the window frozen with all those memories replaying in my head, until when I felt a hand around my shoulder,

It was her mother,

"Vinay! Come sit here she will be fine."

I was surprised that her mother knew who I was upon seeing my confused look she replied "Pratiksha told me about you, she had told me that you would come searching for her, and has also told that if she cannot make it to meet you, please forgive her."

"Why are you saying this aunty, she will be fine, it is just a small illness it can get treated and she will be fine" I said wiping my tears and reaffirming my belief that this separation can never happen.

Later she unravelled the fact behind her health, upon knowing that all this while she was struggling with her life and yet she was portraying herself to be fine before me might have been so tough for her, the series of shocks did not end here, I further got to know that her grandmother was alive and this was an excuse which she made before me and during that time she had gone to Delhi for her treatment. She made up all that story of no networks and everything while she was going a brain surgery.

She gentle caressed me forehead and asked me to not cry, giving me the fake assurance which she was not even sure of.

I sat there on the hospital chair paralyzed staring at the floor with constant stir of tears rolling down my eyes. This was why she was avoiding my calls as she was cleverly hiding her pain so that it may not impact my exams. all those medicines which I found in her might be for this treatment which I assumed as normal medicines.

When the monitors of her vital stats began showing the adverse signs the doctors made their visits to her room more frequent and after a rapid movement of doctors here and there trying different drugs to revive her declining heart rates there were several attempts being made by the doctors to bring her back.

There was internal bleeding which had started in her brain which aggravated the problem and slowly her heart rate depleted.

All of us rushed towards the window peeping inside what was happening to her, she was breathless and it took her trouble to take breathe she was even applied an oxygen mask to help her with that.

After struggling for nearly 10 minutes there was some relaxation in her breathing pattern and she opened her eyes, all three of us rejoiced to see that after 24 hours of struggle she had finally opened her eyes.

Before we could celebrate and take a sigh of relieve of this little improvement little did, we know that it was the last time she was seeing this world before closing them forever.

Her eyes closed again, the monitor showing her heart rate began to show a straight line, the doctors removed the oxygen mask and all other machines connected to her and slowly began walking out of the ICU.

"I AM SORRY, WE COULD NOT SAVE HER" said the doctor leaving us with the most painful and heartbreaking truth of our life.

We went inside to feel her to touch her one last time, the feet felt like they have been tied with weights around which made it impossible to walk towards the bed on which she was lying lifeless.

I was still hoping for a miracle to happen like a wizard she would stand up and say I am fine but it was hardly ever going to happen, I touched her hand which had now begun to get cold they were swollen the canula with the syringe was still attached I carefully held her hand thinking that it would hurt but she had surpassed her bodily pains and had now left to her forever new home up in the heaven.

Those hands which promised to be with me forever, holding them we were ready to tie the knot she had left me stranded alone on this journey where I never thought I would live without her.

The most difficult and hard to swallow pill of my life became the separation from her, the pain left me blank, I went with her family to their house and even to the funeral but seeing her turn into flames burnt the person within me I was with her being in my life.

I was simply a lifeless living being because my life has already gone, I hope I get to meet her up in the heavens because she had left me stranded here but up there will be excuse for the separation.

It has been 4 months since she passed but I am still on the last day when I was eager to meet her. I felt betrayed by her that when we promised one another to be the companion in thick and thin times she kept me aloof in the times when she needed me the most, had I known about it, I would do anything to steal the maximum time I could get to spend with her. I could not forgive myself for not knowing her so well, she concealed her deteriorating health with me, but I claimed to love her when you love someone you can also here what is unsaid but my ears only heard the said lies and not the unsaid truth.

I often get messages from Aditi to keep a check upon me but those also remains unread.

The vacuum that had been created with her name had made realise one thing that her name was indeed a sign from the god from me PRATIKSHA: I will now have to wait for her forever.

www.ingramcontent.com/pod-product-compliance
Lightning Source LLC
LaVergne TN
LVHW041309200726
843509LV00009B/423